CRUSHED
Seraphim

DEBRA ANASTASIA

OMNIFIC PUBLISHING

DALLAS

Omnific Publishing
P.O. Box 793871, Dallas, TX 75379
www.omnificpublishing.com

First Omnific eBook edition, May 2011
First Omnific trade paperback edition, May 2011

The characters and events in this book are fictitious.
Any similarity to real persons, living or dead,
is coincidental and not intended by the author.

Library of Congress Cataloguing-in-Publication Data

Anastasia, Debra.
    Crushed Seraphim / Debra Anastasia – 1st ed.
    ISBN 978-1-936305-74-2
    1. Hell — Fiction. 2. Heaven — Fiction.
    3. Love Triangle — Fiction. 4. Supernatural Romance — Fiction.
    I. Title

                    10 9 8 7 6 5 4 3 2 1

Cover Design by Micha Stone and Stephanie Swartz
Interior Book Design by Coreen Montagna

Printed in the United States of America

To T, J, and D.
You are everything.

PROLOGUE

He pulled his hand through his long hair and lit a cigarette. The rush of the smoke into his lungs did little to dam the pain that poured from somewhere in his center.

"Get dressed," he whispered. His voice was the most compelling thing in the room; he knew she would listen.

Sitting on the edge of the couch, he ran his hand over the red velvet, creating meaningless patterns. The remembering wouldn't stop. The woman behind him, shuffling as quietly as possible into her clothes, would never be the woman he sought to bury himself in.

He knew the speech she was about to deliver by heart. He'd heard it so many times. He took another drag.

"Um, that's never happened to me before. I mean, I've never thrown myself at a man that way. There's just something about you..." Her voice trailed off as the glow of their intercourse bled from her face.

He didn't need to look to know her eyes were darting around his smoky room, looking for a way out.

There wasn't an exit for her, of course.

He reached for the bottle close to his feet and took a swallow. "There *is* something about me, doll face. It's between my legs, and I do believe a few minutes ago you were praying to it."

He stood and turned to face her. The woman's nightgown was ridiculously prissy with a high, ruffled collar.

"Where do I go now?" She clutched the copious skirt in her hand like a child with a stuffed animal.

He took another drag. The ritual was so timeworn there were almost groove marks around his next words.

"Listen, baby, only you know where you go next. Deep inside you." He walked toward her, seducing again because he had no other choice. "When everything around you is quiet, what do you hear?" He placed his hand on her heart.

Throughout their sex he'd avoided looking into her face. But now he gazed into her eyes. They were almost familiar. He hated it there.

"I don't hear anything when it's quiet. Is this a trick? Is it a riddle?"

She was breathing more quickly now. The evil of which he was capable was even more potent than his sexual prowess. She could feel it.

The smoke began to swirl, almost dancing with glee. Her frantic eyes watched it, trying to get a hint as to what was next.

He took his hand away and bought time with another chug from his precious bottle. After he swallowed, he wiped his mouth with the back of his hand.

"You know where you are, and you know how you lived your life. No one is here by mistake, child. You had choices. You made the wrong ones. It's okay, baby. I know what that's all about." He grabbed her arm, because he had to. This was the way it was always done.

He strode confidently through the dark smoke until he reached a very, very old wooden door. There was just a hairsbreadth between its thick planks, and the glowing, lava-colored light that emanated from behind the barrier created a phantom red jail cell on the floor.

She would struggle now—kick him, slap him, bite him. None of the physical violence affected him, but the soft cries did. Her despair became tangible.

"No! Please, no. You kissed me. You wanted me. There must be something else I can do? I'll do anything. Oh God, please, no."

She was hugging his arm now, kissing one of his tattoos to prove her earnestness. He hated this part. Really, he did. The woman's dark curls reminded him of his love so much. It was designed to be that way, he knew.

"God's already passed Judgment on you, honey. This is what you deserve." He opened the door's handle.

The wood couldn't hold back all the light when it was closed, but it did keep the screams from permeating his chambers. Now they resonated from below like demented church bells.

He let go of her arm. He would not push her or torture her like his predecessor would have. He motioned for her to enter. She stood, shaking as she peered into the red-hot abyss. There was no floor, no elevator—just a sheer drop.

He stuffed his hands into the pockets of his jeans. This was the part where he always wanted to save them, the women he'd romanced and pleasured.

He wouldn't, of course.

"I have to go down there?" She pointed a shaking finger at her destination. "What will happen to me?"

He shrugged and looked at the empty space above her head. "You'll receive what you've given in life tenfold. My minions will tend to your doomed soul."

The way her body stiffened was the answer to any regret he felt about her damnation. She'd obviously been a heinous bitch in her living days. Getting back what she'd doled out to others was scarier to her than a drop with no end. It was worse than her fear of the screams from below.

He nodded toward the space again and raised his eyebrows with expectation. The woman turned to run. But his smoke had anticipated her movements and created a wall that she smacked right into.

The gravity began then, the pull from her Judgment. It was as if unseen hands had grabbed her arms and legs. She fought the whole way, and he almost smiled at her spunk—almost.

When the woman he'd just bedded fell into the seething red forever, he closed the door to block out her screams.

His smoke was happy, swirling in delight. He'd done his job again. But for him there was no satisfaction, only the grinding emptiness of his own damnation.

He heard the monsters that guarded the gates engage in battle, and this caught his attention. Someone was coming to him. Willingly.

Leaning against the wall by his metal outer door, he waited for the visitor's inevitable failure. The noises were so rambunctious he almost wanted to take a peek for entertainment's sake.

His gaze landed on the damned woman's slippers. She'd forgotten to wear them to her sentence in Hell. She might regret that later.

The slippers were quite sexy—they hadn't matched her dowdy sleepwear. The noises of the fight beyond his door and the sight of the slippers suddenly set his memory in motion.

Years ago, one of his female minions had come to him with an unusual problem. In this very room she'd requested her release, wearing shoes similar to the ones he now saw on the floor.

"Sir, I need to beg you for understanding. I need to get to the surface."
She was gorgeous, as all his minions were.

"Violent, that's not a possibility. No one goes to the surface. How
about I just give you a mind-numbing orgasm and you forget all about it?"

He'd been smoking, of course. In the haze, her long, red hair and
purple eyes were just hints of her beauty. She was out of focus.

"Sir, with all due respect, it might be possible to get out. Before your
reign, a handful of minions tried it." Violent stepped closer.

Dirty jeans and an old т-shirt never looked so good. After careful
inspection of her ridiculously tempting body, he looked in her eyes. She was
in serious pain. He saw that same pain every time he looked in the mirror.

"Gorgeous, I have no idea what you've been smoking, but I want
some." He offered her a glass of wine that she declined with a flick of her
wrist.

Violent was his Minion of Sleep, and she was tremendously valuable.
When his reign had begun, she was a quivering mess. His predecessor had
abused her in too many ways. As the years stacked up, she began to understand that he would rule differently. This Devil would be more business
and less pointless cruelty.

Violent had closed his metal door and crossed the distance so she
could kneel at his feet.

"Oh great and wise Satan, I have served here in Hell for more years
than anyone can count. I do not deserve mercy or redemption. But I'm
asking you to let me go, to try to make it to the surface." She kept her eyes
on his old motorcycle boots.

He tossed his cigarette and lifted her chin with his finger, "Baby,
since when do I have minions kneel? Please—this is insulting. Sit next to
me and tell me why you feel you need to leave."

She obeyed, as he knew she would, as she always had in the past.
Violent clasped her hands together and sighed.

"Tell me the truth, baby. Anything else is just wasting my time." He
could always spot a lie. No one was better than him at that game.

"I've been visiting dreams—planting evil, as I should. But while I
surfed from one consciousness to another, I found one I needed to keep
visiting." She clenched her fists.

Satan let her form her words while he tried to deduce what had
happened. Violent wasn't any type of avenger, and she would never want
to stop a planned evil event. It could only be one thing.

"I fell in love with a man—a soul—on Earth, and I need to find
him," she confessed.

She turned to face him, and he saw she was deluded with this love.

"He has the most stunning dreams," she continued. "He's a painter, and he lives in his art at night. In his dreams I've appeared to him and we've loved one another. I'll have him in my arms — if you allow it, of course."

The whole encounter was perplexing. This sounded a whole lot like goodness, and that never grew in Hell. "No one's made it out," he countered. "You know that. You'll be extinguished if you attempt it and fail."

He reached for another bottle from the floor. This one was red wine, his second favorite next to rum.

She hopped from his couch and faced him like a fighter. He smiled as she pulled out her weapon, a short dagger. He shook his head and didn't stand. The wine tasted luscious.

"I'm not him, Violent. The Devil before me would have punished you viciously for even dreaming of leaving. And I could." He held out his wine bottle to her.

She sheathed her dagger and accepted the wine. While she took her swallow, he walked deeper into his room and returned with one of his best swords. It was as long as his leg and hummed as he slashed it easily from side to side.

Violent nodded and tossed the bottle. The crash was followed by the gentle sound of glass scattering. She closed her eyes and held out her palms, ready to be slashed to bits for even having hoped.

Satan came close to her and watched her bravery as she waited. She'd rather cease to exist than not feel the love she imagined existed for her.

He leaned closer and whispered in her ear. "Beautiful minion, take my sword. It is your fate to choose. This painter you love? If you make it — and I don't think you will — he gets a piece of Hell for his very own. Is that a gift or a curse, Violent?"

She opened her eyes, and he saw her doubt. "You're letting me go?"

"No, gorgeous, you're leaving. You're not mine to keep." He kissed her on her cheek and motioned to the metal door.

It had been years since that moment, but he could still see her eyes burning with determination. He'd waited and listened to her exit from Hell in the same spot where he now stood.

He'd held his breath as he heard Violent's screaming, the monsters making their awful crunching noises. He'd hoped she'd reach the soil. He'd have paid money to see her red hair in the sun and the victory in her purple eyes when she made it to the same realm as her dream lover.

Years went by, and he had no idea of her fate. He'd tried not to picture her skin slick and red, the color of her hair seeping from her veins while one of the beasts feasted on her. But there was no way of knowing until the day he had encountered his first half-breed damnation.

The girl had Violent's purple eyes and readily showed her fangs to him. After a short interview he knew his minion had indeed made it to the surface. No man alive could deny a beauty as potent as Violent's, and her painter was no exception. They'd mated and created the girl in front of him now. Celeste was the exact opposite of her name. She did *not* have a heavenly disposition, and there was a fascinating hunger in her eyes. Satan did not feel compelled to bed her, and she seemed to be anxiously anticipating her damned forever.

As he walked her to the old door, she smiled widely. Instead of screaming and running, she spoke casually, like they were making conversation in a grocery store line instead of standing at the precipice of all evil.

"I love pain," the purple-eyed girl had panted with sheer pleasure.

Satan looked her up and down and couldn't even imagine the tenfold she would be getting back. She stepped into the drop and squealed with glee on her way down.

He knew a few things for sure now: A soul could get out of Hell. It was possible, even if it was unlikely. Violent had mated with her beloved human and created a new species of half-breed minions, which seemed to be something twisted and damaged and akin to vampires. If the one he'd just encountered was any indication, he'd be seeing a lot more of them on their way to Hell. Finally, he was reminded again that his predecessor would've cut Violent down the moment she approached him — and he'd have done the world a favor.

The noises behind him ramped up. Whatever was coming down had some considerable talent. Satan couldn't help but wonder if it was Violent, coming to collect her offspring after so many years apart.

When the noises ceased, he lit another cigarette. *Oh well, I'll never know what that was about.*

Then just as he inhaled, a knock reverberated off the door behind him. He coughed the smoke out in surprise. He could smell the Heaven before he even opened the door. It was fresh and amazing.

Satan swung back the heavy metal door and chuckled at the sight before him. Completely, spectacularly white, an angel stood in his doorway. He wore an impeccable linen suit, and his wings extended far past the doorframe. He was gorgeous.

"Did you make a wrong turn, asshole?" Satan shook his head.

"Listen, I don't have a lot of time. God's coming to parlay for souls. I have a plan that will change the face of Earth, to our evil benefit. I need you to keep him here until I finish what I start."

The angel was handsome and absolutely crazy.

"The last Devil tried that shit, and he couldn't do it. I think you need to go back where you came from," Satan said. "If my minions get a whiff of you, they'll eat you for breakfast." Satan began to close his door.

The angel stuck his foot in the gap like a pushy salesman. "That was the last Devil. You're different. You're smarter. The half-breeds are your work? Excellent. My hat's off to you. I think you can keep God captive. If you do, I'll bring Hell to Earth. Imagine that, Devil. All that innocent flesh for you and your minions—it'll be a succulent buffet. No need to stick to the evil ladies anymore." The angel held out his hand, businesslike. "I'm Everett, and I'm a huge fan."

Satan regarded the batshit-crazy angel with suspicious eyes. The bastard was lying, he could tell. *But which part was the lie?* This guy was better than a politician.

Satan hated that he had such a longing to feel the sun on his face. The angel would fail, but as the Devil, he was duty bound to do his best to help in a situation like this. An evil plan cooked up by an angel? Satan was pretty sure that hadn't happened but once before. Almost one thousand years ago, and Satan was the last to have the balls to do it.

The Devil took his cigarette and stubbed it out on the winged weirdo's palm. "All right, freak show, I can keep God here like the other bastard couldn't. What's your plan?"

Everett grabbed his lapels and smiled. "I've rigged a Christmas Angel to visit a half-breed, for starters. Can you imagine? She'll be a colossal failure. With her out of the way, Earth and Heaven will be mine—and yours, of course."

"Well, you best scurry along, Everett. I hear my next customer coming." Satan wanted to slam the door for a more impressive effect, but as Everett turned and walked away, Satan just watched instead.

The wings were mesmerizing, shimmering, and huge. As the scent of Heaven lingered, Satan remembered just what it felt like to have wings—back when he'd been more good than bad, back when God had smiled at his jokes and his lovely angel Claudette had let him hold her hand.

When he could no longer see the angel, he shut his door. Things were actually going to change—he could feel it. The Christmas Angel sent to Earth to make a half-breed vampire freak feel God's love would never complete her mission. After all the half-breeds he'd walked to the old door, he knew they were a lost cause, a heinous, self-loathing species.

He took a leather wrap from his wrist and tied back his hair with it. He needed to work; keeping God trapped was delicate business.

CHAPTER 1

*J*ason tracked the falling star on Christmas Eve. Its tail was exceptional and distracted him completely from the task of finding a tree in the forest to decorate for his siblings. The sparking rainbow arch scratched its mark in the obsidian sky as it broke the atmosphere and came screaming closer. Jason watched until he was sure he glimpsed the gentle form of a woman within the scorching, white-hot fire. Then he began to sprint. If he hadn't been a half-breed, he'd have never caught her.

He braced himself beneath the shower of sparks, and she landed heavily, nearly knocking him off his feet. His extraordinary reflexes had awarded him an armful of angel. She was unconscious, and her blond hair covered her face. He knelt, shocked to be holding something so cold that had come from something so seemingly hot.

A steady stream of prism-flavored light sprinkled from her skin like water droplets. She was glowing and barely dressed, her white satin gown singed and smudged away. He laid her gently on the snow at his feet, moving her hair from her face. Her skin was pale, but her cheeks were pink.

She sighed before she opened her eyes, like she regretted being able to do it at all. When her luminous gray eyes took in his face, she shook her head.

"Are you hurt?" Jason would swear he was dreaming, but his mind hadn't allowed that for many years.

"Yes, I'm hurt, *half-breed,*" she said with a bit of a sneer. She winced as she sat up. The girl flicked bits of cloud and stardust off her shoulders.

Jason stood and held out his hand, consumed by curiosity. "Can I be of assistance in any way?"

The girl snorted and ignored his hand. She stood on the ice-cold carpet the sky had provided to cushion her fall from the heavens.

"Sure. Let a vampire help me. That's hilarious, right?" As the girl tilted her head to yell at the stars in the sky, one perfect wing appeared from behind her.

Jason gave up pretending he wasn't in shock. Her wing was a tightly knit gossamer web. Feathers the consistency of hope shimmered as she stomped her feet and glared at unseen opposition.

"Up yours!" She turned from Jason to give Heaven the finger.

Jason could see her back was marred. A single slice, welted with melted silver, lined her shoulder where another symmetrical wing should have been. Gentle drops of liquid metal pooled in the snow, solidifying into a small mirror.

She whirled to look him up and down with disdain. "As if I could make you change your ways. A fool's task. You're an insult to add to my injury."

Jason squeezed his eyes shut against her blinding presence. She was trying to fly when he opened his eyes again, fluttering her one wing uselessly. It was heartbreaking, seeing her efforts foiled. She was a broken, angry angel.

"Damn it." She shook her head so her hair covered her raw, pained eyes.

The quiet way she tucked her magnificent wing from his sight stirred his latent human compassion. "I can give you a toss, if you think it would help," he offered. He hoped humor would buoy her spirits.

She walked toward him. The little sprinkles of leftover Heaven hit the snow, making tiny wind-chime sounds to announce each footfall.

"I'm Emma. I'm here to make you see the meaning of your life. I hope you can mend your ways and rejoice in the glory of the afterlife." Her exalted words were totally conquered by her dragging tone and lack of eye contact.

"Pardon me? You're here to help me? And you know I'm a half-breed?" Jason held up his hand as if he could connect the dots from his questions to some answers with his fingers.

Emma bit her bottom lip and nodded.

"I'm a killer, miss," Jason said harshly. "I need to feed off living things to keep my own selfish soul alive. I'm the worst thing in the world, and there's not a thing you can do to change that."

For the first time since her meteor-like arrival in his arms, she seemed present in front of him. The wind chimes pinged as she walked closer. He could feel his skin tingling in reaction to her scintillating glimmer. *Is she made of sunlight?*

She laughed. "No, silly, aren't girls made of sugar and spice?" She stood in front of him now, teasing him with half-closed eyes, putting a hand to his face. "And everything nice?"

His need climbed from Hell itself. His lust was vicious; he wanted to fill her completely.

You can hear my thoughts?

Emma gave a forced laugh and looked from his lips to his eyes. "Yes. This'll be fun, I bet."

She smelled like something freshly baked...with vanilla. Some sort of cake? *It's a lost cause, beautiful angel. Go back to where you came from.*

She stepped to him, and he felt true danger for the first time in his too-long life. Her wing was out again, and now it glowed red hot, matching the anger in her eyes and scorching the air that dared touch it.

"What's worse than a parasite like you? What's worse than a selfish, twisted half-breed vampire?" Emma seethed as she curled the sweltering feathers of her wing around him.

Instinctively shying from the intense heat, he was forced to put his chest against her breasts to avoid being touched by her wing. Its heat seemed to be a searing manifestation of her anger.

"Killers are allowed in Heaven. Bottom-feeders are allowed in Heaven. All you have to do is be forgiven." Her voice was now filled with disbelief—and something else. She leaned in, put her arctic lips on his, and mumbled, "Can you taste how bad I am?"

Jason couldn't move. She moved her lips from his.

"I'm far worse than anything else, half-breed. Have you ever known someone so evil she was mangled and tossed from the clouds?"

He hungered to kiss her deeply. He wanted to press her hot wing in the snow to cool it. He wanted her desperately, irrationally.

"Men are so typical. Don't you even have the common sense to be frightened?"

Jason wrapped his solid arm around her waist. *No, I don't. Broken angel, I'm not afraid of you. You'll have to try harder than this.*

"Don't tempt me. I've been lowered to *this.* Consorting with vermin for a chance—for a maybe chance at..." She looked over his shoulder and trailed off.

"A chance?" Jason felt her wing cooling.

"I've said too much. Just suck it up and take what I——"

She never finished her sentence. Her knees buckled and she fainted.

Jason caught her, grateful once again that they'd been standing close. He lifted her into his arms to keep her from hitting the ground. Her wing sizzled as it brushed the snow, and a hiss filled the air. Jason's face was reflected in the huge, perfect mirror of her cooled and copious angel blood. It was a pond of mercury made from her pain and shame.

How in God's name do you fix a bleeding angel?

There was no response to his thoughts this time, so Jason ran. The night was filled with the sound of his beating footsteps and her wing trailing on the ground.

Jason wished he could run faster. Emma was unconscious, her head and limbs lolling around in an alarming way. Finally, he burst into his home. His brother and sister stared as he crashed through the door.

"Dean, please, she fell from Heaven. I think she's an angel. I don't——I can't fix her," Jason said, his voice feverish with desperation. "Please tell me you've seen this before?"

Dean at first looked playful, as if his brother was joking. But after a beat Dean's smiled faded.

"Bro, I don't see anything but you," he said.

Jason felt like he was losing his mind, and all the while, his bleeding angel was fading in his arms. *God, she's dying…But isn't she already dead?*

"Maybe you ate poisoned blood," Seriana suggested, her eyes locked on Jason. "Please, come sit."

His siblings couldn't help. Jason shook his head. He pulled his mirage closer. Her wing was dirty from their useless run to his house.

"I need to be alone. Please excuse me." Jason went back out the door he'd come in.

He continued his trek through the woods, finding his way to a familiar creek, and he set Emma down carefully. She looked human now. The pink of her cheeks was draining, her singed dress turning gray. Her skin looked transparent. She was fading away.

Jason pounded a fist into the ground. *God, why can't I help her? And why do I want to?*

It was just a flicker, like adjusting a TV with the slightest touch, but her body had looked more solid for a moment.

What did I do?

Jason pounded his fist into the ground again.

Nothing.

He used both hands this time. Winter birds fluttered from their trees as he created a miniature earthquake.

Still nothing.

She'd become translucent again. He ran his hand through his hair.

Damn it all to Hell!

Quickly she became just a whisper of a memory.

No, please, God, no!

Emma had more definition for a heartbeat. Then Jason got it: When he prayed she became more solid. He slid his hands under the misty outline of the angel, putting pressure right where her wing had once been, and prayed.

God, let me have her, please, just for a little while. I want to be here with her. Please, God.

His thoughts had colored her in. She was vibrant once more. Touchable — even if she was only for his eyes.

Heal her, please, if you exist at all.

Her eyes fluttered open. She took in the sight of him as he smiled.

"What the hell did you do?" She sat up and stretched like a fractured winter fairy. She put the crisp, white snow to shame with her perfection.

He pictured the whole scene from beginning to end — his brother, her blood, the praying.

She read his mind. "I expect you want me to thank you. It won't happen." She went to stand and fumbled a bit.

Jason quickly held her arm. She sneered but let him support her weight. From this angle he could see the mark where her torn and missing wing had been repaired by his urgent prayers. She now had a jagged silver tattoo — like trapped lightning just under the surface of her skin.

"Why were you bleeding? Why can't my family see you? I think I deserve some answers," he said.

She shook her head and turned to face him. "That wasn't blood. It was love. It pours out of you when you lose faith. Only faith can heal, so congratulations, half-breed. I'm still here in this horrific place because of you. Do you want me to pat you on the back, or can you do it for yourself?"

Jason extended his hand to her. "I'm sorry. I just…it was awful. I couldn't just watch you disintegrate."

She shrugged as if to say, *Fine. I'll give you that.*

"And my family can't see you?" he prompted.

She reached down for a handful of snow and cupped it quickly between her palms. When she opened her hands, she revealed a perfect snow sculpture of an eagle with its two wings spread. She trailed her finger over the beak gently before clapping her hands and turning the snow back into formless flakes. She seemed to be doing everything to avoid looking in his eyes.

"Jason, I was sent here to be your lesson. If others could see me, it wouldn't be all about you." She finally let her eyes meet his gaze, and he felt like he'd never look away. "Please tell me your miraculous healing of my wound has restored your hope in an afterlife? Then my work here will be done." She looked from his lips to his green eyes.

Done? No. I'm not ready for you to be done. Not by a long shot.

"I knew it. That'd be too good to be true." She turned and marched off, her bare feet never leaving a footprint in the snow ahead of him. "You have until the end of the year—midnight on New Year's Eve—to find yourself."

And if I don't?

"If you don't, I can never go back." She looked toward the sky. The dawn threw wide-stroked rainbows on the lingering clouds.

Well, I'll do what it takes to get you back to where you belong.

She gave a humorless laugh and whirled on him again. "Aren't you interested in why I want to go back? I'll tell you why. I want to finish the job I started. I want to pull *him* out of Heaven and throw him straight to Hell." She put her hand in the center of Jason's chest, as if to warn him of all she planned to do. "That's why he made sure I got *you*. You're the broken ladder to redemption I'll never have."

Jason laid his hand on top of hers, and they both felt the slow, unnatural cadence of his heartbeat.

"You really know how to make a gentleman feel fantastic." Jason used sarcasm to hide his hurt, though she could probably hear it in his head.

"Glad you like it, tough stuff." She continued her hovering movements, her gown growing sleeves and a longer train as she walked. When they reached the edge of the woods, she looked at her expanding ensemble and raised an eyebrow inquisitively. "Was I cold? That's almost sweet."

Jason shook his head, confused.

"I am as you perceive me." She made a sweeping gesture over her body. "This is how you want me to be."

Are you only in my imagination?

Her eyes had a faraway look as she answered his musing. "I'm still a presence, for now. Shall we get started? Your journey will be arduous—and hopefully enlightening."

"I have to tell my family I'll be gone." Jason ran a hand through his hair and dialed his phone, trying to decide how to explain a trip with an angel to Dean and Seriana.

"…Yes, I'm doing fine. Really. I have a small trip to go on, but I'll be in touch." After Jason said goodbye, he turned to Emma. "They're worried about me."

He liked her new look. Emma was now wearing a pair of white pants, a soft, white sweater, and she had big fuzzy boots to keep her angel feet warm.

She laughed out loud at her new attire, and he loved the sound of her genuine pleasure. "Do you really picture me as cold, Jason? Truly, for a murderer you are quite considerate."

Jason looked at his feet. He wanted to drape her in diamonds and take her to a sandy beach. The thought made him squirm, as he knew he was broadcasting it to the object of his desire.

"I love the beach. But tonight doesn't hold that luxury for us." She looked to the sky and held her arms out, palms up, obviously speaking to someone he couldn't see.

"You didn't even think I'd try, did you? How about this, assface?" She faced her palms to the snow, and it came scurrying to her like trained mice, forming a large pile.

Are you calling God an assface?

She smiled a bit before giving him what she seemed to think was an obvious answer. "Ah, no. I don't think He's even taking my calls anymore. The *angel* I want to pummel is trying to sabotage this mission for me."

The magical accumulation of snow became animated, flickering and flashing like white fire.

"Come to me, half-breed."

Her eyes were sultry, and Jason couldn't imagine doing anything else. She held one hand toward the snow flames, the other out for him to grasp. Emma tugged him close when he put his hand in hers.

"Hang on." She stared at his lips and licked her own.

I want to kiss you. Jason placed a hand on her hip.

"There're worse ways to pass time, I guess." She was daring him, smiling and leaning closer.

Their lips were just an impulse apart when the world slid out from under their feet. Jason tried to right them, but there was no center, no way to orient his body.

"Shh. I'll be your gravity, Jason." Emma's voice was calm.

In the swirling tempest of dark, she was his beacon. Her grip on him was gentle, and he had to trust it. He stopped trying to find a horizon and focused on her gray eyes — the color of angry clouds. She looked a little bored as time and place seemed to cease to exist.

"Prepare yourself, handsome. We're about to hit bottom." She placed her lips on his, keeping her eyes open as his thoughts collided with his need.

Breathe her in.

They materialized in an embrace, and suddenly their private moment felt very public in the blinding daylight. Jason's entire body tensed.

She spoke with her mouth on his lips. "No, half-breed, here you're as invisible as I was to your brother and sister. We're here to observe."

He pulled himself reluctantly from her lips and took in the city scene before him. It was far from present day. He recognized the street, the time period, and the smells of his childhood.

Jason's eyes widened as he realized he'd traveled through time with his broken angel. Disoriented, he stumbled a bit.

"I can't believe what I'm seeing." He squinted as if that might make the scene make sense.

Emma rolled her eyes. "Well, you better wise up and quick. We have a job to do here."

A scene he remembered from his childhood began to play out before him. He'd been about ten years old when he stood up to three older boys who terrorized everyone in the neighborhood. His younger self was walking home from school, and the sight of his clothes took Jason back to the feel of his handmade wardrobe and the memory of his mother's tape measure.

"I know what's next. The O'Dowell boys were a vicious bunch." Jason nodded to the alley his younger self was about to pass.

Jason went to step closer, but Emma squeezed his hand hard and warned him, "You can't let go of me. Okay? No matter what, don't let go."

He nodded and turned to watch again, the fuzzy memory crisping up at the edges.

The O'Dowells had been tormenting an old, blind street dog. The shopkeepers kept it alive because they had pity on its cloudy eyes and tossed out food from time to time. The boys thought it hilarious to throw rocks at the dog. They laughed as it yelped and cowered against the wall.

"I didn't even know what I was doing. What was I thinking?" Jason watched as his younger self made two furious fists as he witnessed the unjust behavior.

First, his younger self tossed his school bag at the biggest one, hitting him in the back with the sack of books. Then he jumped in front of the old dog, taking the next rock in *his* stomach.

The boys were thrilled with the availability of human prey and set out to make Jason yelp as loudly as the dog. Emma put her other hand on Jason's chest as he thought again about helping his younger self out.

They watched as the old dog slinked out of danger and took off running down the street.

Jason knew the ending of the story. He was beaten until he cried. They'd left him with a torn book bag and some sizable bruises. But just as Jason was ready for the scene to end, Emma shook her head and motioned for him to look in a different direction.

His mother.

He'd had no idea she'd been present at the end, and she was clearly enraged, shaking with anger.

"Borrow my gift, Jason. Listen to her mind." Emma stated this like it was the obvious course of action, but he was reluctant.

He'd never heard his mother's thoughts, and right now seemed like a horrible time to take a peek. But he opened his mind anyway, and his mother's essence filled his head.

My boy. God, I love him so much. He's so good and kind. I'm going to kill those O'Dowell monsters. If their mother didn't drink like a sailor...

Jason watched as his mother followed not his small, injured body, but the three boys that had dealt the blows. He and Emma trailed behind her, holding hands tightly. His mother tracked those boys right into their backyard. When they noticed her, they quickly adopted a respectful manner.

"Mrs. Parish! Hello ma'am. Are you looking for our mother?"

His mother smiled, but it didn't reach her eyes.

Filthy little bastards.

"Boys, are you having a nice day?" She held her umbrella in her hands like an offering.

"Yes, ma'am. No, ma'am." They all spoke at once, and Jason could read the fear in their heads as well.

"I saw you put your hands on my Jason." She let the words sink in.

They did, and the boys began to shift with guilt.

"If any of you come near him again, I'll beat you to death with this umbrella. Is that understood?" She looked in the face of each boy.

They were shocked. It was the promise in her eyes that scared them. They were sure she was crazy, but she was speaking in a soft, pleasant voice.

"Yes, ma'am. Of course, ma'am." They mumbled their answers.

"Very well, I bid you good day." She turned to leave, but thought better of it. She smiled at the tallest one, then whipped the umbrella down hard on the top of his head. A sickening *thwack* resounded in the air. "Now I feel better."

She used the umbrella as a walking stick as she sauntered away from the now-whimpering child.

Jason was shocked as he looked at Emma. "I had no idea she did that."

Emma forced Jason to continue following his mother. "Listen to her! Do it!"

His mother's mind was loud now, her worry giving it volume. *Jason would die for a blind, old dog. Where did that child come from? He certainly doesn't take after me.* His mother pictured his face, brave and determined, and she poured her achingly deep love over his image. He was everything to her. She walked faster, almost running in her rush to get home and tend to her son.

Emma pulled him closer. "See? You had love in its most basic form. You've seen what I'd intended you to. Hang on."

The rollercoaster through time with Emma as his safety belt began again. She made sure he focused on her face, which made him wonder what he'd see if he looked away. *Would my whole life be flashing by us?*

Landing softly in the snow, back in the recognizable, present-day woods, Jason found himself grateful for the quiet—the lack of other people's thoughts inside his head. He treasured the solid memory he now had of his mother's face. He'd keep her with him always—the sound of her voice, the strength of her love.

He still held Emma's hand tightly. So tightly, in fact, that had she been human her hand would've been broken. The pure bells of her laugh filled the woods, and he turned to see what was so funny.

Emma was again clothed in crisp white, but now she wore a long, slim dress and a huge hat with a white flower.

"Dressing me in period clothing? Really, half-breed, am I your dress-up doll?" She wiggled free of his grasp and took a few of the small steps her skirt required.

Jason closed one eye, realizing that in his pondering of the time jump, he'd also mused about how beautiful Emma would look with her hair up. And she did look beautiful.

You clearly exceed the standard of beauty for that time. But I apologize. What would you prefer to wear?

She blinked, flattered by his thoughtfulness in spite of herself. "Honestly? I'd love to try out some pajamas. They look wonderful from above — much better than a frilly nightdress I had to wear when I was alive." Shaking her head roughly, she looked down at the hem of her skirt.

What is it?

"I'm here for you, despite my slim chance of success. I still have one wing, and I'm duty bound to give you proper guidance. So I feel a bit selfish requesting something as silly as clothes."

Smiling, Jason gestured to her, and at the same moment she was wrapped in glorious white cashmere. She wore the most comfortable, luxurious nightclothes he could fathom. And he included a pair of bunny slippers.

She squealed at the sight of their pointy ears and hugged herself. She moaned with her laughter in such a way that Jason had to concentrate to keep the clothes that gave her such pleasure on her body.

"Half-breed, you have a phenomenal imagination!" She bent over to examine the bunnies up close.

Jason continued smiling at her joy as he inspected her remaining wing. It looked dingy, tinged with gray. He thought this might be just a trick of the cloudy morning light, but as he watched, a single feather floated to the snow and emitted what seemed to be a tiny explosion on impact. Then it was only a memory, hidden in the snow's glitter.

When Emma stood again, she was no longer smiling, but she held her shoulders proud. He was sure she could hear the panic in his head.

"This is just to remind me that I'm failing here," she explained, motioning to her disintegrating wing.

"You took me to my past. How can you be failing?" Jason wondered if he could fashion a feather out of snow to replace the one she'd lost.

"Your mother was right. You are kind. Have no false impressions, Jason. I'm not a blind dog. I've fought viciously." Her words were belied by uncertainty in her eyes.

How can I help you?

Emma reached over her shoulder and pulled her wing around her like a cloak to inspect it. "I can hear your thoughts, but *they* know your feelings, the state of your soul." She let go of her dingy wing and shook her head with disgust. "Tell me, and be honest, have I changed your outlook? You've seen your mother's love. What else is there?"

She took a few disarming steps toward him. He tried to shield his thoughts, but when the white pajamas caressed the outline of her body, he became a poor editor.

He pictured the old dog he'd been willing to take a beating for as a child. Then he pictured the wretched thing he'd become. He feasted on sleeping humans for their blood. Abhorrence of his parasitic ways engulfed him, along with a crippling despair.

"Oh crap. Seriously? The mom? The love? None of that touched you? Damn it." She stomped her fluffy bunny slipper, and unlike her, its bouncing ears seemed anything but angry.

She looked up as if she heard something. Jason raised his eyes as well and discovered a show of gold-colored lightning that crisscrossed the pink-orange sky like a spider web.

"He's laughing at me," Emma said this out loud, but she seemed to be speaking to herself.

Who's laughing?

She didn't answer, her attention above.

"Send a ladder then, bitch! See if I won't march up there and kick you so hard in the ass that you can count my toes with your lying tongue!" Emma began pacing.

More lightning flickered as an answer to her curses. Finally, with a huge boom of thunder, a slanted shaft of golden light punched through the clouds, stopping just inches from her bunnies' noses.

"He's such an ass. Who sends a ladder? Honestly, anyone could go up now. He flaunts his power and makes stupid choices." She extended a bunny and the sunlight became a translucent step for her feet.

She looked over her shoulder to address him. "Hey, half-breed, sorry about your luck. For what it's worth, I don't think you're so bad."

Jason watched as she ran up the stairs, dingy feathers now falling from her wings like magical rain. He replayed her words: *"Anyone could go up now."*

Anyone could go up the stairs…

CHAPTER 2

Jason rushed up the stairs behind her. Despite his half-breed speed, the little slivers of see-through step were wiggling and unsteady. He knew going back down would lead to a hard fall, so he focused again on the path ahead. Rapidly fading into the distance, Emma seemed close to flying with her speed.

Finally, in a dizzying array of clouds, electricity, and blinding sunlight, Jason arrived at the top of the stairs. The clouds were still pulsating from where Emma had penetrated them, and he ran through to catch up.

Her angry voice stopped him. "You send me down, just to let me back up again? You can't decide what the hell you want, can you?"

Jason stood still, and sure enough the clouds parted enough for him to see her as if through a sheer curtain. She remained in her pajamas, hands on her hips, scowling. The object of her hate stepped into view. He glowed like the sun, waxed and shined. His wings were easily the size of two cars. They trapped light like crystals and threw off rainbows in every direction. He was bare-chested, wearing only a pair of jeans. His rippling muscles flaunted his strength.

"Emma. Sweet Emma. You couldn't turn down a chance to get a good look at me again, could you?" The angel trailed a finger from his neck to his abdomen, licking his lips as he looked at her.

Jason was jealous. The feeling seemed compounded by the altitude. His anger had him shaking.

"Everett. Asshole Everett," Emma said, mocking him. "Looking at you makes me wish I could still work up a forceful puke."

She didn't look scared, but from this angle she did look dirty. These clouds were like cotton candy made from starlight. Emma was a grubby sock in a pile of bleached laundry. The vision that was Everett walked closer, and he made his pectoral muscles dance like a male stripper.

"How's your redemption going?" He gave an elaborate pout.

Emma snorted. "About as good as your erections were on Earth."

Everett flew toward her. Jason wanted to go to her side, fight for her, but the clouds that hid him had become a tight-fitting shroud. He struggled against them, but he couldn't move, couldn't help.

Emma tried beating her one floppy wing to gain some height, but it barely lifted her off her feet. Everett's out-of-place smile grew more menacing as he swooped closer. Jason felt his mind cry as Emma gave up on her wing and squared her stance. She curled her hands into fists. Her defense looked like someone planning to blow out a forest fire with one breath.

Emma!

Her words came to him again as his concern escalated. *"I am as you perceive me. This is how you want me to be."*

Jason shook his head and channeled his mental distress into something useful. As he began to picture her, she transformed. The bunny slippers became thigh-high leather boots. Jason made her a gladiator. He was even able to picture her wing dyed jet black. Her hands were soon wrapped around two coal-colored swords, as sharp as he could imagine them.

Everett stopped his threatening approach and set his feet close to, but not quite touching, the cloud-covered ground support.

"Oh, we're not alone?" Everett scanned the area in mock surprise, pretending to look for Jason. "Did your new boyfriend try to get in the backdoor of Heaven?"

Emma didn't turn, didn't acknowledge the change in Everett's demeanor. She dropped one blade and hoisted the other above her head. She charged at Everett, who merely snickered. A clear divider materialized to stop the blade's downward motion. Emma tossed the weapon and pounded on the barrier with her hands.

Everett began laughing, a deep, false-sounding noise. "Did you really think I wanted to fight? Emma, Emma, Emma. I come in peace. I'm here to offer you guidance in your time of need. Tell me, precious girl, what can I do for you?"

Emma ran a hand through her hair. Jason wrapped her hair in a ponytail for her mentally, appreciating the soft curve in her neck.

"You can go screw yourself, for starters." She paced behind the barrier, her eyes scanning the clouds and pausing on the spot where Jason was hidden.

"You know, I was listening the other day, and it seems there might be some development down on the rocks of Croton," Everett said. "Shame, the eagles will lose their habitat. Such is the way of the world."

Emma became a statue. This seemingly innocuous information about eagles had terrified her. "You won't touch him. You will *not* put your filthy hands on him."

Everett's voice went up an octave, as if he was talking to an infant. "Sammy-poo? Now, Emma I don't need to tell you what my job up here entails. You did it for so many years."

Everett approached the divider and placed a hand flat against it, offering his palm for her viewing.

Her voice came again—quiet and tremendously more threatening than when she'd been cursing. "Mention his name one more time, and I swear on your dirty soul I'll—"

Everett interrupted. "You can't do anything. Please. You have to save the soul of a morose half-breed. Good luck with that. I'm untouchable, and you know it." Everett put his mouth closer to the divider. "If *Sam's* time is up, then I do my job," he whispered. "And if his time is up in his next form, I'll *keep* doing my job."

Emma placed her hand against Everett's palm, then curled it into a fist and punched the divider.

Everett winked and blew her a kiss. "Reincarnation is crazy, isn't it? You die again and *again* and *again* and *again.*"

"You're a vicious bastard. I'll get up here soon. And I *will* rip your black heart out and deliver it to Hell where it belongs." Emma stepped away from Everett.

Only another man would see the longing in his eyes, the want. Jason's eyes widened as he registered Everett's buried feelings.

Everett pulled his hand away from their almost-touch and ran his fingers across his lips. "Your pain tastes like honey. I want more." His angel wings flared vibrant red.

He threw his arms above his head in a vicious cheer. "Run, pretty Emma! Try to fly! Save them all. I'll be waiting."

Everett smiled and twitched his head in the exact direction of Jason's cloud coffin. The bottom fell out and Jason started a breakneck fall to Earth.

Emma dove almost immediately after him, ignoring Everett's rising cackle of volcanic laughter. Jason's remaining cloud confines unwrapped, leaving him free to flail as he hurtled to Earth.

Emma was glad to see him provide resistance to the wind while she maintained her perfect diver's form, her wing tucked so she'd be aerodynamic. When she drew even with him, she wrapped her arm around his waist. He looked worried as she glanced down to gauge their speed.

"Do me a favor, half-breed, when I loosen my wing, grab the end and hang on." Emma concentrated as the wind filled in all the space around them.

Will it hurt you? Thinking was easier than yelling.

"No. Quit being thoughtful — it pisses me off." She sounded tough, but she had a hint of a smile.

Jason took a firm grip on the end of her wing. Her black feathers arched into a parachute above them and their drop slowed considerably. Emma tilted her head back to glare at the clouds above their heads.

"I wouldn't put a tornado or hurricane past that asshole." She was still angry, ready to fight.

Jason readjusted his hand, trying to find a softer way to hang on to her.

It's a long way down. Why don't you tell me why someone so evil is allowed in the gates of Heaven, and you're tossed out?

She focused on him, finally. "Everett knows how to work the system. Always has, always will."

Jason watched as the ground grew closer, more tangible. The morning light had gone from pink to light blue, brightening with its effort of bringing a new day. Emma's lips were so close to his, her body pressed so tightly against him, it was mind-numbing. She smelled like a honeysuckle and clouds. Thankfully she seemed to be ignoring his thoughts, or was completely immersed in her own.

"I hate him. There's nowhere in the world I can go to get away from him. I wish..." She seemed to remember to have a tough exterior as the ground got closer.

Jason's feet prepared for the impact. They were two wishes blowing back down to the land.

He thought in her direction. *Tell me what you wish. Please?*

Then Emma and Jason landed gently. He released her wing, hating how hard he'd had to hold on to make their impromptu landing gear successful. A bouquet of her feathers had come loose in his hand.

"I'm fine, half-breed. Really." She stretched her arms and wing at the same time.

She looked dispassionately at her leather battle armor. He quickly pictured her in a long, white-velvet dress. Simple and warm.

Tell me.

Emma liked her new outfit. He could tell by the way she ran her hand over the fabric.

"I wish I had a forgiving heart." She turned her back on him.

Her scar now looked more silver, like it might start to bleed again. He began to pray. *God, she needs strength.*

The wound became more like a tattoo again, healing.

She sighed and hugged herself. "I can't even pretend to forgive him. I should do better. I know I should."

Jason had no words or thoughts to help her. He couldn't imagine forgiving Everett for a damn thing.

Emma turned to face him, rubbing her temples. "Okay. Let me think here...I need to get you to the next event."

"Aren't we going to help Sam?" Jason stepped closer, imagining her in a downy white jacket and pair of mittens.

She shook her head. "I need to get back up there." She jabbed what looked like her knit-covered middle finger in the direction of her last confrontation. "To do that I need to get my wing back. So we have to fix you. Quick."

Emma began hover-walking in the direction of his house. "How the hell can I show a half-breed something he doesn't already know?" She directed her question to no one in particular.

Jason stopped in his tracks. She continued a few more paces until she registered his resistance. Sighing, Emma came back to where he stood.

"It would really help if you could minimize the diva moments here." She tapped her angel foot, and Jason put the bunny slipper back on it.

She looked at the bouncing ears and almost smiled.

Do I get any input here?

"You're not supposed to. I'm supposed to show you your past, present, and future. Then you suck it up and enjoy your freaking life." She pulled her hair out of its ponytail.

It tumbled over her shoulders. Jason wanted to curl his fist around it.

There's nothing you can show me, angel. I'm going to Croton to find an eagle. Jason stepped in the direction of the town. *You can either come with me or wait here for me to have some sort of massive personal revelation that'll launch you home for your battle.*

She let him get a good distance away before she followed, but she caught up quickly, gliding by his side.

"So are you just planning to stalk birds and look for one in danger?" She glanced at him, batting her eyelashes. When she heard the alarms go off in his head, she blew a kiss his way, playing with him.

Why don't you tell me a little about what we're looking for? I'm not sure I even understand what's happened to Sam. Jason gave her a sidelong glance, proving two could play the flirting game.

"Sam's my love. My best friend. Everett killed him a long time ago."

Jason wanted to think comforting thoughts, but he could only come up with rage.

Everett? From the clouds? With the wings? He's a murderer?

Emma clenched her teeth as she nodded. "He was a murderer before he was an angel. Begging for forgiveness is a powerful tool. God cleans many slates, including Everett's." Emma's mittened fists were tight balls. "When Sam died, he was given the option, as we all are, of reincarnation or Heaven. He chose to return to Earth in another form." Emma's voice was flat, like she was reciting a script she knew by heart.

Will he know you now? Like this?

Pain stabbed through her eyes, and she blinked to tune him out of her agony. "No. He's an eagle. He retains none of his human vestiges."

And you're saving him because...?

She turned to face him fully, stopping their trek.

"Because he still *is*. As long as I know *what* he is, I will do my damndest to protect him." She looked at the sky again, calculating, dreading.

"I'm sorry. I should've been more sensitive. Please accept my apology." Jason held a hand out in peace.

She nodded and resumed their march to Croton. She'd ignored his hand, but accepted his apology.

Why isn't God rebuking Everett for his obviously evil behavior? Jason had so many questions for this ethereal girl.

"God's in Hell." Emma finally reached for Jason's hand, and soon he hovered next to her. They were moving faster than a car on the highway, but exerting no effort at all.

"Are we starting the Apocalypse? Did I miss something?" Jason squeezed her hand.

Emma scanned the tops of the trees, looking for some*one* who'd become some*thing*. Their path ended at a huge, high cliff. The view of the sea was extraordinary.

She was distracted as she answered. "No, don't be silly. God goes to Hell to parlay for souls every great once in a while. He faces down the Devil for any being he feels has a scrap of goodness." Suddenly Emma whipped her head to the left.

Jason followed her gaze to a slowly circling eagle. It seemed to be hovering, using the strong wind off the cliffs to remain like a miracle in the sky.

"That's him." She was quiet, reverent.

She sighed with relief and Jason gave her hand a comforting squeeze. They watched together as the eagle that had been Sam dove for the water. He returned victorious with a fish clasped in his talons.

"Do you see that, Jason? He doesn't have guilt. He just has instinct." She squeezed his hand back, realizing this could be a teachable moment after all.

I should have more willpower. Last longer between feedings.

She turned from the eagle to look in Jason's green eyes. "Do you take more than you need? Do you hunt recklessly?"

He shook his head. He wouldn't dream of doing such things now. But in the beginning, the learning had been vicious.

But my impulses — they're far from pure or respectable.

Emma searched for the eagle again, and upon finding it she smiled. She let go of Jason's hand.

"That just makes you alive, Jason Parish, not bad," she said. "Impulses are only sins when you act on them, even though you know they're wrong."

Emma went as close as she could to the edge of the cliff, her new vantage point giving her a clear view of the bright yellow construction vehicles below. Jason joined her, mesmerized at the merciless slaughter of the trees.

"That's his home. His mate is there." She pointed to a clump of tall trees that were obviously next. Emma touched her hand to her mouth, stricken with grief over the eagles' future.

They mate for life, don't they?

"Yeah, he was a monogamous kind of guy." She watched the bird again perform his aerial show.

The eagle was obviously disturbed by the noises below. He couldn't figure out how to get to his nest. Jason had a thought, and he knew he was on to something as soon as Emma looked hopeful. He reached for his phone and dialed Dean. The investments Jason's mother had hidden around the world for them might finally do some good. The wealth had offered him little emotional comfort until now.

"Hey, I was wondering if you could do a little research for me." Jason gave his brother the exact location of the proposed condos. After a few minutes, he smiled. "Can you go ahead and buy them for me? Tell them all construction is to be ceased immediately… Thanks… No, I'm doing great."

They waited for a crystal silence, an end to the distant rumbling and banging. Jason tried his best not to stare and to stop thinking about what an angel might look like naked, but it didn't matter. Emma's eyes tracked her eagle love's anxious looping path through the sky, and her mind focused solely there.

Ninety minutes later, when the machines ground to a halt, the eagle circled once, twice, and was finally able to land. Emma turned to Jason and hugged him so quickly he was almost thrown off balance.

"Oh, thank you! Thank you! I can't believe you did that. It means the world to me." Emma bit her lip and wrinkled her nose, making Jason want to buy for her every condo ever built.

"I don't need them all," she said, smiling. "Half-breed, you *are* truly kind." She looked at his lips, and he could tell she was thinking about kissing him in thanks.

She looked over her shoulder, watching as her eagle returned to the sea to hunt. "I think he's getting food for the little ones. They have two of the cutest eaglets."

Emma turned to watch the free, flying Sam, safe now.

Jason couldn't help but feel smug. *Take that, Everett. Maybe money can buy some eagle love.*

Suddenly it seemed easy to change fate. He felt powerful and light. Jason wrapped his arms around his personal angel's waist. She allowed it and hugged his arms in her joy.

Then Jason heard a sound that tightened his arms into a restraint instead of an embrace. He put all his concentration into holding her, for he could tell she heard the same sounds as she tensed and flapped her wing. A hunter had stumbled into the clearing below.

The sheer cliff walls amplified the gunshot that rang out. When Sam was shot, his wings folded quickly. He fell like a rock. He fell like a broken dream into the choppy water.

Jason let Emma fall to her knees and claw the ground, sobbing Sam's name.

And he cursed Everett. He cursed Everett to Hell.

Emma heard screaming, but she had no idea the noise was coming from her mouth. The half-breed patted her and quickly ran by, launching himself off the cliff. Emma crawled to the edge, shocked at Jason's apparent suicide. But when she found him again he was already making effortless strokes toward Sam's eagle body.

Of course. He's not human.

She wished she could fly out and hover to help pluck her lover from the sea. Jason disappeared under the water and soon emerged bare-chested. He held his shirt as a makeshift shroud around Sam's body.

Emma knew she would be grateful for Jason's altruistic act, but she was dying inside, cursing and hating. Her feathers fell off in a deluge behind her. Only compassion would stop the flow, and she had none available.

The half-breed was fast, and soon he stood before her, cradling the lump in his arms. He was thinking, and Emma knew she should try to pay attention.

Finally, when he received no response from her, he spoke. "Emma, I'm so sorry."

She sat on the ground. She barely noticed the thick, white blanket that now protected her from the cold. He was imagining things for her still. *Like the elements could affect me.*

"What can I do?" He turned his attention back to the sopping wet bundle in his arms, tucking his shirt around the dead animal so she wouldn't see the carnage.

She put her knuckles to her lips. Seeing Sam cut down in front of her had brought back so much of her human pain. *Just as Everett intended. He set me up. He used Sam to throw me off the path back to Heaven.*

"Half-breed, my Sam is no longer in *that* body. The reverence with which you handle his corpse speaks to your good heart." Emma stood and decided to offer the being in front of her some of the kindness he'd shown.

With a flick of her wrist she forced the snow to form an eagle-sized sarcophagus. Jason stepped to the opening and placed the bundle inside. Emma summoned the strength, the courage, it took to defy Everett's intentions that she crumble, and she walked to the body. She removed Jason's shirt and felt her mind convulse with shock and pain. When she handed the shirt back to him, it was dry and clean. Emma took one feather from the bird's breast and tucked it in her hair. Her talisman. She would use the pain it held as the key to lock Everett in Hell.

She closed the snowy confines over the bird and stepped back. The same fiery snow that had transported her and Jason through time now took the remnants of a once glorious eagle somewhere else entirely. Jason bowed his head as if in prayer. Emma didn't bother to sneak into his mind to see if he actually was.

"Will he go on to the next life?" Jason watched as the smoke from the snow fire glittered and rose.

"I don't know. The time between lives is changeable. Right now Everett is in a place of great power. If Sam comes up for Judgment…" She couldn't put the horror she felt into words.

"He's doing your job? Is that what he said? What did you do, Emma?" She turned to face him, his green eyes so earnest in their desire for an answer.

She felt numb; she had nothing left after working to contain her anger. She could feel her faith dripping from her wound. She didn't want him to notice, to worry again. Emma nodded so he'd start walking. As she began to move, part of her heart tore away to stay with Sam in the last place his soul had felt joy.

They walked a distance before Emma answered. She was looking for something, looking for someone.

"I was a seraph. We're in the circle closest to God. It's a huge honor and a great responsibility. I have failed Him in my weakness. But maybe I can change that."

Finally, she heard what she was listening for: the mind of the hunter. That evil bastard who could take a father out of the sky and deny his eagle mate her forever with Sam—she would kill that man now. End him. Send the hunter to his Judgment.

Jason watched the hunter as well. His mind wanted to heal her, help her. She would use that to her advantage now.

"Jason."

His mind perked up because his name was on her lips.

"Can you run back to your house for a moment? I think your brother is having a problem. I'll meet you outside soon."

No, he's fine. What are you up to?

"Nothing. I just need a minute alone with that hunter." Emma touched the feather in her hair, and her plan made perfect sense: If she murdered this man, she'd go to Hell. If she went to Hell, she could tell God what was going on. And she could save Sam's soul from Everett's delusional wrath.

Jason's thoughts revealed his hurt. He'd figured out her intentions. "You can't. I won't let you," he said. "I'll take him down myself." Jason was on the hunt immediately.

"Half-breed, stop. You feed on humans, but you don't kill them like the others do. I know this. If you murder him, I won't be able to redeem you or myself."

He stopped and turned to face her. *You're in so much pain. You're willing to go to Hell to make things right. Will God take you back to Heaven if you murder this man?*

"That's nothing you need to worry about right now. Just don't be here for it. I don't want you to see what I can become." She hovered closer to the hunter. She could hear the man's thoughts now:

I can't believe I did that. I would never hurt an eagle. My God. Maybe I had a seizure?

Emma lost her nerve. Everett had touched this man's free will. He'd made the hunter do something he normally wouldn't.

"Everett's going to tear this joint up. God help me. Seriously." She turned her back on her almost-victim.

Jason followed at a respectful distance, letting her burn off her pain and anger. She heard him thinking of her dripping wound and praying for its healing.

She sighed deeply. Finally, in a clearing in the woods with the sun high in the sky, she tried again. She wasn't a quitter—never had been.

"Maybe I need to try something more immediate," she pondered. "I need something in the present I can take you to that will make you see the beauty of your soul."

Emma looked down at the fresh snow, seemingly littered with diamonds in its quiet. Only Jason's footprints led to the spot where they now stood. She listened to his mind. At the word "beauty" he'd pictured her in his arms. She arched an eyebrow, coming up with a quick fix. A sure-fire way to bliss? Sex.

"Kiss me, half-breed. Make me want to wrap my legs around your waist." She gave him a sensual stare.

Instead of melting him, her words gave him confidence. He closed the distance between them and pulled her to him with one strong arm. Jason kept his eyes on her lips as he let his unfiltered fantasies dance from his imagination to hers. She gasped at his creativity.

He trailed up her arm with his fingertips, stopping at the hollow of her throat. "Are you doing this because you want me? We just buried Sam."

Sam's name was a knife. Pain.

And then it was exactly what she wanted. She wanted this half-breed vampire to pound the torment out of her. She wanted him to bite her neck and feel every part of her body. Pleasure to combat agony. Kisses to heal the bleeding.

Emma hovered a bit higher so she could take his bottom lip in her teeth. His mental moan exactly matched the one he breathed into her mouth. She grabbed a fistful of his hair, tugging on it, demanding everything from him.

Say my name, angel.

"Jason...please."

CHAPTER 3

Her lips tasted like vanilla and something—he laughed a little when he realized it was angel food cake. He hadn't thirsted for anything other than blood and knowledge for so long that wild passion kicked him in the teeth.

She wrapped him in her arms, massaging, insisting he join her in her frenzied arousal. His body was more than willing to cooperate. But his mind could still hear her crying for her lost love. Her wails echoed in his conscience. He opened his eyes.

Maybe he could have taken her, slid the soft velvet away from her legs and felt her thighs with his hands, but then he saw the tear she was ignoring.

It shone with touches of metal, leaving a dusting of gold leaf on her cheek. He stopped kissing her and pulled her arms away from him.

She opened her eyes, angered. "Stop stopping! Kiss me again. *Don't you pity me!*" She stomped her foot, and the snow below her propelled into a little cloud.

He couldn't stop the kindness coming from his mind, but he knew she was misconstruing it.

I don't pity you, but an angel who's used to endless time might need a moment to breathe after…that.

He saw the eagle falling into the ocean again, before he could remind himself not to remember. Emma looked over Jason's shoulder, avoiding his crisp recall as best she could.

Meanwhile, Jason got busy putting her in something a little less tempting. He visualized her in a pair of flannel pajamas, complete with covered footies and zipped all the way to the top. He added whimsical bunnies, making sure each had a sweet face and pointy ears. *Maybe she'll smile at the bunnies.*

But she didn't even register the outfit change. Her gaze over his shoulder solidified from pain to hate. Revulsion and anger rolled off of her in waves. It was the same way she'd looked at Everett in Heaven.

Everett?

Jason spun and sure enough the angel, resplendent in a white tuxedo and fire red wings, was advancing on them. Jason had to shake off the blurring, uncomfortable feeling of being in the dark, being weaker. Everett headed for Emma with a single white rose.

Is he really here? Can he hear my thoughts like you?

"Yes and no." She stepped next to Jason.

She wanted to move in front of him, to put herself between the delightful-looking evil and her ticket to Heaven, but Jason held out a hand, warding her off.

"Well, jackass, sorry to see you here. What'd you do to Seraph Gabriel?" Emma was full of moxie, but as Jason looked at her, she and her new footie pajamas rapidly became transparent.

The sight of Everett on Earth was causing her to lose faith—again. A quick glance behind her revealed a pool of mercury, expanding by the second.

Everett smiled like an excited groom. "Emma, sweetheart. Don't lose all hope. Surely you can still stop me, right? Right?"

Everett swooped closer as Emma fell to her knees. She was fading. Anger whipped through Jason. He hated Emma kneeling before Everett. Jason placed himself between the angels.

Can I hurt him?

There was no response from Emma.

"Jason Parish. Look at you! Are you chivalrous or were you just looking to get laid?" Everett's expanded his wings even further, showing like a peacock.

"Step back from us. How are you here?"

Jason needed time. He needed to restore her hope, get her advice.

"That's the reason your pretty angel slut collapsed. She knows I'm in charge now. Which is pretty hilarious, because God is in Hell. And the Devil? He's hanging on to God for a bit." Everett ended his tirade with a victorious chuckle.

"Emma?" he continued. Everett leaned to his left so he could look at her.

Jason didn't dare take his eyes off the thing in front of him.

"Sweetheart? Come with me now. You can sit at my right hand. I'll give you whatever you want. Sam back by your side? Done. World peace? Done. You naked with me? Done."

Jason punched Everett so viciously in the face that his red wings rippled with the force. Jason didn't wait for relief that he could touch the angel to set in, he just jumped on Everett like he was prey. The white rose tumbled from Everett's hand and was lost in the snow. Jason used his speed and ridiculous strength to land several punches, but he knew he was outmatched.

Darting away, Everett flapped his massive wings and rubbed his mouth. Jason backed up to reassess. Everett hovered just above the height to which Jason could jump.

"You pack a wallop, parasite. I hope you enjoyed those hits, because you'll never get another," Everett growled.

Jason had to fight the urge to run as Everett powered up. Energy pulsated around him. His wings and hands crackled with lightning and dominance.

Stand still, he told himself. *For every second he fights me, she's safe.*

Jason risked a look at her, wanting her beautiful form to be the last thing he knew in his mind.

Emma was gone.

Oh God, please, no! She's already gone?

He turned. The jet-engine noise emanating from Everett demanded cowering, but Jason stood proud. Suddenly Emma hovered in front of him, arms thrown wide, using herself to protect him. She was hit instantly — a river of hot blue current lighting her like the electric angel on top of a Christmas tree.

Though she deflected the current Jason still felt like he was being electrocuted; he was powerless to move at all. Then it stopped, and the silence was as loud as the cracking sound the deadly angel had produced.

Emma collapsed at his feet. Jason moved as soon as he could, knelt and pulled her head into his lap. Everett flew angrily above their heads, the beat of his massive wings causing Emma's hair to blow away from her face. Her gray eyes opened slowly, painfully.

"I wake up to your face a lot lately." Her voice sounded strong.

Are you okay? What the hell just happened?

She shook her head, as if to say "not now." Instead she said, "Heads up."

Everett was lower now, reeling and angry. "You stupid, stupid girl! Well, guess what? That won't work either. You protect *him?* That thing? It's like a tick, a gnat, a sponger."

Emma lifted her hand to give Everett the finger. Jason leaned over and gave her insulting gesture a light kiss. She switched her focus from the outrage above her to Jason's face. Emma let her other fingers join the middle one and laid them on his cheek.

As she spoke, her eyes filled with the same gold-colored sheen that had been in her tears. "Don't listen to him. You're a miracle. If nothing else, I'm so very glad we've met."

Fire began to rain down, with little flames in place of water drops. Jason covered her body from the onslaught.

"My half-breed umbrella, it's okay. He's already done the worst he can do."

Jason tried to reassure himself with her permanence, her solidness in his arms.

Everett hollered with rage, the ground shaking from the verbal onslaught. "You think so, Emma? I offer you everything and you think the worst I can do is send your soul to Hell?" Everett arced the sky with lava. "Wait until Sam comes to Judgment! Ha! It'll be spectacular — the pain I'll give him to live through, over and over again. Your heart will explode in your chest, Emma. You don't even know what pain tastes like yet. But you will. You will."

Jason was mesmerized by Everett's just-out-of-reach anger. He looked ludicrous in his tuxedo now, the veins popping in his rage-filled neck.

"Don't look at him, Jason. Kiss me. Nothing will hurt him more." Emma moved her hand to Jason's neck and pulled his face to hers.

Jason felt like he was trying to ignore a natural disaster, but he did so because she asked.

"That's right. Good. Now kiss me *hard.*" Emma smiled and licked her lips.

Jason pulled her whole body closer, supporting her back and cradling her head. She'd told him one time too many in his book, so he took great care to kiss her deeply. She still tasted like angel cake, which delighted him — and his loins — immensely.

He could almost forget that Everett was cracking the atmosphere like an egg above their heads. Jason held her close, pulling her into a hug. He ended their kiss and looked at the blood red sky. Everett's fury had tinted the blue out of the horizon. Emma's breath was hot on his skin, and she cuddled deeper into his chest. The wallop of Everett's wings echoed as he beat them against the air, taking himself back to Heaven.

Where's he going?

"I don't know." Her words moved like a pulse along his neck.

What gave you back your faith? Your anger that God's a prisoner in Hell?

She pulled away from him, looking into his face with more softness than he could ever have hoped for.

"No. But that does suck." She put both hands on his face like he meant something, like he was precious and fragile.

Was it the punching? If he didn't fly away I would have pounded him some more. Jason smiled, pleased.

"Not that either… No, don't be sad. It was thrilling, really." She sat up straighter. "It was when you thought about saving me a few seconds of his wrath. That made me whole. That made believe."

She leaned forward and kissed him because she wanted to — not to piss off Everett, not to forget Sam. She kissed Jason to kiss Jason.

He stroked her hair and smiled. It felt so much better this way.

With the evil angel gone, the blue crept back to the sky. Everett's anger was far away, at least for now.

What did that blast do to you?

She stood up and dusted off her footie pajamas. "Although I love these, can I have something else now?" She held her hand out to help him off his knees. He didn't need assistance, but indulged in her touch anyway.

He kissed her hand once he was standing. *You're avoiding an answer. Please tell me?*

She looked reluctant, but maybe it was her nature to be honest. Maybe she didn't have a choice because of her wing, her physical connection to Heaven.

"That blast was meant to take you to Hell." She pulled his fingers to her mouth, taking a turn at kissing his hand.

And you stopped that? I'm surprised he gave up so easily.

She nodded and motioned to her outfit. Jason put her in white jeans and a soft sweater, topping the outfit with a soft faux-fur coat. Her hiking boots were white with gold shoelaces.

She held out her foot, laughing. "These are pimp."

Angels are allowed to say "pimp"?

"Probably not." She stepped into his arms again.

He held her, kissing the top of her head.

What did the blast do to you?

She sighed, and he waited.

Finally, she gave him the answer he sought. "When my time's up here, I'll be taking your place in Hell. Everett was determined to send someone there, and since he hit me, rather than you…" She took a deep breath before continuing. "He left because he'll need to power up again."

Jason squeezed her tighter. "Why did you do that? That's not fair. *I* was trying to protect *you.*" He switched to thinking, a little afraid to hear his next question out loud.

Emma, what are we going to do now?

"I don't really know. This is unprecedented. Seraph Gabriel was the failsafe. I don't know how he lost control." Emma sighed and stepped away from Jason's comforting embrace.

Is Everett planning to end the world? Could it possibly be that bad? Jason wanted to keep her in his arms. This talk of Hell and angels made him want her close.

Emma let her feet touch the ground. Her hiking boots left scrolling, star-shaped treads in the soft snow as she began to walk. Jason followed as if she had his heart on a leash.

"Everett wants Earth to be Hell. He wants Heaven to be Hell. He's like a Devil's minion." Emma tilted her head back, and her long, blond curls skimmed her rump. She held her hands to her mouth as if the simple motion would deliver her words to the clouds. "Everett is the Devil's bitch!" She turned her hands into tight fists. "I can't think of a way to stop him, Jason."

Jason hated his next question, but the filter his mouth gave him did not apply to his thoughts. *Will you know when your time is up?*

Emma reached behind her almost thoughtlessly and stroked her remaining wing. Her hand was covered with glitter when she pulled it away.

"My wing will be gone, and after that I'm on the express train to Hades."

Jason tried to ignore the fear in her eyes. *Everything seems normal now. Is your task with me finished?*

"No! No, it's not. You're a genius. Of course! We've been to your past, and we're looking at your completely sucktastic present."

Some things here are very fantastic. He interrupted her with his thought. He pictured her kiss again — the last one, the one that had tickled his barren soul.

She walked forward and put her glittering hand on his. "The future! The future's next. We'll get to see if we're successful or not!" She curled her wing around him.

Before he could become enveloped in her scent and her power, Jason shook his head. *Can Everett stop this?*

"Everything's up for grabs, but the mission is always the same: three capsules of time to be investigated. We have to try."

He held on to her hand more tightly, knowing the disquieting time travel was about to hit. She put her lips on his and they watched as the snowy, blue day inked up with darkness. Twirling, whooshing, and the feeling he might come out of his skin surrounded him. The thud was violent this time, and Jason fell onto his back. Emma landed on top of him. The smell from the future was overwhelming. The odor of rotting bark filled the air.

The winter scene was a topsy-turvy kaleidoscope of color. The snow was greenish with gray tints. The sky was a deep, red velvet. The silence hurt their ears.

Where are the animals? Jason thought as soon as he placed the abnormality.

"There are none. No life. Oh my God." Emma didn't get up. She looked around, her hair brushing across his face like lace.

A slow, dragging slither captured their attention and broke the alarming silence. From their prone position, the two time travelers watched Dean dragging the corpse of a woman through the snow, leaving a rut.

Jason could not believe his eyes. *Dean has killed? He's not covering his tracks? What the hell?*

Emma pinned him down at the shoulders. "Hold tight, we're going back." She started to curl her wing again.

"No, Emma! Stop. I need to see where he's heading. Please? We came all this way—maybe finding out about here will help us then. Or now. Or whatever. Come on, we've got to hurry. He's picking up his pace."

Jason held tight to Emma's hand, remembering he had to maintain contact, and dragged her unwillingly behind him. *He's on his way back to our house. How far in the future did you take us?*

"One hundred years." Her voice was flat.

"Well, my brother's still here, so that's got to be good, right?" Jason turned to take in her face as she answered.

"No, sweetheart. This won't be good." She seemed resigned that Jason would see the vision through to the end.

Jason followed Dean, puzzled. He answered all his own questions using Emma's power to read Dean's thoughts. He heard the frantic panic in Dean's mind.

*"Not fair. Not fair. All that's left is this one, and she's been dead for days.
There may not be enough to feed one of us. Never mind all three. How do I
pick which of us gets to eat? That's not fair. Not fair. Not fair."*

Jason was surprised at the clatter in Dean's mind. The repetition
seemed so out of character for his meticulous, organized brother.

The half-breed finally arrived at the Parish residence—or what used
to be the Parish residence. The exterior was now in complete disarray. There
were no cars in the driveway.

"I can't believe they still live here—after all this time," Jason said,
gazing at the house in confusion.

"Is there anything I can do to keep you from going in the house?"
Emma squeezed Jason's hand, but he was single minded.

Dean bent and picked up the corpse, throwing it over his shoulder.
His strength seemed diminished. He opened the door to the living room,
and Emma and Jason slipped in behind him before the loud click closed
the half-breeds in their horrible world.

Dean tried halfheartedly to instill some manners in his brother. "If
we take small sips, we can each have a little." Dean held his hands out as
he spoke, an offering and surrender with one gesture.

Jason had the bizarre experience of standing in the same room with
his future self. The eyes of the self he saw were vacant. His hands had
formed permanent fists. Seriana was barely moving, strewn on the couch
like a forgotten doll.

Then the sickness in his mind filled the room. Jason had to guess no
longer. His diseased future brain was on a loop. Interspersed with nonsense
and children screaming were the events that had brought the Parishes to
the squalor in which they now lived. Future Jason ran through the list of
appalling events like a mantra, over and over:

First Emma was my angel.

Angel went to Hell.

Sky turned red and animals died.

Then we ate the people.

Then we eat the people.

Emma pulled on his arm. "Please, please? Can we go?"

Jason watched his own face as if it were a carnival mirror. Future
Jason spotted the cold body and a toxically competitive look crossed his
face as the smell of dead meat hit him between the eyes.

Dinner.

Future Jason jumped with an agility his brother seemed to lack. Seriana held her throat; she was too weak to move. Being crazy made future Jason strong and selfish. He tore into the neck and growled when he discovered the blood no longer flowing and hot.

Jason let Emma pull him from his future self. She brought him outside, but the sight would stay forever in his mind.

He stood still as the beautiful angel went through her motions, kissing his lips and wrapping him in her wing as if it were a toasty beach towel. But not even her magic could warm him now.

They landed softly in the present, in the clearing where they'd fought Everett together.

Jason stood in shock. Emma bit her lip and looked toward the sky.

"You son of a bitch! You knew what we'd see. That's why you didn't stop us, bastard!" Emma beat on Jason's chest, trying to pull him out of his instant depression. "Don't let him win, Jason. Please? Can you understand that the future's always subject to change? Those things you saw? Those were weapons for him."

He felt her hands warm on his face. Finally he looked into her deep gray eyes. She was frantic and determined.

"That wasn't you. That wasn't you! You couldn't ever do those things. I know you." Emma put a kiss on his lips, trying to get him to see it her way, feel it her way.

Beautiful angel, don't you see? That's already lurking inside me. I'll outlive my brother and sister and everything on earth. It'll be me eating cockroaches like popcorn at the end of time.

"I won't let that happen," Emma swore. "You have to trust me. I believe in you. Honestly, you're good. You are! They wouldn't have delivered me to you if you weren't worth saving." Emma tried to touch more of his skin, warm him from the outside in.

Jason strained to keep his mind from spiraling downward. *All I have is now. All I have is right now. That's what I believe in.*

Emma took a steadying breath. "That'll have to do."

She stepped away from him again, pacing just above the snow. Goodness flickered from her like a firefly's glow.

I'm selfish. God, you went to Hell, and all I can think about is me. Tell me what I can do to help you.

"Heaven and Hell are changeable. Hell might be the best place to be right about now. If I was done instantly, if my wing disappeared right now, maybe I could get to God." Emma reached over her shoulder and gave her glistening wing a hard yank. She yelped with pain.

"Wait! Emma, can you rip your own wing off? Stop." Jason rushed to her and held her arms. If the wing was gone, so was she.

"What about me? Can you kill me? Surely I'll go to Hell, and I can try to save God." Jason tried to imagine himself saving the world, and his vision fell flat.

She shook her head and looked down. Jason had changed her outfit again. This time to an elaborate strapless gown. The shimmering fabric reached her ankles. She now wore impossibly high-heeled glass slippers.

Are you cold? I'll fashion you a wrap.

"Glass slippers? Truly Jason, the way you see me makes me blush." She clicked the heels together and smiled at him. "I'm not cold."

Jason loved how the dress fluttered around her as she came near him. He held an arm out, and she offered him her hand. Jason twirled Emma so her skirt flared. She was a glorious dancer, as if he'd expect anything else.

"No, you wouldn't go to Hell," Emma said. "What did I tell you? Heaven isn't safe right now." She let him wrap her in his arms, dipping her to complete the impromptu dance. "I need to go, and I know what you have to do for me now."

Anything, beautiful angel, anything.

"Someone very, very strong can rip an angel's wing off. Someone who just promised me anything can hasten my trip to Hades."

Jason forgot to pull her out of the dip. *I can't. I won't. I will not do that.*

"You can and you will. What if this is the whole reason you're the kind of half-breed you are? What if you're meant to help me save the world?" Emma put her hands on his chest, trying to smile.

Send you to the Devil? What's he even like?

Emma rolled her eyes. "Satan makes Everett look like a boy scout."

She was serious once more. This choice was up to him. He was the only one who could see her, the only one who could touch her.

"Jason, I'm positive Everett would never see this coming. You have to rip off my wing."

Jason pulled her to standing, confused and angry. *How could I possibly ruin someone so majestic? How can I protect you if you're in Hell?*

Emma ignored his questions. "We have to move — and fast."

Do you have a plan?

"I'm going to have to trick the Devil to save God." She bit her lip as if this was no more irksome than an unpaid parking ticket.

She held her small shoulders straight, and Jason almost believed they alone could carry the burden of rescuing the world.

CHAPTER 4

*J*ason clenched his fists. *This is a decision I can't make at the drop of the hat.*

He tried to picture holding her down to tear off her wing, and it was heartbreaking. He put his troubled eyes on her beautiful face. *How can you ask me to hurt you?*

She smiled. "Shh. Don't be sad. It's just you and me against the Devil and Everett. What's scary about that?"

Jason put his hands to his temples and rubbed, trying to come up with a great excuse to keep her, a solution that made sense. *I wish I could just stop everything for a minute and focus. Everything's so scattered right now.*

His feelings for her were intense and quick, but she obviously loved someone else. Falling for this angel would only break his heart.

She squinted and tapped a finger on her lips. "I wonder…" She held her hands out and the snow came to her. She molded it with a few graceful swipes and soon held what looked like a sparkling white remote control, with diamonds in lieu of buttons. She smiled; apparently its appearance made her genuinely happy.

"Jason, I could be wrong, but Everett might not have control of my gifts as a Christmas Angel. They were gifts from God." She looked closely at the remote she'd made.

"Well, you've taken me to the past, present, and future. What else is there? Either I have an enlightening moment, or you've failed." Jason hated how the logic fell into place. Each coherent thought made her slip further into transparency.

Please, don't leave. You feel like air to my soul. Please. God.

At the word "please," she clarified. And the word "God" she shimmered again. Her eyes softened.

"I have a few more tricks up my sleeve. Well, I'm not wearing sleeves now, but if I were…"

Jason wrapped her in a soft, white trench coat. He took his time tying the knot at her waist. She had generous sleeves now, with plenty of room for as many tricks as she needed to keep her with him.

She chuckled. "You have all my bases covered, huh?" She walked closer to him, his intense eyes watching her every movement.

He shrugged, as if imagining her every comfort was nothing at all.

"Well, not all of the Christmas Angel's tools, if you will, are publicized." She tapped the remote with her other hand.

Jason raised an eyebrow. She held the remote up so he could see it. Despite its unusual construction and adornments, it looked like a simple TV controller.

She put her hand on his smooth jaw. "I have a pause button. We can think here, with privacy." She twirled so her back was to him. "Hold me tight, half-breed."

Jason complied, grabbing the knot on her trench coat. Her wing fluttered harmlessly. He put his mouth close to her ear, wishing he could whisper something meaningful, but he had no words that fit his dreams.

She held up the remote victoriously. "Suck on this, Everett, you panty-wearing little girl!"

She pressed the pause button as Jason laughed. He felt lighter, further away from the fate he'd glimpsed. He still held her when it happened, and it was such a shock he almost jumped. His heart beat quickly and steadily again, like it had when he was human. She laughed at his reaction, covering her mouth because she knew she was being rude.

The snow eclipsed the trees and the blue sky bleached away, leaving the travelers as the only color on a completely clean, white canvas.

You paused the whole world?

"I did. Well, you did. Your wish for more time to consider your options was granted." She slid the remote into her pocket and turned so her mouth was dangerously close to his. "We're here for a bit, but not for long. It's like pausing live TV, sort of. Eventually, we'll be snapped back to the present moment."

She turned in his arms like a ballerina in a jewelry box. "Breathe, Jason. Take a breath."

Jason looked at her like she was crazy but complied. Air rushed into his lungs, and he remembered how necessary the reflex had been when he was... *human?*

"You feel human, and so do I. Touch." Emma opened her coat and took his hand. Her heart thumped against his palm. "But it's kind of like a mirage. I wanted you to feel the relief of taking a deep breath as a human. Was it worth it?"

He could concentrate on nothing but her warm skin under his fingertips. Breathing her scent was suddenly not about evaluating prey, but about another sort of sustenance, flavored with her.

Yes. Absolutely.

"So, think. You can create here like you have with my outfits."

The empty space was instantly black as night. The ground and sky were littered with stars, and in the center was a huge, four-poster bed covered in silks and velvet. Music fell around them, a piano picking out emotions and setting them free like butterflies to soar.

Jason smiled as she gasped. Red rose petals fell like autumn leaves around them. The moment the petals touched the ground they faded away.

The knot in her belt slowly unraveled until the ends hung separately. Emma started to giggle and held out her arms. He took charge of her jacket like a magical gentleman. The bottom button pushed itself through the hole that had held it captive. She stopped giggling as his mind moved to the next button. Each one was set free in an achingly slow process. The material slid off her arms and soon she was before him in her strapless gown again. She winked at him and blinked like a genie granting a wish. His casual clothes transformed into a finely tailored tuxedo. He stopped mid-stride.

Two can play at this game here?

She held a hand out and caught a rose petal.

She put it to her face and sampled the fragrance. "Heavenly, and I should know."

Jason licked his lips and held out both hands — one filled with a bottle of champagne, the other held two crystal glasses.

Would you care for a drink?

She nodded, thrilled that he was embracing the pause. The world might be about to crumble around them, and he was dreaming up alcohol. He handed her a glass and kept his eyes on her lips as he filled it. When he was done, she reached for the bottle and filled his glass.

Jason held his crystal up for a toast. "To never waking from this dream."

Emma touched her glass to his, the clink echoing off the night sky that was their backdrop.

She looked pleased and added, "To using this break in the spirit it was intended."

They swallowed the bubbling liquid, and Jason turned down the music and conjured up a large, red couch. The pillows were huge and inviting.

Have a seat. As much as I would relish ravishing you on that bed…

They both looked at it, the testament to his lust that it was.

…I can't take you. Your pain's too much.

She blinked hard, the emotion he'd brought to the surface punching her in the now-beating heart. Jason disappeared the glasses and bottle, and they both sat.

"Tell me why Everett seems so fixated on you." Jason reached out for her hand.

Emma let him comfort her with the simple gesture.

"I'm here for you, not the other way around." She leaned back into the couch.

Things change.

She sighed and tilted her head to look at the fake stars.

"Everett was my fiancé a long, long time ago. He didn't take kindly to his property being with another man," Emma said.

Jason squeezed her hand gently and tried to quiet the jealousy in his mind so she could think. He hadn't expected such deception from a woman who'd become an angel.

"You judge me so quickly?" She pulled her hand from his. "You and Everett should have a chat. You might be good friends."

She was angry. More than that, she was hurt—his opinion of her must mean more than she was letting on.

I don't want to insult you, but wouldn't it be better to stay true to the man whose wedding proposal you'd accepted?

"Men. You're all just suckers for putting your stamp on something. Peeing on your trees. You know what I say to that, half-breed? Up yours and your sanctimonious, self-serving bullshit. Hot damn. I even wanted to kiss you." She paced on the stars, stomping through the black sky.

I'm just saying I can understand why Everett was angry—not that I agree with his actions at all.

She was furious. "Where the hell's my jacket? I'm leaving you and your throbbing bachelor pad. Take your flower petals and stick them up your ass."

Jason rose from the couch and stepped bravely toward the vexed seraph.

I don't want you to leave. Please. I want to know what happened so maybe it can help us save God. You do want to save God, right? This isn't all about your dating style.

She put a hand to her forehead and closed her eyes. She looked like she might cry. Jason stood in front of her, wishing he could kick himself. He was jumping to conclusions instead of listening, letting her talk.

She heard his remorse and finally opened her eyes. "Everett asked my father for my hand in marriage. My father agreed. I never had a choice."

She hugged her arms around herself, and Jason noticed her wing was gone. In the mirage they were exploring, she'd left it out. She wanted to be human with him, just a girl and a boy.

"I was the only female in our family. Even though I'd been treated and acted like one of the boys, when I was sixteen my father demanded that I garb myself in my fanciest dress and curl my hair." She stepped to the couch and sat back down.

Jason hurt for her. She'd been just a child, commanded to be something she wasn't.

Emma clasped her hands in her lap. "You're right. I wasn't a fancy lady. I wanted to swim in the river with my best friend. I wanted to ride my horse all day. Sam was with me for all those things. He was my childhood, and then he became the only reminder I had of who I used to be." She formed a bird with her fingers as a child might, a sweet comfort for a lost soul. "My father let the engagement linger for a few years, and Everett was happy to see my dowry grow while my father prospered. Those two years with Sam, I pretended I wasn't engaged. I pretended Everett didn't come by once a month to stick his tongue down my throat and whisper exactly what he expected from me as a wife in my ear." Emma shuddered, and Jason raged.

"The night before our wedding, Everett stopped by for what he felt was his due," Emma continued. "He called it 'The Test.' I told Sam not to show up. I told him I was ready to take it, but he wouldn't listen. He crawled in the window when I was fighting Everett off, begging to have my innocence last one more night. Everett won that battle when he shot Sam in the chest. He claimed he was defending me. I held Sam's head while he died. Imagine my surprise when I saw that bastard, Everett, wearing a set of angel wings in Heaven." Emma clenched her fists again.

Jason took a deep breath. *How did you die?*

Emma looked off into the distance for a while, stuck in the night of Sam's first death. "I put off the wedding. I wanted to bury Sam, and I used that as my excuse. It even worked for a few months. I spent a lot of time riding Feisty, my favorite horse. Everett noticed that as well."

Emma stood again, riled up from remembering her human years. "One night the barn mysteriously caught fire. I died trying to save Feisty. Neither of us made it out." Emma hung her head.

I am so, so sorry. You lost so much.

She shrugged. "It's old news. When I got to Heaven, I was able to ride Feisty in the clouds. So that was nice."

"And Sam? Were you able to be with him?" Jason patted the couch, encouraging her to sit.

She didn't. She closed her eyes just a fraction too late, and Jason saw the betrayal there.

"You get a choice when you cross over to the other side: eternity in Heaven or reincarnation. The options are clearly laid out for you by Seraph Gabriel. I picked eternity, of course. Sam's path was a different one." She turned her back to Jason.

Oh.

And then it made sense. This beautiful, cursing angel was full of love for a man who kept choosing life again and again over an eternity with her.

He made the wrong choice. You're worth all the time in the world.

She shrugged. He could see her shoulders shaking. The mirage of being human finally allowed her to cry for a love that might have been mostly one sided. Jason stood behind her, ghosting his hands over her shoulders. He was not willing to touch her without her permission — not after that tale.

"Even if I did love him more than he loved me, I'm dedicated to him. I'm in a position to protect him and any soul he loves. Well, I was in that position." She sighed and turned, her tears still tinged with gold from her magic.

"May I hold you? Please?" Jason opened his arms.

She answered by stepping into them, cuddling deep into his tuxedo, and putting her head against his chest, over his enchanted heart.

How much longer do we have, Emma?

"Enough."

"So tell me why I'm here," she said. "I've been around you enough now to know you're a stand-up guy — although technically not a guy, I guess, half-breed. Why did you need a Christmas Angel? You must have been on the docket before Everett started all his stupidity. You're a legit assignment, just a really difficult one."

Jason shrugged. "Of all the things that have happened over the last handful of hours, that's the part that makes the least sense."

"Really? An angel falling from the sky? Time travel? All of that is more believable than God being concerned about you?" She traced his lips with her fingers.

Jason's jaw tightened, and he released her from the hug. "Don't you know what I am? Where I come from? Surely the history of half-breed minions reached even your lofty perch."

"Well," Emma said slowly. "Angels do seem to think poorly of Earth-bound half-breeds, but I was never one for gossip." She pulled Jason over to sit on the couch again. "I don't know of any half-breed angels personally, but — how can I explain this? That doesn't mean they couldn't exist. When souls come to Heaven for the afterlife, they're whitewashed of their previous sins, and angels are supposed to focus on them just as they stand in front of us. It's considered rude to inquire about the past. We all start anew."

"Which would explain why Everett got so far after having been cruel to you in your time on Earth," Jason said.

"So why should you be last in line for kindness, Jason? Tell me." Emma sat on her hands and leaned toward him.

Jason smiled into her attention. "And what if you hate me after I explain? Telling you what you don't know might be the biggest mistake I could make."

She looked away. "It takes a lot for me to hate someone. More than you could ever do, I promise."

Jason exhaled audibly. "Okay. To honor what you've shared, I'll tell you why I'm destined for Hell whether Everett sends me or not. Long before I formed my first words, I was evil." He rose to give himself some distance from her distracting goodness.

"My mother was alone when she raised Seriana, Dean, and me. We were told our father died in a mining accident. We thought that's why we were different. If only it had turned out to be that simple…"

Jason paused to look warily at Emma, who seemed enraptured by his story and made no move to speak. He had no choice but to keep going.

"My mother was really beautiful, and she was always good to us. But there were nights when she turned pale and shaky on her feet. We called those her 'episodes.' She'd leave the house to find a 'doctor,' who we never met, and a few hours later she'd return with rosy cheeks and an almost manic happiness. What did we know? We were children. We moved from place to place a lot—usually when the whispers about mother's nighttime activities hit the rumor mill. I heard the word 'prostitute' on regular occasions long before I knew what it meant."

Emma stood and crossed her arms. Jason was relieved to find she still looked sympathetic.

"She always told us, 'Home is where the people you love are. And you children will always have each other.' She left herself out of the equation when she spoke of our future. Eventually, school became too tricky, I guess, so Mother schooled us at home," he continued. "She supplemented our education with trips to museums and foreign countries. As we got older, we started to realize she was really uncomfortable around people, and we figured this was why we always traveled at night. But even though she wasn't able to interact with them very well, she wanted us to love humans—I see that now. We stopped by hospital nurseries all over the world where she'd lecture us about how each soul should be valued, how each human had intrinsic worth."

Jason paused for a moment, lost in thought. "The other thing I remember about our travels was her long, red suitcase. It was always with us, but we never saw her open it, and we were forbidden to touch it.

"Then it all made sense a few months after Dean's nineteenth birthday. My brother had been getting paler and weaker every day since the anniversary of his birth." Jason nodded and sat back down. The tale made him anxious and restless.

Emma sat down as well and let her hand cover his.

This part of the story was the part he feared—the part that changed his perspective about good and evil and his rightful place on that scale.

"Mother sat us down on the beds in a boarding house in France and told us we weren't just exploring the world, we were escaping our grandfather's clutches. At first, I was excited to know we had more family, but then she explained how our grandfather was also the man who murdered our father. Our father had been a miner before he met my mother, but he didn't die in an accident.

"Mother told us she was a half-breed minion, as was her mother before her, and on back for generations. She told us how she'd screamed in horror as Grandfather—also a half-breed—drained the life from Father right in front of her. She said he told her he'd be back for us after we turned nineteen, and she'd better train us as killers. If we weren't, he said he'd just breed us and have us killed."

"Breed you?" Emma gasped.

"You might not want to touch me during this next part," Jason said. He glanced at her and bit his lip.

Emma squeezed his hand hard and shifted so she could put her arm around him as well. "I'm not scared."

"Very well. Nineteen generations ago, a minion named Violent escaped from Hell and mated with a human. The child created from that union was a tiny, twisted half-breed—like a vampire except born that way, not created. Violent was able to feed it the blood it craved, and so generation after generation, Violent's legacy has lived on to bring horror after horror into this world. We have no way of knowing how many descendants she has, but right now, you're holding one of them."

Emma touched his face and understanding filled her eyes. "But you say you had a normal childhood."

"Oh, yes. Each new generation gets one more year to live a seemingly normal human life before their true nature overtakes them and they become parasites. I even had a few friends, back in the day. I didn't change until I was nineteen. My childhood was actually fairly stellar, considering Mother was a vampire. The only example she had for a parent was her father, Vittorio, who sent her to boarding school until it was close to the time for her change. Then he brought her as an almost-eighteen-year-old back to his lair to introduce her to all the half-breeds he'd collected. He said he was starting an army. He wanted to dominate the humans and take over the Earth. He and his half-breeds were feeding on miners, particularly the ones that worked at night. The caves were a perfect hunting ground.

"Mother endured her eighteenth birthday and the change it brought, and she was presented with her first victim as a prize. Vittorio carried my future father's unconscious body to her and closed her bedroom door. Despite Mother's dark thirst, when my father opened his eyes and smiled at her, she couldn't bring herself to feast on him. She let him escape from her window and promised to find him in the mines the following night.

"Vittorio was furious when he discovered what she'd done. He'd expected her, as his own child, to be even more ferocious than the specimens he'd collected. He also believed the twentieth generation of half-breed minions descended from Violent and her human love would be the strongest of all—the ones to lead the species to domination over humans.

"But then it was my grandfather who inadvertently made my mother realize there was another way. He tried to explain his disappointment in her by telling her half-breeds could subsist on just a little blood from a human, but if she didn't kill her victims, the humans wouldn't fear her species. 'Fear wins half the battle, Rebecca!' he told her.

"When Mother found Father the next night in the mine tunnels, she shared with him everything—everything she shouldn't have. Lo and behold, my father had a deep interest in science, and together they figured out how much blood she needed and how to get it without killing her victim.

"One evening, they threw caution to the wind, and Mother and her red suitcase escaped with Father. She married him in a quiet chapel the next day. The poor priest had no idea the sacrilege he was performing—wedding a monster to humanity."

Emma looked appalled. "Surely you can't call your own mother a monster? After all she'd done?"

"All she'd done?" Jason asked, eyes wide. "Mother had not one, but three babies with my father, even though she knew the plans fate had in store for us. No matter how diluted the minion genes become, where there's even a hint of them the outcome is always the same: vampire. She claimed my father was looking for a cure. But Dean, Seriana, and I were just babies when my grandfather and his clan caught up to my love-struck parents and killed my father—his way of proving to my mother that humans were worthless after all. So there was no cure for my brother and sister, no cure for me," Jason said, his eyes glassy now. "Just the promise of a grisly demise if we didn't become the worst type of evil."

"I guess Mother prepared us as best she could," Jason said more softly after a moment. "She taught us everything she and Father had learned about feeding without killing humans, and Dean has continued their work. He's obsessed. He's practically put himself through medical school, one book at a time." Jason laughed, but then fell silent.

"She also told us how to kill other half-breeds, in case Vittorio found us like he'd promised. Do you know we need to be crushed?" he said, suddenly addressing Emma directly. "How appropriate—just like a bug. And it takes a great deal of strength and weight to get the job done. But we never had to do it. Even after we'd all changed over, we followed Mother's rules and avoided drawing attention to ourselves. And all the while—even more after we knew we weren't human—Mother kept reminding us of humans' value. She wanted us to interact with them as much as we could, not just use them to stay alive. She also always wanted us to stay together. Partly to help each other feed without murder and partly so we'd have enough combined strength to save our own miserable lives if Grandfather—or any other half-breeds—ever found us."

Emma reached up and ran a hand through Jason's hair, trying to ease the torment she now knew his mind held.

"The last night we saw Mother, she hugged us tightly and warned us to run," Jason continued, giving her hand a quick squeeze before sinking back into himself. "She said Grandfather was closing in. She just sat in her room next to the opened red suitcase, holding a very old blade. She told us the weapon had been forged by the actual Devil in actual Hell, and it was all she'd need to protect herself. Then she told us again to go, so we left—because she begged us to.

"We finally saw what was inside that suitcase. That was my mother's family heirloom. Nice, right? Since that night we've been running—surviving, but not killing. I've wanted to die at times. But then how would my sister and brother fare without me? I was nineteen in nineteen thirty-seven. I'm aging, but slowly. I could live forever in this limbo. Waiting for my grandfather to find us and end it all or waiting for something to make all this pain worth it."

Jason looked at the floor for a moment, then turned to face her. "How do you feel about me now, Emma? How did you like this little story?"

Emma rubbed his back. "I hate this story. I can hear your hope dying in it, and that's so sad. But now I understand why I'm here all the more."

Jason scoffed. "Why you were tossed from Heaven by a psycho? You see a plan in that?"

She shook her head. "Jason, you were already going to be visited by a Christmas Angel. I just got—how do I say it?—*nominated* by Everett, that bastard."

She stood and pulled Jason into a hug. Instead of words, she offered her embrace. Emma tilted her head to look in his eyes and smiled, her cheeks gold-leafed with empathy and her own pain. "Let's show each other we're worth all the time in the world, Jason. Please."

She stood on her tiptoes to give him the sweetest kiss, asking for little and, he realized, willing to give everything.

CHAPTER 5

*J*ason couldn't help himself. Her taste was intoxicating. He nipped at her bottom lip, and she sighed.

Are you sure? Because I want to give you pleasure, not add to your pain.

Emma took her lips just a breath away so she could talk, so she could convince him. "Jason, my next stop's Hell. These moments might be the final ones of my choosing. Delight me."

She tilted her face toward the endless, black faux-sky, offering him her neck.

Instead of lusting for blood, his instinct was only to kiss. He trailed his lips from her jaw to her throat, nuzzling the hollow with restrained reverence. *I'll savor the way your skin feels forever.*

She lifted her hair, piling the blond curls on top of her head. The slope of her shoulders captivated him. The graceful curves of her breasts teased him — her nipples were so close to the edge of the fabric. His hands barely touched her waist, but he could feel her shaking.

Are you scared?

She lifted her face to his and outlined his lips with her tongue. Jason tried his best to say passive, but she pressed her breasts against his chest.

"Do I feel scared? Give me what I want, half-breed." She seemed almost angry.

Their pretend hearts beat wildly and in time. The pounding filled Jason's ears. Her desperate, massaging hands started at his chest. She boldly traced his stomach, pushing against the tuxedo's fabric. He wanted her hot hands on him. She reached lower and grabbed a firm handful of him, and he moaned into her mouth.

She pulled away and looked at him with sultry eyes. "You'll say my name by the time I'm done with you."

God damn you.

"He already has." As she reached behind her to take off her gown, Jason smirked and imagined that her had zipper disappeared.

Emma was puzzled as she felt for the zipper's tag.

If someone takes it off, it'll be me.

Emma clenched her fists and sighed impatiently. Jason skimmed her body lightly, ending with his hands on her face. He kissed her nose and her lips chastely.

"What do I have to do to convince you to stop being a gentleman?" Emma's voice was raw and soft.

I'd like to see you try.

The dare brought some fun back into her posture. Jason held his arms out, throwing down the gauntlet. She squinted at him and smiled. Jason felt a chill and found himself bare-chested. Emma had left him with just his tuxedo pants, his suspenders hanging at his sides.

You think I turn myself on?

Her giggle made his beating heart cry to be next to hers again. The thought of how warm she must be inside nearly melted him.

"No, half-breed. But I figured…" She took the few steps necessary to close the distance between them. "I figured the feel of my skin…" She turned to press her back against him. "Against your skin…" She looked at him over her shoulder. "Might convince you to let me out of this pesky dress."

Jason was speechless. Even his mind was silent as she slowly licked her shoulder.

"We're wasting time pretending, Jason. How many ways do I have to beg you before you give it up?"

She twirled around again and ran her hands over his chiseled muscles. She opened the button on his pants before he could give her an answer.

I'm trying to think about you. And that's not helping.

She traced his waistband while biting her bottom lip. "Think about me then, and don't stop thinking until you're inside me." She hugged him closer and spoke into his chest. "Take my mind away, Jason. I don't want to be in my head anymore."

The starlight streaked silver through her hair. Without her wing she was so real, so human. The blood pumping swiftly through his own veins made him feel like a human man. Filling his lungs again made choices and time feel important. He wanted her. Now.

All she wanted was a moment of peace, of human joy. He could do that. She smiled, hearing his decision.

Jason pointed at the backdrop and sprinkled the air with thousands of levitating candles.

She gasped. It was romance on the grandest of scales. He reached behind his back and produced a huge bouquet of red roses. She accepted them, gave them a sniff, then chucked them over her shoulder.

A wall.

Emma looked confused, but Jason knew what he was doing as he advanced on her, grabbing her tightly and pushing her back against the newly imagined barrier. He wanted leverage as he ravished her. With his hands on either side of her head he pressed against her with his body, kissing her until she stopped shaking.

He skimmed her breasts with his fingertips, and she moaned. Jason heard his brain snap as he picked her up. All at once she could feel his need between her legs, and she drew in a breath.

"This is going to be good." She put her arms around him and began biting his neck, then switched, tickling his ear with her tongue.

Jason pulled the wall out from behind her and carried her, kissing all the while, to the bed. He was beginning to envision exactly what lingerie he'd put her in before he ripped it off when a loud beeping invaded their starlit paradise.

Jason put Emma down on the bed and covered her while scanning the space for danger.

"Shh…" Emma touched his cheek with sad eyes. "Time's up, handsome. Hold tight to me." She pulled on his shoulders, and he made himself a blanket for her.

"Kiss me." She breathed into his lips.

As he kissed her, Jason watched their paradise evaporate from the ground up. Soon he was lying on top of Emma in the middle of the clearing. He ended their kiss sweetly and took his weight off of her. His heart slowed erratically in his chest as the world caught up to them. Jason wanted to soothe her. He wanted to stay in the stars with her for hours, for days.

But as they looked to the day-lit sky, fireworks began illuminating the atmosphere, and Emma shouted in fury. "Son of a bitch! This is between you and me. You and me! Leave the rest alone. Come down here and fight me, woman to woman. Everett, you pussy!"

Then it dawned on Jason what the anomaly in the sky was. As surreal as it seemed, he watched falling star after falling star. *He's tossing angels from Heaven?*

Emma was too busy launching snowballs at the sky to answer. Jason looked closer and could see glimpses of hands or a flow of beautiful hair in the stars' trails.

Let's go. I'll catch that one—you run for that one.

She shook her head. "We can't. There are too many. Crushed seraphim..." She trailed off, lost in sadness for a moment. "We can't help them here."

Lightning sparked across the sky. Everett was laughing. Emma turned to Jason and noticed he was wearing his casual clothes again. Everything was as it had been. Scary and threatening.

She reached for his hand. "Half-breed, I need you to man up and quick. The only hope we have is getting me to Hell. Pronto." She took one last look at the sky. "Do you have a car? I need you to drive me. I need to recharge my power before I can transport us both again."

Jason and Emma made excellent running time to Jason's house. Soon they were in his hot little sports car and speeding toward town.

Can't we just wait until your time's up? Jason begged silently. *Maybe we can think of something else.*

"No. See, I figured that bastard out," Emma said, shaking her head. "He wants me to stay here indefinitely. He was trying to send you to Hell, so he could keep me out of Heaven. When I stepped in front of the blast meant for you, I screwed him. I couldn't go to Heaven, but if I go to Hell I could cause problems. Here, in between, I'll be powerless. I'll just fade into nothing, Jason."

She looked scared again, and Jason felt the burning need to protect her.

"Make a left. Pull into this parking lot. We're here."

We're here? A discount store?

Emma took some deep breaths and shook her head, as if to clear it. She seemed to be psyching herself up to go inside.

"All right. Now or never. Let's go, cutie pie. Bring those big muscles."
She dusted invisible dirt from her gown.

Jason got out and looked up. Star after star fell, the tempo like a
metronome of pain. Emma held out her hand and begged him to hurry
with her eyes.

I'm not ready to let you go. And why are we here?

She hurried ahead but stopped just inside the store and joined the
fairly long line for cash register nine. She surprised Jason with her vulner-
ability when she used the wait time to cuddle into him. He kissed the top
of her head as she explained, "This is it. The gateway to Hell."

Jason tilted her face to his with a finger under her chin, not caring
that he probably looked like a crazy person to those around him who
couldn't see Emma. *Pardon me?*

"This place is the doorway to Hades. I thought that was obvious. Please,
like anybody would pay that kind of money for the crap they sell here." Emma
stepped backward, still wrapped around Jason, as the line inched forward.

The whole day had been unexplainable, but the cashier couldn't have
looked less like Beelzebub if she tried. She was a grandmotherly woman with
thick, blue eye shadow and a huge, teased beehive. Despite the fact that
the register was equipped with a scanner, she moved excruciatingly slowly.

I can kind of see it now, Jason thought, deciding to play along. *But
is she the Devil?*

Emma gave Jason the gift of her laugh. "No, she's just got a lot of
makeup on. Will you do this for me?"

They were close to the magazines and candy now, and Emma motioned to the mints on the shelf. Jason picked up the wintergreen ones
and set the small item on the belt.

I have to buy these?

"You just have to buy something. Those will do." She stroked his arm
sweetly, and Jason had never wanted to be surrounded by stars so much
in all his years. "When she scans them, when it beeps, that's the moment.
It'll open the gates. Please tell me you can do this?"

No. I can't. Not in a million years. Never.

Emma touched his face and smiled. "You're stubborn. I bet that's
why you didn't have sex with me. When I get back, I'm getting some."

There was only one more customer in front of them, and Jason was
still dead set against doing anything other than keeping her. He listened
to the humans talking as they entered the store.

"That's a bitch-load of falling stars," one man told the woman who
accompanied him. "As soon as we get done in this horrible store, I'm getting my camera out."

"Those are all good souls, Jason. Everett will ruin the whole world." Emma kissed his lips. "Think of Dean. Think of Seriana."

The unfriendly cashier, declared by her nametag to be Marge, scooped up the wintergreen mints.

Oh God. I have to do this for you.

She nodded and smiled sadly. The mints twirled in Marge's hands. She was seeking the UPC symbol like she'd never seen one before.

Jason put one arm around Emma's back and placed the other on her beautiful, glittering white wing.

Marge was finally victorious in her hunt for the small symbol and aimed it at the red lasers that flashed up from the black glass void.

Jason kissed Emma but kept his eyes open. She held his gaze, brave and true until the last possible second. Then she closed her eyes tightly, preparing for the pain, and broke their lips' touch.

Jason gently pulled on the feathers and her wing tore away effortlessly. Like wet tissue paper, it disintegrated in his hands.

She opened her eyes. "It didn't hurt. Jason, it didn't hurt because you did it with love."

He felt her light touch on his cheek as she whispered, "Jason."

She was disappearing. Jason pulled her closer, as if he could keep her from drowning. *Please, no. Don't leave. What can I do? What can I do!*

She was just an outline, a ghost of who she was. Her scent was fading.

The cashier demanded three dollars and fourteen cents over and over in a repetitive drone. Jason tuned her out and focused on Emma. But his arms soon circled nothing but a puff of glitter. He could hear her last words, just a hint of a hushed "Pray for me, Jason. Pray for me."

Jason stood in shock. His hands were covered in gold. But Emma was gone.

CHAPTER 6

Emma forced herself to keep her eyes open, but the rollercoaster-drop feeling was testing the boundaries of her reflexes. She was standing, but going so very fast. His arms were gone. She was glad Jason couldn't hear *her* mind because he would have known how scared she was, how hopeless this plan was.

The amusement-park sensation came to a sudden halt, and Emma found herself standing in a cement-bricked hallway. She felt blazingly human again—full of fear, sweat, and pounding terror. She didn't know much about Hell, but she knew damn well she wasn't likely to get out of it. She looked down at her bare feet. The cement floor was freezing cold.

Aren't I in Hell? Where's the heat? Where's the hot?

The huge metal door at the end of the hall creaked open. When Emma looked behind her, she saw only a gaping void with occasional red lasers flashing in the nothing. The noise of a loud, banging machine made her jump. The door looked like the most inviting option. A soft, red light spilled toward her like a welcome mat.

She watched the floor as she went, checking for trap doors, and she realized her outfit had changed again. She was wearing a red union suit. She reached behind her and felt her lower back. *Complete with a fanny flap. Fantastic. Nothing makes a girl feel more powerful.*

It was red, so she knew Jason hadn't changed her in their final seconds together. He always picked white.

Jason.

Emma tried not to remember his strong arms around her waist as he'd put her against the starry wall.

She took a deep breath and kept walking to the door, each step hitting her like a blow. Instead of fear as she walked through the entrance, she found herself consumed by lust. It was a wave of need—out of place and totally inexplicable. The want focused just inside the door. She knocked on the metal, wondering what exactly was considered proper etiquette in Hell.

That's where I am? Right?

"Come on in, Emma. I've been waiting for you."

Emma stepped in and felt the door close behind her. She let her eyes adjust. There were dim red lights and a cloying smoke smell that made Emma's thoughts blurry.

"Hello?" Emma could barely make him out, the one who'd spoken.

He straddled a simple wooden chair. As his image sharpened in the fog, she realized he was an absolute treat for the eyes. With shoulder-length brown hair, deep brown eyes, and high cheekbones, he smiled as she took a swallow of her courage.

"Well, aren't I being rude? Would you like a glass of wine? A cigarette? I roll them myself." He lifted a cigarette to his kissable lips and took a slow drag, watching her while she watched him.

I want him. Please. Now. Emma covered her mouth, though she hadn't said anything out loud. It didn't make any sense. Her intense ardor for this man must be false, manufactured.

He blew a heart-shaped smoke ring into the air and stood, poking his finger through it playfully. He wasn't as tall as Jason, but his presence was dominating. He wore the perfect pair of torn-up jeans and a white T-shirt. His forearms were covered in tattoos. He wore leather cuffs and layers of necklaces, and he walked carefully through an empty army of liquor bottles strewn on the floor.

As he came through the fog, a coat rack with a single hat appeared. He pulled the hat from where it rested and flipped it from his hand to his elbow, then tossed it onto his head with the utmost style.

He came closer to Emma, and she closed her eyes. She tried to rein in the crazy impulses created by the acute lust that washed over her. She could smell him now—the musky, sweet-smelling cigarette smoke had become his cologne.

His breath was hot and just inches from her ear when he spoke. "Angels are rare in these parts. Maybe it's the Heaven that sticks to you still, but I bet you taste like cotton candy and rum."

She shivered and her nipples hardened, the flimsy union suit showing him her body's reaction. She kept her eyes sealed, knowing that looking in his eyes was wrong. Somehow she had to keep her wits about her.

He lifted a handful of her hair and spoke his words to her neck, his breath searing her skin. "Don't be frightened, Emma. I only seek to fill your needs."

She opened her eyes then, when she could stand the imposed night no longer. *I'm such a failure.*

The man in front of her embodied pure, walloping sex. He let his eyes sparkle in victory. "See, beautiful Emma, I knew you'd come around."

He had a scruffy goatee and his jaw line was insanely defined. The word *come* on his lips made her legs tremble.

Hump him.

"Imagine what happens when the Devil kisses an angel. Don't you want to know?"

His lips were so close to hers. She just had to lean into them. She shook her head. "You don't seem scary enough to be the Devil." Emma bit the inside of her cheek. *Am I asking to be more scared? Am I an idiot?*

He backed her against the metal door, stepping forward every time she retreated.

"I'm the Devil," he said in his sexiest voice. "But I prefer to be called Satan, if that's okay with you."

She felt her back hit the door. He stroked his chin and raised an eyebrow. His hands were so tempting, his fingers so strong. She could tell by the look on his face he knew exactly the effect he had on her.

"And I guess being scary depends on what you're frightened of, doesn't it?" He put his hands on her hips. She could feel his demanding fingers through the soft fabric.

Jason. Think about Jason. Or Sam. Or Everett. Anything…anyone.

He inched his hands to her lower back. "Did you get one with the buttons in the back?"

She put her hands on his, stopping him just before he could pop the fasteners. "I feel like we've only just met. Maybe my ass hanging out is a bit inappropriate right about now?" Emma closed one eye.

Satan took a huge step backward and held up his hands in a nonthreatening way. "Of course. There go my manners again. You really better keep me on a tight leash, pretty child. I can't be trusted when it comes to you."

Emma was engulfed by disappointed when he moved away and kicked herself mentally. *Horny bitch! Get your head in the game.*

"Emma, I can't help myself. Surely you understand. I'm merely the warden to souls that need to be imprisoned." A coffee table appeared just as he needed it. Satan plucked a half-empty bottle of cabernet and a wine glass from its surface. He poured the glass to the brim and walked back to her, holding it out. "Please partake. You must be parched after your journey."

He held the stem of the glass with an easy expertise. Emma had never experienced such thirst. Her tongue was made of sand, tainting her oxygen with dry, crackling desire. Mentally, all her alarm bells were sounding, but her hands weren't listening to her head anymore.

I need to wet my throat.

Emma reached for the wine. Satan bit his tongue and watched as she hurriedly guzzled the alcohol. She handed him back the empty glass, disappointed that she'd crumbled so quickly. A slow smile spread across his face. His teeth were perfect and blindingly white. He took the glass and held the bottle up in a mock toast, then proceeded to drain it.

"There. Wasn't that nice?" Satan walked backward until he could again straddle the wooden chair she'd first spied him in.

He set the glass and bottle on the ground, where it joined the other empties. Emma's eyes had adjusted completely now, and she could see that there were hundreds of bottles — no thousands of bottles.

How big is this room?

"Please, angel, have a seat." He waved a hand in front of him and another chair emerged from the smoke.

She so was weary all of a sudden, exhausted. The seat looked like a fantastic place to just rest. She padded over quietly, her bare feet making next to no noise. She turned the chair around so she could straddle it, mimicking his leisurely pose. The wine muddied her thoughts. He folded his arms on the top of his chair, as if he had all the time in the world.

Emma pictured the sky alight with her falling friends. *Urgent. This trip is urgent.*

"Do you mind if I have another smoke?" He was already lighting the cigarette.

Maybe something in that smoke is making me lust after him? "If I said no would you stop?" Emma was proud that her words weren't slurred.

"No, princess, I'm just trying to be polite." He took a drag and held it for a moment. He blew the smoke in her direction as he exhaled.

"So how many girls have you offered a glass of wine in this room?" Emma looked pointedly at the empty bottles that were the room's main decoration.

The silence held the air tightly. Emma was concerned she'd asked too much.

Finally he looked at the floor and gave her a soft answer. "Thousands, Emma. Thousands." He looked up from beneath his lashes.

It was a practiced move, she knew that, yet it hit her between the legs.

"But you're the only one here with me now," he continued.

He stood, still straddling the chair, and as if walking around it was too much work, and he knocked it flat as he moved forward. When there were no more obstacles, he stepped slowly until he was in front of her. He let the awkwardness of her face in his crotch build for a moment. Then she had to look at his eyes; staring at his package was just too bizarre a way to hold a conversation.

"Devil, I'm not here to stroke your…ego," she finished, raising an eyebrow. "Or anything else, for that matter."

He chuckled, and the noise was deep and instantly addicting. He reached up and took his hat off, placing it on her head.

"I would be the one stroking your…" He put his thumb to his lips and clasped it in his teeth. When he had her full attention, he pulled it out and finished his sentence. "Ego."

Emma wanted to say something sassy. She wanted to deflect him with sarcasm, but her mouth refused to do anything but hang there like drying laundry. This was a chess game—the most important one in the world. He was tempting her, and he was obviously a master. Based on the sheer number of discarded bottles, Emma knew he'd played this game many, many times. And won. He always won.

Time to place my bets. "Let's cut the crap, you corrupt cupid. You have God. I want Him back. What's it going to take to get my way?" Emma stood as well, gripping her chair and looking him in his sensual eyes.

His pleased smirk revealed the hint of a dimple. "I knew you'd be different. Pretty child, I knew you'd be the most fun of all."

Emma had trouble getting her lungs to fill. Danger was layered between each of his words. *I'm so scared.*

He reached out and fisted a chunk of her blond hair. Although there was no pain, the threat was as clear as water. Emma could feel the ions of power coming from him. He let go of her hair and ran the back of his hand down her cheek, finally resting his hand on her throat. He leaned in, and she focused on his lips, determined to hold steady as he came so close.

"What makes you think I don't get to have you *and* God? There's no getting out now. I thought you knew that."

He grabbed the chair separating them and yanked it away in one violent motion. The wood clattered far from the place they were standing when it finally hit the ground.

Terrified, Emma knew she had to picture something, someone to help her focus. She tried Sam in his eagle form. *I'm still shaking inside.* She tried Sam in his human form. *No change.* Jason with her in their star-laden pause? *Still panicked.* And then she found it, the image she could hang onto, the thing that would strengthen her spine in this no-win situation. It was Jason with crazed, selfish eyes, turning to face his brother in the future.

You're not getting him, Everett. Not today. Not tomorrow.

"Maybe you do get us both. Must be nice to have somebody with a little power up in this joint after all these years." She reached up, tipped the Devil's own hat at him, then tossed it like a Frisbee.

Satan stepped closer, his beat-up motorcycle boots close to her toes. The nearness of him was its own drug. His skin was tanned and flawless. He parted his lips and drew in a breath through his teeth. Emma held herself steady, keeping her gaze locked on his mesmerizing one.

"You've decided to disrespect the hat? Bold move." He leaned even closer to her face, breathing her scent and smiling like the predator he was. He slowly, deliberately gathered her wrists. His fingers became her handcuffs. He pulled her arms behind her and secured her hands with one of his. "I want you to want me, pretty child. Is that so much to ask?"

He barely touched her cheek with his index finger. She shivered. He traced her jaw and slowly trailed his finger down her throat. Emma's knees began to shake. Satan put his lips as close as he could to hers without touching them. Emma's breathing became erratic.

He continued his merciless assault on her senses, popping the first button on her union suit clean off. She swallowed hard. There was no use pretending she wasn't turned on. He already knew; he always knew.

He moved his mouth to her ear, making promises that made compromises sound fantastic. "No one knows you're here with me, Emma. Wanting me isn't a sin. I'll give you pleasure, pure and simple."

He snapped the second button of her union suit. It clattered to the floor and rolled on its rim, taking some of her virtue with it.

"Pure." Her ears were so sensitive, and the deep vibration of his voice drove her wild. He licked her lobe gently, then whispered again. "And simple."

Satan changed tactics and dared to start licking and nipping at her neck. Emma felt her eyes roll into her sockets. He popped the next button. His hand forced her wrists together more tightly. He was losing some control of his own.

Give me a clear head. Make him give me a second to think, to breathe. Oh my Hell.

The Devil popped the last button, and her pajamas were open in the front, the seam just skimming her breasts. With a flick of his wrist, she'd be standing before him for all she was worth.

He lifted his head to put his forehead against hers. Emma had to close her eyes. He smelled so perfect. He was fresh-baked evil, and she wanted a bite.

"See how you won't even try to fight me off? You want this." He leaned down and sampled her lips.

He tasted of his alcohol and such intense desire. His mouth was so skilled. Satan dragged his hand slowly up her body, stretching out his fingers as the material of her pajamas parted. He splayed his hand on her heart. He let go of the hands he was holding, just to prove she was completely taken with him.

"Emma, don't you want to be just a little bad? No one'll know. Just me. And I can keep secrets. You'll come for me, pretty child."

Her morals told her to run, or at least back up a little. He pulled her close to him and let her feel his excitement.

He's huge. Holy crap. She opened her eyes in surprise. He was smiling again; the expression told her he knew she was shocked.

"Please, baby, you had to know the Devil would be well endowed." He decided then to bite her bottom lip.

I don't have the strength to fight him. God help me, Satan will own me and hard.

CHAPTER 7

Jason stood looking in horror at the spot where Emma had disappeared. Marge, the over-powdered cashier, had no sympathy for the handsome, suddenly distraught man in her lane.

"Three dollars and fourteen cents. If you don't got it, move on. I don't have all day here."

Jason turned to face her. He snatched the mints out of her hand and rushed for the door. *No matter. She's gone.*

Jason slammed himself into his car, staring at the box of candy as if it held the answers. *What the hell should I do? Go back there and plow through the scanner?* He held his hand up to the car's overhead light; he could still see tiny specks of her wing's glitter. *She was real. She is real. I sent her to Hell.*

He peeked at the sky. It was empty. No more stars falling like horrifying fireworks. No more crushed seraphim—or mangled angels of any kind—for now. *I don't know what to do. Maybe I am crazy.* He licked his lips and tasted angel cake. *How can I help her? Who'll believe me?* Jason started the vehicle viciously and slammed it into gear. Speed sometimes cleared his head.

He was soon out of the asphalt maze that made up the town, and his car ate pavement voraciously on a long stretch of road. *Think. Damn it.* But a plan wouldn't come. He kept seeing her fade away at the power of his hands.

Jason slapped the steering wheel with the flat of his hand. He could still feel her skin hot on his own as he'd pushed her against the starry wall.

His own heart seemed to be quivering now, remembering its farce of beating. *Her lips. Dear God, her lips.*

Jason pressed the pedal harder. He was going as fast as the car would allow, but it wasn't fast enough to outrun the pain, which clung to him like a metal spider web. *I want her back.*

Maybe it was habit, but he soon found himself flying up his driveway. He threw the car into park and sat behind the steering wheel. He needed help, and there was nowhere else to go.

He heard Dean toss the snowball, so the slap on his window wasn't a shock, but it made Jason angry anyway. He hopped out of the car and launched himself at his brother. Dean immediately assumed a wrestling stance, ready to play like a Labrador retriever. When Jason hit him with all the force he had, Dean began to protest.

"What's up your ass? Your new invisible girlfriend won't put out? I'm pretty sure if you hump the air you don't need a condom, Mr. Saintly."

Jason hurtled his fist into Dean's stomach.

Dean assessed the anger rolling off Jason and changed tactics. "Bro, what the hell went on today? Simmer down and tell me. I can't help you if I don't know what I'm fighting."

Jason would have kept punching if he hadn't heard Dean's next words as well.

"Jason, even if we're fighting a bucketful of nothing, I'll never leave your side."

Jason stood still and looked hard at Dean. "I'm sorry. Truly. That was uncalled for. I could very well be losing my mind, but it feels so real. It tastes so real."

Dean sat and patted the snow next to him. "Have a seat, bro. I can't read your mind."

Jason hesitated, but Dean's open face invited a confession. Jason started from the beginning and ended his tale with sending Emma to Hell.

"That's crazy stuff," Dean observed.

Jason rolled his eyes. He was wasting time trying to get some perspective from Dean.

"Bro, you know what I've learned from chicks?"

Jason sighed. *Advice from Dean about women?* He might as well spit in the wind. Although their mother's love for the people on Earth had piqued their interest in human women, because of their bizarre diet of blood, the brothers had limited their dating to short, casual relationships—and in Dean's case to one-night stands. Probably not exactly what Mom had in mind.

"Listen to her. A lot of times chicks tell you what they need you to do. But half the time, it isn't what we think they want, so we ignore them."

Despite spouting what at first seemed like inane blather, Dean had a point. Emma had asked one thing of him, and he'd yet to even try it.

Pray for me, Jason. Pray for me.

"Thanks, Dean. I think," Jason reluctantly offered.

"You *are* welcome," Dean said and waggled his eyebrows.

"I think you have a point," Jason added. "I mean, it seems ridiculous, but I'll try it. She did ask."

Dean stood and pounded Jason on the back. He headed for the front door of the Parish family home.

"I'll leave you to it." Dean winked at Jason and shut the door behind him.

Jason knew his brother and sister would be peeking out at him from every available spot in the house. He trotted off into the woods to give himself a bit of privacy for a conversation he'd never expected to have.

Hey, God. I, um... You and I have never been friends... But even though you made me a monster I...

Jason slammed a fist into the closest tree. He couldn't get it right. He didn't know who he was talking to or what the hell he was going to ask for. He needed perspective. Inspiration. He tasted his lips again.

Her.

He pictured her flowing blond hair. He hated how it squeezed him inside, but he pictured her last moments with him. It was like she was right there again. She was closing her eyes, waiting bravely for the pain to come when he tore away her wing.

God, please do this for her. Where she is now I can't even imagine. I need her, and that's selfish. But she makes me believe in love. She makes me believe in magic. If she comes out of this okay, I might even believe in You.

The snow around Jason began to glow and swirl. He concentrated again.

She's real in my heart. She needs strength right now. Take mine—I have too much. Take it all. God, please give Emma strength.

The snow around Jason became a tornado, whipping his hair into his face.

Amen. And thank you, Jason Parish.

When his eyes opened, Jason was surprised to see his hands clenched together, as if he'd prayed a million times before.

The tornado pulsated and grew stronger. Jason looked up through the center and saw perfectly blue sky.

This makes no sense. Is this God's response?

An explosion of falling stars erupted in the patch of sky he could see, then a horrible rainbow arched, and he knew it contained thousands of angels. Everett was purging Heaven of all its good.

The wind around him emptied like a drain, and soon the woods were calm—but the sky remained far from it. He looked over his shoulder and saw his brother and sister standing close by. When his eyes met theirs, they nodded in acknowledgment. They couldn't possibly understand the falling stars, or Jason's trip into the forest for a moment of prayer, but their greatest fear was losing him. They'd come to support him—or at least keep him from hurting someone if he'd turned to the dark side of reason.

Someone with Everett's massive power should have made more noise. But as Jason turned from his family to see the sky again, his vision was suddenly blocked by Everett's huge, red wings. His face was angry and sneering.

"Well, half-breed, you've pissed me off and sent my girl to Hell. Now you expect an evil thing like you to have God's ear? Think again." Everett's smile was not one of welcome.

Jason crouched and motioned for his brother and sister to do the same. They remained standing, so Jason stood up as well. They couldn't see any of the threat in front of them, he realized. If sending someone to Hell was the worst Everett could do, Jason would take it for his siblings. *At least I'd be back with her.*

Jason waited for the blast, but Everett wasn't powering up like he had in the clearing earlier. He hollered up to the hovering Everett. "Hey, overgrown pigeon! She's not your girl. She's mine."

Everett's hands began to shake, as though he was fighting the anger inside him. "You're dead, half-breed," he spat. "God doesn't care what you do, but the Devil has his eye on you." An evil grin spread on Everett's face, and intent sparked in his eyes.

Here it comes. Hell.

Instead of feeling the blast, Jason began to levitate. He watched in surprise as Everett pulled him, as if by invisible strings. Closer and closer Jason rose, his arms pinned to his sides again, as they'd been when he was in Heaven. Soon he was far above the woods, looking Everett in the face. He could hear his brother's shock and alarm from below. Dean had lunged to a tree and climbed it quickly, but he wasn't even close to Jason.

Everett flew closer so he didn't have to raise his voice. "She's so stupid. How could she think you could be anything but a murderer? You remind me of myself, half-breed."

Without warning, and so fast only a minion or a half-breed could see it coming, Everett punched Jason in the jaw. The invisible bindings held Jason tight, refusing to let him reel from the impact. Everett tilted his head like an interested pup and threw another punch. This time Jason's head was allowed to snap back. After a round of alarmingly fast fists, Everett put his hand on top of Jason's head. Like a reverse baptism, Jason was bathed in pain. He began screaming, but he heard it only in his mind, because Everett had sealed his mouth shut. The agony should have made him black out, but his mind remained agonizingly present. Everett was boiling Jason from the inside.

"Let me hear you scream. Scream for mercy, half-breed. Beg for me." Everett closed his eyes as if listening to a beautiful concert, and Jason's mouth was finally free to move.

Jason concentrated on keeping quiet, but when he could take it no longer, his loud, hard voice echoed through the woods. Jason put into words the only wish he had in the world and sent it into the universe:

"Emmaaaaaa!"

CHAPTER 8

God help me, Emma thought again.

The word "God" gave her clarity. It was like a brief glimpse of candle-light in the darkest night. She couldn't fight Satan—he was too good at this game. But maybe she could join him. Force his hand.

Emma smiled, trying not to let on that she had a plan at all. She took her newly freed hands and wrapped them around his neck. She grabbed two handfuls of his hair and kissed him with every bit of desire he'd fabricated in her.

He laughed—a rich, deep rumble—and kissed her back. Victory was his.

Then she pulled his head away from hers and lowered her lashes. "Devil, I don't want pure and simple pleasure. You've been doing this for eons. Surely you'll be creative?" Emma pressed her breasts against his chest and licked her lips.

"Of course. I'll be the best you ever had. No fear, just sin." He lifted her leg and grinded against her.

She tilted her head to expose her neck. "You'll have to be better than Everett. Good heavens, he makes me quake."

She shivered at the thought of Everett—particularly *that* thought—but she hoped the Devil would take it as leftover ardor.

Satan stopped his assault on her senses and squinted. "You screwed Everett?" He looked like he might want to back up.

Emma snickered and gave him her best doe eyes. "Of course not." She didn't want him angry with her...yet. Emma kicked herself mentally as she pulled out her ace card, her left breast.

The sight of her nipple washed the apprehension from his face, and he bent his head to suckle. His tongue was everywhere and so fast. She wasn't pretending when she arched her back to force him to be rougher.

He lifted his head to watch her excitement. "There you go, pretty child. That's the way." The Devil pushed Emma onto a chaise lounge that had appeared from the smoke.

She wanted the weight of him on her; she clawed at the red velvet. *Think, Emma. This is about more than what's in his pants.*

He pulled his T-shirt off in an uncomplicated motion. He had just enough tattoos to appear dirty, but not enough to be confusing. He unbuckled his belt while he watched her writhe on the lounge. The Devil smiled because he liked what he saw.

Emma swallowed and pictured future Jason's eyes. *For him. Do this for him.*

The Devil unbuttoned his jeans, certain he had her full attention. He left them undone as he crawled up her body, placing his lips on any skin he found. He began speaking to her between luscious kisses. "I'm...going... to...savor you...like wine...like Heaven...comes...to Hell."

All Emma could do was moan.

He straddled her and pulled his hair into a ponytail while she watched the muscles in his arms work. He used a piece of leather from around his wrist to secure it out of the way.

"You see, I've been down here far too long, toiling with women who've lived a life of wanton carelessness. Whores."

The word "whore" coming from his lips as he leaned down sounded wonderful. He caressed her face. "But you, Emma, you make this whole room glow. The scent of you is just...intoxicating."

His eyes were so brown she could see her reflection in them. She knew she'd have to give him more than her heart wanted to, but for him to believe, her morals had to be shredded. She put her hand around his neck and spoke into his lips. "I've been so good, Satan, but I think I need a lesson in wickedness." She kissed him again as his hands moved under her union suit. He was exploring her and murmuring horrible perfections from his Devil lips.

Do it now, or your mission has failed.

Emma could barely put together her words; they kept falling like beads from a string.

Make him jealous. Make him worry. She ran a hand over his hard stomach.

"You want to be bad, angel? I can teach you every position it comes in." He pressed his fingertips into her thighs.

"I need something to take my mind off the evil Everett is tossing around up there." She boldly grabbed a handful of him.

He stopped his pursuit of her pleasure to grit his teeth and growl at her. His eyes looked primal, timeless. She kissed his scary, sexy mouth. She took time to trace his bottom lip with her tongue before she made her next point. "God's here, and now that I've met you, I think I'd rather be in your company."

Is this a promise I'm making? Am I making a reservation to be here with the Devil for all time?

She knew going to Hell was a risk. Crap, forever in torment was almost a sure thing. But with God here, maybe He'd provide some protection?

It seemed that right here and right now, in this room, it was just Emma and the Devil. He shifted to lie alongside her. He caressed her face and neck like he'd molded them carefully himself.

"Sexy woman, you want me to believe you're here with me because you think I'm your safe haven from Everett?" He began nibbling her ear again.

She nodded and found that putting a hand on his chest was way too easy. He looked at her lips and then her eyes. She saw anger flash across his face, but before she could react, he had her hands together. The handcuffs appeared, hanging in the smoke from an invisible hook. He skillfully slapped them onto her wrists, and soon Emma was bound with her arms above her head on the chaise lounge.

He relaxed at her side again once he'd imprisoned her. He reached over her to a table that held his beloved cigarettes. He picked one up and lit it with his finger. She watched as he drew the smoke. He closed his eyes and rubbed his forehead with his hand as he exhaled, thoughtfully, away from her.

Emma knew he was on to her. *Trick the Devil to save God. Who can do that?*

"Smoking kills, you know." She could afford to be cheeky now—her jig was up.

The Devil looked almost pleasant again. "One can always hope."

With the cigarette between his lips he buttoned all the buttons she had left on her union suit, covering her. When he was done he nodded, like he knew he'd done the right thing.

"To think you would give me the gift of your body." He shook his head and gave a humorless laugh. "Maybe my age has made me weak, angel."

He sat up and turned his back on her. From midair, he plucked a bottle of rum. She watched the muscles in his back shift as he indulged in a swig from the bottle. When he stood up, his jeans were buttoned again.

"I want you to stay here. I want you to *want* to stay here. That'll take time. I understand that. I've jumped the gun. But can you blame me?" He took another swallow of the alcohol.

Emma needed some perspective, so she voiced her thoughts. "God doesn't make mistakes. You're here because you belong here. Nothing you can do will make me want to be in Hell. I've known the pleasures of Heaven."

Emma shifted to try to make her arms more comfortable.

He tilted his head a bit and looked down his nose at her. "God doesn't make mistakes? Are you sure about that, princess? Are you *positive?*"

Emma hated the doubt that crawled into her heart. *Everett is a mistake. Everett's pure evil.*

"I see your answer. You think you can get one by me? I pass my days with the best liars that have ever *existed*, Emma." He swirled the golden liquid in its bottle.

Emma was so thirsty.

Jason.

"And what of a seraph handcuffed to the Devil's bed? Is that in God's master plan? He's as useless as a mortal. Your faith in Him is a sick mistake." The Devil found a red velvet chair to sit in. He propped his boots up on Emma's lounge.

The distance and the clothes were helping a bit. She felt more in control. She tried to test the strength of the cuffs and found they were impenetrable. *I can't lie to this bastard? I'll be honest then. What else do I have?*

Emma looked at her bare feet. "I feel cheated. Everett has no place in Heaven; he wasn't even a little bit good. And yes, I guess I'm ticked off at God. I don't want to be here fighting a losing battle against you." She looked at his face.

He took another drag and released it before replying. "And now you tell the truth. It suits you."

Emma shifted again. His gaze was deafening. It made her heart pump so loudly.

"Well, I do have resources," he said. "If you think God made a mistake concerning Everett, I'll punish him. Your hate would put him under my jurisdiction." The Devil put his boots back on the floor and leaned forward. With his elbows on his knees, he gave Emma an uncompromising stare.

"Punish who?" Emma asked. "Everett? God?" She felt a rush of power.

He rubbed a hand on his lips for a moment before he spoke. "Both, princess. Imagine that—giving Everett exactly what's coming to him."

He gestured to the room behind him and suddenly there was a projection on the smoke. It was flashes of Satan's power: humans enduring the most horrendous of tortures. Emma closed her eyes, horrified and sick to her stomach.

"I'm sorry. Too much? I guess I have a high threshold for that type of thing." He leaned over and ran a knuckle down her jaw line. "It's gone. You can open your eyes."

She did, and he was telling the truth. Just smoke and the dim, red lights remained.

"Why did God let him in?" Satan asked. "Did Everett pull the forgiveness card?" He sat back in disgust.

It was truly bizarre having a heart-to-heart with this man—or what had once been a man. Emma was playing games now that were totally out of her league. She wasn't tricky enough. All she had to offer was herself, her honest opinions.

"Everett killed my love. He tossed me from Heaven. God's captured here. Yes, God made a mistake. He wouldn't listen to me. I knew Everett was bad!" Emma realized she'd raised her voice. She had shouted this anger at him.

The Devil smiled. "If God would just listen once in a while," he said, "maybe there'd be fewer mistakes." He shrugged.

Emma had flown at God's right hand, and here she was venting to the Devil, of all people, talking about God behind His back. She tried to remind herself of the beliefs she'd held dear for so long.

"God has a bigger plan," she said, trying to make her voice strong. "It's not for me to judge Him." But saying the words didn't make her any less angry.

Satan moved from his seat to her lounge. He flicked his cigarette into the vast, empty smoke and ran a comforting and equally sensual hand up and down her leg. "That's a good seraph. Take your opinion and choke on it. How're the lies going down now?" His brown eyes seemed to know everything.

"Everett got in on a technicality. 'Ask for forgiveness and ye shall be granted access at the gates of Heaven.' But Everett never apologized—well, he never meant it anyway. His eyes never changed, never softened. He was hate from top to the bottom. He *is* hate." Emma's eyes filled with the annoying tears that formed when she was angry.

"And your love, he's in Heaven waiting for your return?"

His massage was so calming.

"No. Sam chose reincarnation. He chose endless life."

Satan was so understanding. If she wasn't handcuffed, he might even convince her she had the makings of a friend.

"So *that's* how it is." The Devil switched his positions so he could sit at her feet.

He applied his effective massaging there. Emma sighed; the mix of tight cuffs and relaxing touch were overwhelming.

"You and I have more in common than you know." He looked over her head, either playing with her mind or, possibly, indulging in a real regret.

"Tell me your story. I'll listen." Emma wanted to imagine that this was part of her plan too—being generous with Satan—but the distance in his eyes called to her good soul.

He stopped massaging her feet and stood, as if she might be poisonous. "People don't ask *me* about *me*. They want to hear themselves talk."

Emma tucked her feet closer to her body; they were chilly without his strong hands. "Maybe I'm different. Spit it out, Satan."

He found his floating bottle of rum and took another drink. Emma was so thirsty. When he locked his gaze on her again she saw a tiny bit of hope. Perhaps finding kindness in Hell moved him. He returned to her chaise.

"Would you like a sip?"

She nodded, hoping he would unlock her cuffs. He didn't, but he held her head and tilted the bottle. She drank deeply, though the taste made her cringe. He took the bottle away and let it float again into the smoke.

"Not a fan of rum?" He was close again, and his power and sexiness filled her whole body. He smiled wickedly before kissing her gently. "Rum tastes better on your mouth than in my glass."

He licked his lips. Her heart battered her chest.

"I'll tell you, beautiful Emma, the story I share with no one but live every day in my head." He began to pace, agitated by his old anger.

"I was a good man on Earth. A true man. I was rewarded with, as you put it 'the pleasures of Heaven,'" he said, nodding in her direction. "I fell in love with a virginal angel. She had brown hair and fawn-colored eyes. And we would laugh. I was never so witty as I was around her. I was never as strong as I was with her. And I wanted to make love to her, desperately."

He stopped and ran a hand through the smoke. It complied and formed the picture of his lovely paramour. But when he tried to caress it, the smoke scattered. He punched the air where she'd been.

He turned to his left and bellowed, "Can I not even touch the memory of her? You have everything!"

Emma assumed he was yelling at God. She tried her handcuffs again. They seemed a bit looser, but she still couldn't wiggle out of them.

Satan continued. "But Gabriel had designs on her as well. He set me up and taught her what it was to despise someone—because she didn't even know how to hate, my beautiful inamorata. She was so pure." Satan looked at Emma again and closed the distance too quickly for a human.

He grabbed a handful of Emma's hair and rolled it in his fingers. "I saw her tender hair first. I was there to apologize, to explain the tall tales Gabriel had fed her about me, but then I heard her moaning. I thought she was hurt. Can you imagine? I ran in there to *save* her. To *help* her! I was so stupid. No one cries in Heaven—unless they're so *fucking* happy." Satan's eyes were wet. He was vibrating with anger, reliving his horrific discovery. "Guess what I saw, Emma? Tell me, because I want to hear *you* say it." He was close again and heady lust clouded her emotions.

"He was with her," she whispered, and the evil one began nodding.

Satan straddled Emma again, aroused. *"He* was with her. *He* was in her. She *wanted* him!" He clenched his fists, and Emma wasn't sure he'd remember where he was. "So you see, angel, I did what I had to do. God asked me to forgive Gabriel." Satan punched his own hand. He barely moved his lips when he added, "I refused."

Satan said nothing as he ran through the old battle in his head for a moment. "And then I plotted, like the bastard I knew I was." The smoke pulsated with his anger, like a trained pet. "So after I tore shit up, I got *this* lovely promotion. I get to live amongst unimaginable savageness. And I get to fuck every girl that walks in my door. I *have* to fuck every girl that walks in my door. They can't resist me, nor I them. Fitting, isn't it?"

He looked again at her face. He wasn't seeing her anymore. "But *you*...you came here, and you're fighting me like you shouldn't. You look like her, a little tiny bit. And you've got that same heavenly smell. And I want to do to you, Emma, what I never got to do with her."

He put his lips on hers. His scruffy face tickled as he poured his ardor over her like syrup. His passion tasted fantastic, like honey and spice. Emma could scarcely breathe. He *was* an angel, just a bad one.

Angel. Angel! Everett's plan hit her like a bolt of lightning.

"Oh my God!" she shouted.

The Devil took her exclamation for desire. She had to shake her head violently to get him to back up. He cocked his head, puzzled.

"Is she still there? Your angel?" Emma tried to sit up, but he wouldn't let her move.

He nodded and swallowed some pain.

"Satan, Everett is throwing angels from Heaven. You know that, right? Even the seraphim—destroying them one by one." Emma watched as he came to the same conclusion she had.

"What?" He hopped up from her and stood at the foot of the couch.

Emma tried to give him the information softly. "I'm so sorry. I don't know if she's been among them." Sympathy surged through her, greater even than the passion she'd felt.

"What?" He seemed to be struggling to get his mind around Claudette's possible destruction.

She hated herself a little because this could help her, but she pointed out the obvious. "Everett could be holding on to her as a bargaining chip. Seraph Gabriel has also been thrown from Heaven. I saw him among the falling stars."

Satan was enraged. "I'll make him cry. I'll kill him so many times." He began plucking a horrible array of weapons out of the choppy smoke.

The room reflected his darkening mood. The red lights grew blacker, and the smoke began churning into tiny hurricanes.

"Wait! Let God go. He'll help you." Emma had managed to sit up, though her hands were still above her head. The handcuffs were chained to something.

Satan stopped cold and turned his head slowly toward Emma. "You think I'd trust Him? After all He did to me? My Claudette is safer with *me* to protect her."

He began strapping an ammunition belt around his waist.

"Well, at least let me come with you," Emma said. "I don't have my wings, but I'll have your back. I want Everett for my own reasons." Emma missed her wings and hated her hate, but it had come on fast, like a force of nature.

Shaking his head, Satan strode quickly to a wooden door that appeared in the smoke and locked it firmly. Then he turned and in an instant was headed out the metal door Emma had entered. He paused for a last glance at her. "God stays put because I don't trust Him. You stay put because…" He gave her a reverent nod. "I know you're safe here." He waved a hand in her direction and closed the door behind him. The smoke followed him out, seeping through the cracks between the hinges.

"Gah! Damn it. Damn him!" Emma kicked and noticed the Devil had changed her outfit. She now wore a full, red-leather dominatrix get-up and a matching pair of neck-breaking stilettos.

She was useless. She yanked on her handcuffs.

"That's just hilarious. The Devil thinks he's protecting *me*." Emma stomped her foot against the red velvet of the lounge chair. A bit of dust made a tiny cloud. "And he dressed me like a slut! *Humper*."

She tried the handcuffs again. Nothing moved. She bit her lip and tried to think of a way out. She heard a crackling, like a faraway vintage radio had been turned on and tuned in. A voice drifted into the huge room.

"God, please do this for her. Where she is now I can't even imagine…"

Emma knew his voice. It was sweet and silky. He sounded so sincere.

She shouted into the deep room. "Jason? Where are you? Can you hear me? Jason! I need help!"

"…She needs strength right now. Take mine—I have too much. Take it all…"

He wasn't in the room, but his words were. "Jason. You remembered me." Emma felt a lump in her throat. It took so much courage for an unbeliever to pray. She was so proud of him.

"…Amen. And thank you, Jason Parish."

"No, thank you, Jason." Emma smiled at the sound of his voice.

The transmission stopped, and the crackle faded away. She tried her handcuffs again, and they tumbled off in a noisy clatter. She pulled her hands in front of her, astounded. Jason's prayers had unlocked her shackles like a key.

"Yes! Yes!" She stood on the wobbly heels and waited.

She wasn't sure if the Devil had an alarm system. It could be anything really—a dragon, a giant spider, anything. A shiver went down her spine. She took a huge breath and hoped it contained some more of Jason's strength as she sprinted for the metal door.

"If this is locked, I'm screwed." Emma yanked on the handle, imagining every type of evil at her heels.

The door opened with a loud creak. She closed it behind her and looked around. In front of her was the thick void she'd fallen through to get here in the first place. To her left was a long, cement hallway. Satan had hollered in that direction when he was speaking to God.

Emma had a choice: she could try to find her way out and join the Devil in fighting Everett, or stay true to God and seek Him out to try to release Him.

CHAPTER 9

The Hallway *had* to be her choice. When would she ever be left unattended in Hell again?

The void was pierced with screaming. *Was it someone coming in or the Devil getting out?*

There was a loud bang and a sharp flash, and the screaming stopped. Being wingless and human made Emma feel weak. She wasn't used to her body reacting to fear, stress, and worry. Being an angel had been the most delicious drug. It was pure good, radiating all the time.

She whispered "good luck" to the Devil, wherever he might be, and tiptoed to the Hallway's entrance. It looked so plain — just cement walls and more metal doors, each with a window to peer into. Then she noticed the note handwritten in a hurried scrawl and tacked to the wall.

Can only open one door!

Emma could see at least thirty doors, but she could look through the window in each before making her choice. Right? The fluorescent track lighting flickered malevolently. *This looks easy. Too easy.*

Satan would never safeguard God behind just a door. There had to be more to it, but for now she could hope for ease. Her heels click-clocked as she took a few steps. She was busy trying to figure out where the Devil would put God strategically, and she eyed the last doors in the Hallway as the first plague hit. Nothing in the Hallway changed visibly. The cement was still cold, and the doors were still a rusty gray. But inside. Oh crap, inside.

It was hunger. The most crippling, inane need to eat. Emma lost her focus entirely. She staggered forward, dreaming of food. Perhaps a delicious hunk of cheese… She began gnawing the flesh of her arm, just to give her ravenous teeth something to chomp on, but they were unable to break the skin. Even self-destruction offered no relief.

Door. Look in the window. She tried to make her feet move, but the pain of the famine crowded her brain, short wiring it to picture apples, bread, watermelon. *Feed me. Please feed me.*

The searching, primitive instinct to find prey finally brought her to the door—not any reasonable plan to find God. She pressed herself against the metal and the desperate hunger eased.

Tricky bastard. She maintained contact with the door and peered in the window. The room beyond it was pitch black. There was a light switch to her left. She knew she had to turn it on. With complete ease, she flicked it into position. The inside of the cell was instantly visible, clear and sparse. There was one small, horrible-looking bed and no inhabitants.

Emma was about to turn off the light when something dropped from the ceiling. *Holy crap!*

She had to consciously focus on getting her now-human heart to beat again. Adrenaline lit her eyes on fire as she took in the bizarre, stringy being. It was mostly teeth and saliva. Like a nightmare set to a body, it banged its head against the glass and snarled. Emma turned off the light with a childish hope of making it go away.

The room went silent.

Emma stepped back from the door and shook her head. The hunger attacked her immediately and she staggered on down the hall. Between the doors was another respite from the hunger pangs. In the calm, Emma tried to orient herself. The relief from the hunger was likely worse for her resolve than the plague itself. Her brain and body begged her to stop, and a part of her began to doubt her devotion.

Clearing her head, Emma shook out her arms and stretched them as if preparing to run a race. With her next step, she encountered the Devil's second challenge.

Depression overwhelmed her, smothered her. There was no escaping it, so why bother to try? It took Emma forever to convince her eyes to blink. It seemed like a waste of energy to keep them wet. Steps weren't worth taking. She would never be able to do this anyway. Each new criticism seemed to smack her head before it took root in her body.

Stupid. She was so very stupid.

Hated. Everyone who ever saw her hated her.

Guilty. Every choice she'd ever made killed her all over again.

Unloved. No one loved her. Sam didn't even choose to be with her.

She was stagnant. There was no primal instinct to propel her forward now. Depression had stopped her completely. Her taunting brain showed her future Jason's selfish eyes. Demented eyes that had changed a good soul into something he'd rather die than be.

She dragged a boot forward. The other came after, but it was slow going.

Boot drag, boot drag. Slow, not steady, dull.

Her progress had no focus, but finally she collided with the second door. It touched her instead of the other way around. Nevertheless, when her fingertips felt the metal, the wet, heavy cloud of doom lifted.

Emma now had trouble keeping her eyes open—the emotional marathon had left her exhausted. She flipped the light switch and braced herself for a jump-inducing scare. Instead she had a shock of a different kind. Her father sat on the bed in the cell. He was holding his chin, looking right at her, but he didn't smile.

Daddy's in Hell?

His piercing gray eyes, so like her own, showed recognition, but no pride. His face didn't light up like it did for his sons. She could hear his voice clearly when he decided to talk.

"Emma, you won't open this door. I can't trust you to watch out for me. *You* take care of *you* best. Go on with you. Go open someone else's door." Hate emanated from him, and each word rippled from his mouth, like water after a pebble is thrown in a pond.

By the time the ripples reached Emma, the words were crashing waves. This wasn't a Devil-manufactured emotion. She felt real disappointment that she'd let her father down, let her brothers down.

"I'm so sorry, Daddy. Everett was a bad man. I couldn't make myself be with him after what happened to Sam." She had trouble touching the door now; his words had made it hot. She wanted to cuddle her knees and be far, far away from her father's judgmental eyes.

"Agh. Yeah, sure. Piss on me. Did Sam feed you? Did Sam give you clothes? Who bought your goddamn horse? Sam? No. You treat your own family like shit because you wanted to whore it out to that horny asshole." Her father stood and swaggered to the glass.

It's not him. Daddy loved Feisty, and he never cursed. His voice seemed too high-pitched, different than she remembered.

But she treated him as she would her father. "Daddy, I forgive you for your words, even though they hurt me now. I love you. The decisions you made were a product of the information you had then. I forgive you."

With her forgiveness, the lifelike hologram of her father warbled and changed. He was distorted by her love. Soon his resemblance dissolved like sugar in hot water. Emma felt peace. Her father wasn't in Hell. She wouldn't have to choose to save him or save God.

She stepped back into the depression again, slowly, agonizingly. When she got to the next respite of peace, she knew she had to change her tactic. The hall was so long. Her gut told her God would be at the end of the hall. That's where she'd put him if she were the Devil. The expanse of cement looked to be far from an easy passage now.

Internal obstacles. That sexy bastard.

She couldn't experience whatever Satan had laid out for her at a walking pace. She needed to run—take a chance that she could get through whatever lay ahead. Common sense said to go slowly because the test was surely too much. Whatever she would face in the next hundred feet would collapse her sanity like a broken tent—especially if she took it on all at once. But God was trapped, possibly being tortured by the same things she was feeling.

I'm going to take the strength Jason prayed to give me, and I'm going to run—no matter what. I'm not going to stumble. I won't fall. I'll run.

She rolled her head on her neck and took a deep breath. Her heart pounded, and her palms were slick with sweat. The space looked so innocuous, but she'd learned quickly that looks were deceiving.

Go!

Emma took off sprinting in her high-heeled, red leather boots. An observer would have been fascinated by the way she twitched and flailed at apparently nothing, but despite it all, she kept running.

In her mind—in her quaking, reeling mind—there was only disaster. First was fear. Paralyzing fear. She ran even when she started to shake. When the reprieve came, she ran through it as well, refusing to relish the peace.

Up next was anger. Devastating, murdering, raging anger. Her fingernails dug into her palms and she screamed as her wrath demanded she hit something, kill something. The moments of peace were growing shorter or she was running faster. She prayed she was faster.

The confusion was horrible. *Who am I? What am I doing?* Emma was only able to keep running because she had so much momentum. Surely she'd have forgotten how to breathe had she been walking.

She was close to the end of the hall now, and finally her brain made her feet stop. There were two doors against the back wall. She looked over her shoulder and wiped her mouth. Emma convulsed as if she'd been electrocuted.

My brain is melting. Oh God. Please, just make it stop.

She stepped toward the door on the left because it was closer.

Love. She was filled with such overwhelming love. She felt like flying. Everything was prettier. She took a deep breath and felt replenished, rejuvenated.

This is God's door. It has to be.

She reveled in the love and flipped the light switch, excited to see His face, open His door.

Sam sat on the bed in the cell. The love overwhelmed her. *Sam! Of course I'll save Sam. My love, my sweet. His arms were so warm when I hugged him. His skin always smelled so sweet. Sam. Sam.*

She touched the door before reaching for the knob. Her fingers against the metal broke her spell, and the infatuation subsided a bit.

He stood and came to the window.

Sam, my Sam.

"Emma, beautiful Emma. I've missed your face so much. Please, please let me out. I love you. You're all I've ever wanted! I'm so scared in here. I love you."

His hair was the perfect color, and his deep brown skin begged to be touched. He looked so relieved and waited expectantly to be released from his cell. "But why didn't you come to me?" Emma began. "You chose reincarnation—"

"You can only open one door," Sam interrupted. "You can't leave me here. I can't stay here. I'm in pain all the time."

To punctuate his dilemma, a gunshot roared in her ears and Sam's chest exploded in blood. He died all over again—the gasping, the gurgling, the light fading from his eyes.

Emma screamed like she had when she was human—like she had when his death had killed the part of her that was innocent.

The blood on his chest receded like the tide, the hole closing up like a film being rewound. He began to blink and wince. As he staggered to stand up, he put a hand to his chest.

"Emma, that keeps happening. I get better just long enough to be afraid again. Please, I'm so terrified. Only you can save me, Emma."

The gunshot rang out again, and she grabbed the knob with both hands. Again he crumpled, again he died, again he bled. She could barely stop herself from flinging open the door. She had to think.

Sam was getting up again. "Emma, take me with you. Let me be with you. I keep having to die." Then her beautiful, brave Sam started to cry. After a moment he continued. "You're not going to save me. I can't keep dying. It's Hell. It's Hell."

Gunshot.

The whole cell filled with his death again. It was a relentless loop of the worst seconds of his life.

It's Hell. It's Hell. She tried not to watch as Sam breathed his last again and again. *Daddy wasn't real. Sam's not real. This isn't real.*

Emma hated her nagging conscience that told her it could be Sam. If his spirit had risen and received Judgment from Everett, this could be Sam.

And what if the sign was a fake? What if I can open two doors?

Gunshot.

Sam experienced his death again before he came to the window and looked in her eyes. "Do what you have to. I do love you, my sweet girl. You've always been my warrior."

He was himself then, in that moment. She knew it in her soul. He really was behind this door, and she had to open it. But not yet. Carefully Emma stepped back, keeping her fingers in contact with the door.

"Emma, don't leave me! I'll come with you." Sam clawed at the window, trying to get to her, desperate to get out.

"I'll get God first. Then I'll be right back. I promise. I won't leave you—"

Emma gasped as the gunshot intruded on her pledge. He fell again. She let go of his door. The only thing giving her courage now was that God could do anything.

She heard the Devil's voice in her ear. *"Then why isn't He out of Hell, pretty child?"*

The overwhelming love hit her again. She clawed at her chest; her heart was so full of love for Sam. She dropped to her knees so she couldn't hear his gasps or see his never-ending death. She had to crawl because she couldn't trust herself to be level with the doorknob.

The gunshots came faster, over and over and over. Soon it sounded like machine-gun fire.

Sam, Sam, Sam. I'm so evil to leave you here.

She crawled into the reprieve, the peace. But there was no silence here. The life-ending cracks kept her on her hands and knees.

One last door. And if she was wrong, she'd have to go back to each of the doors she'd run past. There were so many. She'd never survive it on her own. She had to pray. She had no one else to turn to.

In this time of need, strengthen me. You are my strength and my shield.

Her mind filled with Jason's face, and she saw his despondency at his future. She stood, and although the gunshot kept sounding, she focused on the last door. She reached her hand out in front of her.

She screamed and pulled her hand back.

It was fire. Invisible, perfect fire.

Before she'd died, she'd gotten Feisty to a small hole in the barn's shingles so they could breathe. It had been a useless bit of relief. The fire was so furious and hot. But Emma wouldn't leave without her horse. She'd clung to Feisty's neck, soothing the horse while her own heart pounded. She'd focused on her animal's beautiful eyes. When the fire roared over Emma, her skin had melted.

She looked at her hand now, and it was perfectly fine. This fire, though just as painful, was not going to burn her. It was just going to force her to relive her final moments.

What if I get stuck? What if the door doesn't open? What if my Hell is this Hallway and I never leave?

She pictured Everett, the angels falling from the sky, the Parishes at the end of time. The gunshots kept sounding, fraying her to almost nothing.

I'm going to lose my mind, and soon. I need to do it.

She readied herself.

Just touch the door. Touch the door.

Emma pictured Feisty's eyes and centered her fear. She took off, but the pain engulfed her immediately. She was burning. Emma couldn't scream because the fire was in her mouth. She was dying again. When she took a breath, the flames filled her lungs. She clawed at her throat with burning hands. She was being incinerated, yet she would never die. She could walk no more; the bottoms of her feet were scorching. Emma fell in the direction she hoped mattered. She stretched her arm out and felt a finger come in contact with metal.

The burning extinguished. Emma lay on the cement floor and sobbed. The gunshots still kept sounding. Her Sam stood before a firing squad again and again. Her skin felt fine, but her mind was like a petrified rabbit hiding from a ravenous fox. She could hardly use it.

Emma kept her skin touching the metal and tried not to imagine the "what ifs." She could never go through the fire again. If this wasn't God's enclosure she'd open the door and stay in the cell herself. She couldn't face the fire.

Her legs were wobbly, and she had to convince her hand to flip the switch. Seated on the cot was Santa Claus, complete with a jolly red hat. She cursed like sailor. Santa looked and smiled at her.

She felt boneless with relief. It was Him.

Only the memory of the fire would outweigh the instinct to fall to her knees. She pulled the door open, and it groaned in protest. She made sure to keep contact with the metal until her boots were fully inside God's cell. He was peace and calm in the middle of agony. His brilliant blue eyes welcomed the sight of her.

God removed His hat because a lady had walked in the room, but He didn't get up, which was odd for Him. Short, blond hair spiked in every direction. He was gloriously good-looking, but Emma didn't notice anything but His generous smile.

She wanted to be cleaner, wanted to not be dressed like a hooker. She wanted to maintain all the decorum she so loved in Heaven. The best she could do was stagger. She fell in front of Him and held out her hands.

He took them and kissed her palms. Her brain solidified from the quivering mess it had been, and she could breathe.

God's voice was honey even in Hell. "Seraph Emma, how did I know yours would be the face I'd see? Come from your knees and let me comfort you, my child." He pulled her next to him and engulfed her in his arms.

She snuggled deeply into His fuzzy red coat. "I was so afraid, Lord. I didn't think I could do it. Sam? Is that really Sam? Please, we have to save him."

God petted her head and lifted her chin so He could smile at her. "Of course, Emma. Just sit on my bed and don't get up. You have to stay put. No matter what."

Emma nodded, and God lifted himself from the mattress. He was out the door and back before she could even process why sitting on the bed was so important.

"Sam is free, my selfless seraph. He's been returned to his spirit and has taken flight." Emma nodded and tried not to feel hurt that Sam had left again. He probably hated her for leaving him to be shot over and over.

God sat next to Emma and put an arm around her shoulders. She sighed. Being under God's care took all the pressure away. Now everything would be all right.

"Okay, Sir, I need to update you on what's been happening. Everett went ballistic and has been throwing angels from Heaven. I was sent, with only one wing, to be Jason Parish's Christmas Angel. The future is grim and scary. We need to get back up there and put an end to this nonsense." Emma stood and held out a hand.

God gazed at her offering softly. "If getting up was that simple I'd never have let you experience the Hallway, Emma."

God pointed to a meter on the wall. Emma looked over her shoulder. It appeared to be a scale.

"Sir, I'm not sure I understand." Emma walked over to the device and tried to see its purpose.

"My presence is required to preserve that soul. If this bed is empty, the Devil gets one of my children."

Emma wanted to pull her hair out. The situation was so dire, and God was worried about one soul? She knew there was no reasoning with Him. Every single entity was His to love. She had no choice. She crossed the cell and sat next to Him.

Emma took His hand. "Sir, it would be my honor to take Your place. I'll not move from this spot. Please go forth and save the world. Please."

Emma had a feeling that her specific Hell would be fire, the one she hated most. She was disgusted with herself when she thought maybe the Devil would free her from time to time to make passes at her.

God touched Emma's face. "I would not have you do that. This is my burden."

"Sir, whose soul is it?" Surely she could withstand the pain for an innocent child. She could pretend it was Jason's soul she was saving, coloring his future black eyes green.

God was reluctant to tell her. She could tell. "Emma, do you remember how often you begged Me not to play Santa at Christmas and be the one to parlay for souls?" God imitated her voice: "Sir, it's a safety risk for You to descend to Earth, and You have no place in Hell. At least let some of the seraphim accompany You."

His kind blue eyes made her smile. He was playing with her. His attention was the most soothing balm.

"And, Sir, You would always say…" Emma made her voice deeper to mimic His. "Seraph Emma, the risk is minimal. I need to feel the love of the season. The positive energy is such a warm bath. And Satan is a child of mine as well."

God held her hand again. "You were right, of course. I gifted you with so much common sense." He looked in her face and for once she felt like someone was proud of who she was.

"Sir, how could we deny You the beauty of being near Your children? I can deny You nothing. Never. But our time here must be short. You have to go, please. Remember my common sense?" She looked at Him expectantly. "It's telling me You need to leave me here. Only God can fix the mess above."

Emma realized she had to put in a plug for Jason, this being her final face-to-face with God. "Sir, I'm not sure I finished my task with Jason Parish. But he's a good man—well, a good being. He needs to be made to believe He's worthy of You. Please, if it's Your will, please let him know what he's worth."

God closed His eyes and shook His head. "Of course I love Jason. But you, Emma, your bravery does not deserve to be rewarded with an eternity in Hell."

"I wasn't brave, Sir. I was scared and I cried and I didn't have a good solution for Sam, and I almost gave in to the Devil. And I cursed. A lot. I think this might be exactly where I belong." Emma hung her head.

"So much doubt, beautiful child. Do you not know the face of God?" He tilted her chin up and she looked at Him.

"Maybe I've never been good enough at all. I mean, I got into Hell." Emma's doubt flamed in her heart. Was that this cell's power or was her weakness her own?

"You came here to save Me and the world. You are more than good enough. I can't leave you here, and I won't." God seemed to settle in.

Emma sighed. She loved that God thought she was so important.

They sat next to each other for a moment. The cell door was open, inviting them both to leave the soul to the Devil and claim their escape.

There has to be something. There has to be something.

All of the sudden, Emma smiled. God turned to the goodness like a flower to sun.

"Sir, will You be making me an angel again? I know it's a lot to assume. I'm sorry for being forward." Emma stood from the bed.

God nodded. "Of course. I'll return your wings and restore your glory before you leave Me here."

Emma nodded. "I was hoping You'd say that. Please, Sir, can I have them now?"

God motioned for her to come closer. The ceremony was so much more beautiful in Heaven. The clouds would have been tinted with gold and the other angels would be standing by, resplendent in their nobility.

God kissed Emma's forehead, lips, and cheeks chastely, in the sign of the cross. She opened her eyes and looked into His benevolent ones. He recited the formal ritual.

"I claim your soul back under my care, beautiful seraph. Your unique perfection was created under my watchful gaze, and now you have been returned to me. I have always been proud of you, my child. But right now my praise will become wings for your shoulders. Angel Emma, you *are* loved." God hugged her to his chest, gently forcing her to bend.

His love shot through her heart and bloomed. Pure, crystal love straight from her maker raced through her and solidified into wings on her back. Her glorious, white wings became an oversized feathery frame for her body.

Tears fell from her eyes and she went to her knees before God. He smoothed her hair out of her face. The last time He'd performed this spectacular miracle, the stars had collided in huge, cosmic fireworks. The sun became brighter and rainbows danced in the sky. It had filled Emma with awe.

This time it was just her and God, but the awe and gratitude were just as potent. She tested her wings, and God laughed as she caught the glitter that fell like fresh snow from her feathers.

She looked down and her hooker outfit had disappeared. She wore her angel garb again. The white silk was butter soft. She was reinstated and proud.

Emma shook her head because she would miss this, very soon. She knew it took a lot out of God to create a seraph. He had to restore His energy between each angel.

"Sir, thank You." She bowed her head and wings to Him.

He nodded like the regal king He was.

"May I ask another question?" Emma twisted her hair into a knot.

She stepped a few feet away from God so couldn't reach her from the cot. God nodded. He seemed anxious for her to leave so she could get back to His pained, fallen angels.

"The half-breed, Jason, prayed to give me his strength. Was that emotional strength or physical?" Her hands started to shake.

God knew what she planned then. He connected the dots. He gave each of His children free will, and it was a gift He never demanded back.

He answered her because He would never lie. "Both, my child. He gave you both."

God's eyes filled with tears. Emma tried not to pause as she reached behind her and grabbed her brand new soft, white wing. She pulled as hard as she could and ripped it from her back. The pain caused her to scream and collapse. She hefted the wing in front of her. While she panted with agony, she tested the weight. It didn't seem heavy enough by itself.

She started to cry and God reached for her, His arms open as if for a hug. But she shook her head. Before she could lose her nerve she ripped the other manifestation of His love from her back, her screams filling the room again. The transformation was quick. She reverted to human in an instant. Her heart began to beat, and she took a deep breath of the stagnant air.

Her wings were too heavy for her to carry, so she dragged them as she crawled back to God. He lifted her into His lap, hugging her hard and touching her wounded back. Judging from the puddles of silver on the ground, God was healing her.

"My child, I love you so. Your pain is my pain." God's tears combined with hers on her cheek.

Even sitting in His lap, she felt farther from Him than she had when she'd been an angel a world away. "Please, take my wings and let's see if they're enough, if they can hold the bed down for us," Emma begged. "I'll come back to stay here and take my wings' place if the Devil demands his due, but first let's right the world."

Emma would have laughed at the image of a full-grown woman sitting in Santa's lap in Hell, but her soul had just been ripped in half by her own hands. She scooted down to sit on the mattress, and God reluctantly got up. He lifted her wings with ease and set them behind her on the bed.

"Your sacrifice will hold, my child." God gathered the crying Emma in His arms, holding her close to His chest.

She snuggled into His fuzzy red jacket and closed her eyes. God would carry her to the surface, and then they could make plans together.

CHAPTER 10

Emma reveled in the comfort of God's arms. His waves of pure, undiluted love could heal any wound. She stopped shaking as the mental and physical torture she'd endured faded away. She felt God kiss her hair, but she refused to open her eyes, not wanting to see what was making the horrible noises in Hell. Her hair came loose and tumbled around her shoulders again.

The void.

She knew they were now traversing the space she'd fallen through to get to Hell, and that the Devil had just been through in his quest to enter the world. He'd no doubt fought a raging battle, but God would jump, dodge, and send out beams of power to protect her, as well as Himself. She loved it like this. He made all the right decisions, and she was safe. Safe in Hell with God. Soon God's love was so warm it felt like sunlight on her face.

She realized they were at the surface when God chuckled softly. "My daughter, my sweet seraph, you must wake. I can't carry you forever."

She snuggled deeper in his arms like a sleepy child on a Monday morning.

"We have work to attend to, but holding you makes me feel so proud. I did a wonderful job with you, if I do say so myself." He set Emma on her feet, and she reluctantly faced the present.

She remembered her manners and nodded at Him. "Thank You, Sir."

God took in the sky above them, looking for falling angels. When He gazed at her again, it was with infinite patience. He would never rush her, even if the world were threatening to upend itself.

"Sir, may I make confession?" Emma knelt before Him. His fuzzy red pants and black boots became her confessional.

God put his hand on her head. "If it will give you comfort, my child."

"Sir, I've done a lot wrong lately, but the worst, by far, was doubting You." Emma clasped her hands together more tightly. She was almost used to her human form again, with its thumping blood and rhythmic breathing. "How can You hold me in Your arms when I failed to believe in Your power?" She needed His forgiveness. Whatever would come with the rest of the day, she could face it knowing she was right with God.

God took her prayer-filled hands and pulled her until she stood. Still, she kept her head down. "Emma. I forgive you for doubting me." He wouldn't let go of her hands. "Will you do me the same courtesy?"

She looked to His face in shock. "Of course not! I could never—"

God touched her cheek. "You would never imagine that I could make a mistake. I know, seraph. You're so hard on yourself. I gave my children free will, and that gift may have wrought more pain than I would ever want for you."

Emma leaned into His chest. He was the softest sun. He pulled her into a hug.

"Imagine what it was for me to watch you run into the barn to save your horse. As much as I love you, to let you step into that inferno?" He stroked her hair. "I never wanted to see you in pain, but I had to let you make that choice, Emma. Without tough choices there would be no souls entering Heaven at all. It's an incredible burden. I fight with myself every moment of this world's existence. To hear the prayers and let some go unanswered—sometimes it still feels like a mistake to me. My children come to me with open hearts and needs, and yet…and yet, they must live their lives as they wish." He gave a deep sigh, the burden of a thousand forevers.

Emma smiled into His Santa coat. "Okay, God. I forgive You for trusting me. I promise to trust You in return."

He patted her back, and she had to convince herself to step away from Him.

"I think I'm back to full power. Emma, are you ready for more wings?" God smiled into her face, like it was just a regular old day.

"No, Sir. We have too many angels to reinstate and save. We have to locate Everett. I think it's best if You save Your power for the next angel." Emma tried to ignore her body's craving for God's goodness.

He nodded, always respecting her decisions. "I'm not surprised you put others before yourself," He said. "You do have free will as a human again. Please be gentle with yourself for me."

Emma smiled, waiting to see what God would do next.

"My time here is limited, as you know," He said. "A full twenty-four hours and I'll start an apocalypse that won't stop. I think your time would be best spent finding Jason." God patted her shoulder.

Emma nodded. Her heart wanted to find the half-breed. She wanted to thank him for praying and releasing her from the Devil's snare.

God smiled and began to glow brightly. Emma tried to watch Him as long as she could as He transformed from a man to so much more. The light He emitted created green grass, flowing life from underneath the snow. The faces of countless lovely souls passed through the light as God rounded up His most recently departed children.

Her human eyes had to drop to the ground. When she looked back up, God was gone. Emma sighed. The loss of His power was devastating. She looked at her feet and saw that God had added snow white boots, a coat, and white leggings to her silky gown.

Both God *and* Jason had a penchant for dressing girls in warm clothes. She tried to orient herself. Jason's house was to the west, so she began to make the trip, walking like the mortal she had become.

It had been not even an hour when she encountered a random mist—a patch of smoke. The moment she walked into it, the smell was undeniable. It was the Devil's sweet cigarette smoke that acted as his pet. Then Emma saw his forearm and hand poking out of the snow. *Son of a bitch. He's like a never-ending virus.*

She let the rage of her Hallway Hell consume her. Emma would not help him. She probably couldn't help him. She took purposeful steps past his seemingly disembodied hand. The sidelong glances she begged herself not to take told her his hand was stiff and dead-looking.

But he can't die—he's already dead.

She vacillated between choices. Satan had been on his way up here to hurt Everett. And Everett needed hurting. She stomped on. The angel in her refused to let Hell come to Earth. Emma was here to defend it, even if her wings were weighing down a horrible scale, far from her body.

First she'd find Jason, then she'd figure out what to do about the Devil. She'd not gone a hundred steps when she heard God's voice so clearly in her head: *"I did a wonderful job with you, if I do say so myself."*

God would want her to save Satan. Emma knew He would. He loved all His children. *Even the freaking Devil.*

"You know what? It sucks to be me." Emma stomped back to the dead-looking hand.

His forearm bore a detailed tattoo of a cross, music note, and a knife. He must have known beauty at some point and wanted to keep it on his skin.

"This is so stupid. Honestly, this guilt I put on myself is crazy," Emma said to no one in particular. She used her hands to dig the snow away from his arm. "His twisted ass is going to toss me right back into that cell."

Emma gulped at the memory of the fire. It should have been enough to stop her cold, but she kept digging. When it became clear that his arm was buried deep in the soil, not just the snow, Emma had to pause to find a long stick. She used it to loosen the dirt and wiggle his arm free. She uncovered it all the way to his shoulder, then shook her head at his lack of movement. *He got so close. Just a few more feet and he'd have made it. Bastard.*

Suddenly his hand popped to life and grasped her arm tightly. She gasped. "Holy crap!" Her heart thudded wildly.

She grasped the arm that grabbed her and pulled and pulled. The Devil was vomited forth from the soil as if it was a great mouth. Emma stumbled backward, and the Devil landed with his face in her lap.

She started slapping at his evil head, but grew concerned when he didn't respond. One of his ankles was still buried in the ground. Although he'd spent an unknown chunk of time entombed, he had not a speck of dirt on him. Emma flipped him off her lap and onto the ground. He was limp. His leather jacket fell open to reveal his bare chest. Emma felt for a heartbeat and, of course, got nothing.

Damn it, he was moving just a few seconds ago. She threw her hands in the air and began mouth-to-mouth resuscitation. After three gusty mouthfuls of air, she felt his hand grab the back of her head. He turned the rescue maneuver into a deep French kiss. Emma responded before she remembered she hated him. Then she pulled herself away, and he let go of her hair. His eyes remained closed as he touched his fingertips to his lips.

"Emma the angel — that's what this set of lips tastes like." He opened one eye and smiled. "How in Hell are you here?" His delight reached his eyes.

She stood up. "No thanks to you or your Hallway of Horrors."

Satan remained prone and looked to the sky. "It's been a long fucking time since I've seen that."

He sat up and checked his guns and ammo. His ankle was still buried and Emma wasn't quite sure why it bothered her so.

I've saved him from the ground. My work here's done.

Emma pulled her hair away from her face and twirled it into a knot. "Well, I'm not sure where Everett is, but God's free and He's in Heaven, so you're here for no reason at all." She set off toward Jason's home again, internally cursing Satan. Then she felt his hand clamp around her boot. She stopped and waited.

He apologized quietly. "Emma, I wanted you to stay put. I never wanted you to face that Hallway."

She whirled to glare at him while thinking of Sam's gunshots, the hologram of her father, and God.

"It was designed perfectly to break me, so I find that a little tough to believe. You're the Devil. All you can do is lie." She tried to kick his hand off, but he would have none of it.

"Please, look at me?" he asked.

She stubbornly looked everywhere but his face. He waited. She gave an annoyed huff and glared at him.

The regret was tangible on his face. "Princess, I *have* to do a thorough job. You have free will? I don't. Not usually. You have courage? I don't. Not usually. Believe me when I tell you I didn't want to see you hurt. Not you."

He was so sincere. But Emma hated to concede him anything after what he'd put her through.

"You got out." She tried not to let her softening heart get into her words.

"No, I *almost* got out. Without you I would be here for all eternity waiting for someone to have sympathy for the Devil. I tend to think it would have been a long time." He had not released his iron grip, but his face was relaxed. "Can I say thank you?" He fluttered his alarmingly sexy eyelashes.

"No. Up yours. I pulled you out for my conscience, not to save you. That was just a byproduct." She wiggled and fidgeted, needing to find Jason.

"You're human now. God didn't see fit to keep you on His guard?" He looked worried despite his taunting words.

"No, Devil. He did. I ripped my wings off to keep the soul in balance so God could leave with me." She remembered the pain of her loss and snarled at him.

Then she was seized by regret. Maybe she shouldn't have told him that. Maybe he could snap his fingers and have her back on the cot.

He let go of her ankle and nodded. "I should've known. Of course you'd give your very redemption as freely as you gave your heart in life."

He pulled out his flask and took a deep drink, wiping his mouth with the back of his hand when he was done.

"If we're done here, good luck with Everett. Kick ass and all that." She readjusted her boot. His ankle being stuck still bothered her. "Are you going to be able to handle that?" she asked, gesturing toward it.

The Devil smiled at her concern. "Yes, pretty child, there's nothing I can't handle." He raked her body with a leering stare.

She hugged herself and shook her head. "Okay, then I gotta go."

"Wait! Please stay for a few moments. I need to free myself before I'm comfortable with you leaving my side. I can feel Everett's evil, and he's not in Heaven anymore." Satan pulled out a knife and started hacking at the soil around his foot. "Actually, he's knee deep in half-breeds, if I'm judging correctly." The Devil was using an extraordinary amount of force to try to free his ankle.

"Well, to Hell with you. I've got to get to Jason." Emma began backing away from the scene.

"Emma? I have one last battle to fight before I'm allowed here on Earth. And this last beast? He has a taste for hope. He likes to eat it for dinner. When he busts through, which I gauge to be in about thirty seconds..." Satan pulled his foot free from the soil. His ankle was wrapped in a slender, green tentacle. "He'll go straight for you. I'd prefer he had to go through me first. So if you'd be kind enough to stay behind me..." The Devil smiled and gestured to his side like he was offering her his spot on a crowded bus.

The ground began to rumble. She staggered closer to Satan only because he was armed and seemed prepared. He caught her around the waist and pulled her against him.

"Have no fear, beautiful. He'll have to kill me to get you."

Satan kissed her lips gently, but Emma hardly noticed. Behind him a tremendous dragon-shaped evil emerged from the ground. It was at least twice the size of the tallest tree Emma had ever seen.

Satan watched the beast reflected in her eyes. "Emma, look at me, don't look at him. He searches for hope and kills it. You're the brightest beacon for him. Stay behind me. I'm hoping my hate will mask you."

She tore her eyes from the bone-chilling beast and looked at the Devil's handsome face.

"Princess, if he gets to me and I fall, promise me you'll run—" The ground began curling and forming mounds from the force of the monster's first earth-bound steps. "Run and pray to your God the whole time. Promise me. Do it now!"

Emma swallowed hard. She couldn't get her voice to work, so she nodded as fast as she could.

Satan still held her. "Kiss me once more, angel. It will give me strength."

Emma grabbed both sides of his face and kissed his lips softly. "Bless you."

The sun was eclipsed now by the monster who seemed distracted by his non-fleeing prey. Satan smiled at her once more, then turned to stand between her and the scariest thing she could ever imagine.

He drew a pistol and in one motion pointed it at the thing's head. "Were you looking for this, asshole?" Satan had fantastic aim and in a flash he'd hit it right between its massive, rolling eyes.

Emma hated gunshots—especially after Sam, after the eagle, after the Hell Hallway—but right now it was a comforting sound.

Right after the echo of the firearm cleared, she heard Satan mutter, "Oh shit."

The monster didn't flinch. The bullet bounced off it like a fly encountering a speeding car. She stepped closer to Satan's back, clung to his leather jacket, and started to pray.

CHAPTER 11

Jason knew he was screaming her name, but he hardly recognized his own voice. The pain he felt was more than he should ever be allowed to survive. This horrible angel was holding him high above his brother and sister and cracking his skull.

He clawed at Everett's hands because he had to, and he managed to kick the evil angel during his flailing. The pain in his head lessened a tiny bit. Jason kicked him again. Everett grew wise quickly and spun Jason around. Now Jason faced away from Everett. He tried to kick again and his foot connected with nothing but air.

Everett whispered in his ear. "Wouldn't it be hilarious to watch a vampire bleed to death? Such irony."

Jason's brain was going to crack; he felt liquid seeping from the fissures he knew were forming.

Emma, he's going to kill me. I'll see you soon. Jason tried to take one last peek at the world he'd had so much trouble living in. He could barely open his eyes. When a tree appeared in the sky and arched above his head, he thought it was a delusion until it hit Everett with a thud.

He heard Dean bellow, "I'm coming up!"

Jason tried to wriggle free and found he could open his eyes a bit more.

Dean appeared on the same flight path as the tree. He hurtled through the air like a rocket. After first throwing a tree like a javelin, he'd climbed to the top of the highest tree and jumped with all his might to defend his brother.

The minute his brother's body hit Everett's, Jason was in free fall. He had no sense of space and time, but was caught by his sister before he could hit the ground. Seriana laid Jason gently on the forest floor.

"Jason? You're bleeding." She sounded confounded.

Jason nodded. "Dean?"

Seriana gave Jason the play-by-play. "He's pounding on the thing that had you. We can't really see it. Every once in a while we catch a flicker of something, but what *is* that?"

Jason propped himself up on his elbow. "Dean. Get Dean down. You have to get away from here. It's me he wants."

His sister ignored him. "This is human blood coming from your wounds. This makes no sense at all. What are we dealing with?"

Jason watched as Dean pounded away on the angel he couldn't see.

"It's power like we've never seen. *He* was draining *me!*" Jason pulled himself to a sitting position.

Just then Dean was knocked out of the sky like a tennis ball. Her reflexes faster than light, Seriana dove quickly and caught him.

When they were all together again Jason decided out loud, "I have to help." He tried to stand.

"The hell you will. Stay put. I have no idea what this monster has done to you." Dean pushed Jason backward so he was lying flat on the ground.

Jason's head swirled as he saw his family fighting valiantly against what seemed to them to be mostly thin air. Only he could see this most majestic of threats. Then his vision blurred as he began to drift between consciousness and blackness. *Everett could end us all in a second. He's just playing now.*

As the horrible thing shrieked again, Emma buried her face in the Devil's leather jacket.

Satan tried to be comforting. "Don't worry, angel. I think I know how to kill it…just might take a few tries."

He opened fire again. Judging from the earth-trembling screams, he was just making the dragon angrier. Satan backed up slowly, as if he was leading her in a dance. Emma's frightened feet complied with his sure ones.

This thing would surely tear them both to pieces, and she was only human. She was useless and helpless, nearly paralyzed by her terror. Her eyes snapped open. She was hiding behind the Devil.

She was hiding behind the *Devil.*

What the hell am I thinking?

Ignoring the fear that threatened to pull her under, but she unclenched her fingers from his jacket. The animal hide held an imprint where her hands had been.

"Sweetheart? You okay?" Satan had taken to throwing knives at the monster. It snapped its huge jaws, spittle flying in every direction.

Emma took a breath of the panic-soaked air. *I'll be more than this. If these are my last moments...*

She stepped out from behind his protection. The evil dragon was whipped into a frenzy, his body rippled with muscle and pent-up aggression.

"Emma! Get back here. Please!" Satan began firing ammunition into the beast again to draw its attention away from her.

"No." She took sure steps in the direction of Jason's house.

"Stay put—I'll get to you!" Satan tried to move toward her, but the dragon snarled at him.

"No, I won't. This is *your* battle. Not mine. I'll not hide like a coward."

It was a huge risk, possibly the last she would take.

"You're human!" Satan pulled the pin on a scary-looking grenade, then tossed it in the beast's direction. The bomb bounced harmlessly off the dragon's armored skin and exploded somewhere behind the dragon.

"Crap." Satan rolled his eyes in frustration and made a move.

He tried to forward-roll in Emma's direction, but the dragon's massive tail swept back to knock him off his course. It had Emma in its sights, and with three thundering stomps it was breathing its horrible breath inches from her face.

She was just a lone girl standing in the white snow. Emma had nothing in her hands. She had no protection. The creature's tail kept the Devil at bay, knocking him flat on his ass anytime he looked like he was making progress. Everything in Emma was quaking. Everything but the one tiny light that always stayed bright no matter what she faced.

Instead of screaming in horror and alarm, she whispered to the dragon. "You don't feed on hope. I don't believe that. Hope makes me stronger." She began to sweat. The beast still hadn't touched her, though it was so close. "I think you feed on doubt. I think you feed on fear. I'm afraid. I know I am."

The thing began an awful, impatient snapping. Its jaws could easily rip her head from her neck.

"But I know better. I know even if you kill me, God loves me. He'll never leave me. I have hope. And I believe." She kept her shoulders straight and proud.

The thing still hadn't acted on the instinct for violence it seemed to have. Satan threw himself onto the dragon's back, but it just shimmied until he tumbled off.

Emma got braver. She felt the pure touch of goodness warm her from within, and it gave strength to her words.

"Go!" she yelled. "Get. No one fears you here. Go!" She moved her hands like the dragon was a stray dog she was sending home.

It didn't move anything except its Devil-beating tail.

"I forgive you, beast. You know not what you do." Emma felt like she was talking to a dinosaur—all teeth and no brains.

But it began to slink backward. She stepped forward as it retreated, emboldened by her possible success. Then one of its arm-like tentacles grasped the Devil around the ankle again. The dragon was fully intending to drag Satan back down to the void.

Emma's wanted to have a harder heart. But Satan's defeated sigh made her fight for him, too.

"No. Leave him be! He has hope too. Drop him!" Now unable to disobey, the beast became smaller and smaller until it liquefied and funneled itself into the hole in the ground from whence it had come.

The Devil sat in the snow, looking at the spot where the beast had disappeared. Emma nodded at him and turned her back. She could save his miserable life, but she didn't have to tend to his wounds. She started the trek to the Parish house. She hated herself, but after a few paces she turned to look over her shoulder. Satan was limping along.

No good can come of this—of him. But she watched as he struggled to catch up and stood still until he was next to her again. His brown eyes assessed her. She put his arm around her shoulders and supported some of his weight.

He was the first to break the silence. "You defeated it without me. Here I was thinking I'd be your hero, and you didn't need one."

"I needed you for a few minutes there." Emma tried not to look at his too-close, handsome face. "Do you have some sort of evil-sensing GPS? Do you know how long it will take us to get to Everett?"

Satan readjusted his position, slipping his hand further down on her collarbone. "I do know. We have a while."

Emma decided to use him as a sounding board. "I know sweet-talking won't stop Everett, like it did your pet lizard."

"You think you sweet-talked the dragon? No way. It must be those sexy lips. I think anything would do what you told it to." His voice was husky and smoky-sounding.

His hand slipped lower.

"You have an insight on Everett," Emma said, plowing forward. "You worked with him on this evil he's trying to accomplish. Give me some information. I *did* save your ass." Emma shrugged her shoulder so his hand was further away from her bosom.

"That seems fair. Tit…for tat," he said.

She didn't need to look at his face to know he was smiling like a bastard.

His hand inched lower again.

Emma stopped them both and pushed his hand off. "Listen, you horny asshole. You touch my boob and I'm going to hit you in the hairy larrys so hard you won't be able to see straight."

He put his hands up in innocent surrender. "I had no such intentions, my sweet." His devious smile came out to play. "Did you just call my testicles hairy larrys?"

Emma shrugged. "Yeah. Whatever. If you hold them dear, you'll steer clear of my parts." She gave Satan a onceover and realized he was completely healed. "And it looks like you're fine. Let's walk and talk."

Satan mumbled as he shuffled along. "Surprised you got out of Hell at all with that potty mouth of yours."

"Tell me what Everett told you." She ignored his barb, staying focused.

"Everett? What's there to tell? He wants to take over the world—that's obvious. Got to admire how nefarious that winged fairy is." Satan popped his flask open again and took a swig.

He offered her the metal canister with a raised eyebrow. When she went to slap it out of his hand, Satan pulled it out of her reach, all the while tisking her behavior. Emma closed her eyes and shook her head. After a few deep breaths, she was still overwhelmingly angry with him.

"You have admiration for the beast that ripped off my wing? That killed my love? You disgust me. No, worse than that. You disappoint me." Emma decided to try her luck with a jog, hoping her human form was ready to be put through its paces.

But soon she heard his annoying footfalls, combined with the squeak of leather and jangle of various chains and weapons. She refused to look at him.

He spoke up, just as she expected him to, but he didn't say what she'd anticipated.

"Let me apologize again, Emma. I'm a jerk. I—" He wasn't even short of breath.

She interrupted him. "No 'jerk' is too kind a term for your crazy ass. I think I'd go with 'freakshow' or 'loony bastard' or—"

"Okay! I get it. No, really. I do." He held up his hands when she glared at him.

Emma growled like a tiger.

"See, I'm going to be an adult and not mention how much I want to make you growl like that when you're naked." He smiled. "I'm learning, right?"

Emma gave him the finger—easier than talking. Her breath wasn't coming as easy now, though her body seemed to be in good shape.

"Everett has a huge case of jealousy. He wants what he can't have. Right now, if God's truly in Heaven, I'm betting He'll allow the fallen angels to handle Everett," the Devil continued. "You know you're harshest to one of your own. So if you can keep Everett from killing those half-breeds and, well, you, I'm sure your angel friends will keep his other destructive accomplishments to a minimum." Satan turned to run backward, apparently so he could look at her face and show off at the same time.

Emma wanted to curse him, but she had to concentrate on running. If she remembered correctly, the Parishes' house should be coming into view soon…maybe. Satan stopped abruptly in front of her with his arms wide open. Emma's momentum ran her right into him. He clamped her close to his chest. He smelled delicious.

"We need to move a little faster, princess, though your effort's commendable. I can't convince you to stay put and let me take care of this fucking thing?"

His mouth moved in the most delightful way when he cursed. She looked at the snow and shook her head, still panting from her run.

"Very good then. Hold tight. You do remember how this is done?" He kept one arm around her waist and snaked the other up her back. "I'm still an angel, baby, just a naughty one."

She barely trusted him, so she looked at him to try to see his intentions. Satan's face was so tender. His eyes were soft as he freed her hair from its knot and let it curtain around her shoulders.

"Pretty child, the only reason I wished you were still in Hell was so I could have someone to look forward to." He tilted his cheek in her direction and motioned for her to kiss him.

Emma touched his face and hated picturing him in that smoky room again. "Can't that change? I mean, if you help me?"

Satan took her hand and set it on his chest. His heart was beating.

"If I go back, that stops. Again. I'm about to thrust us in the middle of a battle. Everett won't know whose side you're on." Satan ran his hand from her face to her hips, changing her outfit with his motion. "Appearances are everything."

Being this close to him made her skin tingle. He was so punishingly good-looking.

"Pretend to be on my side until the angels show up. I can keep you from taking a beating." He touched her cheek gently.

She looked down to find that her outfit very much matched his: a leather jacket, low-slung jeans, and a tank top.

"Thanks for not making me topless like you, at freaking least." She brought her lips close to his cheek, nearly ready to angel-warp with him into the battle. But she had to settle one last thing. "I believe you're on my side. When push comes to lightning bolts, I know you're my friend. Right?" Her lips were so close to his skin.

Just as she made contact with his cheek, she heard him breathe, "I've never had a true friend before."

The forest became blurry. She grasped him tighter, feeling off balance in her human body. He took the opportunity to get two handfuls of her ass. As they were dropped in the middle of the clearing, Emma began slapping at his chest and his face. His rumbling laughter brought a sparkle to his wicked eyes. He set her carefully on her feet despite her ongoing assault.

He leaned forward and whispered, *"With* me now, remember?"

She gave him a dirty look but nodded as she turned to the cacophony of noise behind her. The forest seemed to be moving. Two half-breeds were putting up a great fight, leaping through the trees and throwing boulders, but often missing the fiery-red Everett that Emma could clearly see.

"Can't they see him? I can."

"God must have left you a few angel's gifts," Satan whispered in her ear. "He usually does."

Everett had a huge, sickening smile. He looked like a mean cat holding a mouse with four broken legs in its mouth.

Jason? Jason? The half-breeds were definitely Jason's siblings. No one else would fight for him like that—especially not other half-breeds. Then she had an idea. But how could she tell Satan? She couldn't let Everett hear. Just then he spotted the new arrivals and waved at Satan like they were school-aged friends.

Satan smiled and gave a friendly wave while talking out of the side of his mouth to Emma. "Crap, he's an idiot."

Emma licked her lips and threw herself back in the Devil's arms.

He lifted her happily. "Change your mind? We can go somewhere and drink while the world collapses around us. Oh, and we can fuck too."

"I think your smoke that follows you around is *so* sexy. Where is it?" Emma asked.

From Everett's point of view, Emma looked insatiable. But as she gazed at the Devil, her eyes were wide and begging him to understand. She looked from him to Everett and back again.

The Devil looked from her lips to her eyes and back again. "Clever, little princess. Great idea. Smoke it is."

He clicked his tongue like he was calling a horse, and his smoke obeyed. Soon the clearing was enveloped in a hazy cloud. Everett was perfectly outlined, the only crystal clear, angel-shaped hole in the smoke. Dean and Seriana now began throwing with punishing accuracy.

"That'll piss him off and soon," the Devil commented as he grabbed her ass again. Emma stomped on his foot after she wiggled out of his arms. He smiled, but his brown eyes looked sad. He touched her face one more time, then motioned with his head. "Your half-breed, pretty child. He's in a bad way. Right over there."

Emma whirled and spotted Jason lying under a tree. He was motionless and covered in blood. Her role playing was forgotten. The Devil fell from her radar. The havoc above her was meaningless.

She was there in an instant. Emma's hands skimmed over every part of Jason's skin she could touch. "No! No! I've come so far," she yelled. "Please. No! You don't die!" She pulled her jacket off and covered his body, as if she could warm him.

Jason didn't move, didn't register her presence. Emma leaned down and kissed his lips softly.

She begged him quietly now. "I could only picture you. You got me through Hell. Jason, be here with me. Please." She laid her head on his chest, her tears falling on the jacket the Devil had clothed her in to convince an angel she was bad.

Emma clutched Jason so tightly that even when Everett sent the sonic boom that knocked his half-breed attackers from their feet, she stayed secure, hugging her heart's dearest wish.

CHAPTER 12

The Devil braced himself, legs planted firmly, as Everett unleashed his sonic wrath. A sidelong glance told him Emma was okay. With a flick of his wrist he'd shielded her, unseen, from the worst of the flying debris because he couldn't stand to see her hurt. But now he wondered if she'd thank him if she knew. She held the mostly dead body of the half-breed like it was anchoring her to life. She was still crying, draped over him, as the other half-breeds picked themselves up off the ground.

Her cries were heartbreaking because the Devil was willing to bet she'd never cry that hard for herself. If his heart could hold emotion anymore, which he didn't think it could, she would move him. The two mostly alive half-breeds seemed to be sorting out who, exactly, Emma was. He heard them introduce themselves to her. Emma quickly explained she was Jason's Christmas Angel, sent to help him see his worth and feel God's love. Sending darting glances back and forth and speaking in hushed tones, they seemed to connect the dots between their brother's "imaginary" friend and the girl in front of them. Emma ignored them and sought to find Jason's wound. Then Dean knelt and concisely explained what he'd seen of Jason's battle.

Satan pulled a cigarette out of his jacket pocket. He flicked the tip, and it glowed orange. He took a long, steadying drag. He noticed that Everett still hovered high above the group, like the pussy he was. He likely overheard Emma explaining Jason's injuries after Dean's report.

"No, of course you don't know what's wrong with him. Everett used a technique on Jason that's only intended for souls," Emma said.

The Devil rubbed his nose with his knuckle and took the chance to peek at her again. She was using snow to wipe the fallen half-breed's face clean. From the fierce look on her face, he judged that her despair had turned to fiery anger.

"Everett! You mouth-breather. You never, never do this to a body! And guess what? God's back, bitch." She dug her hands into her thick hair in frustration.

The Devil took another pull of his sweet-smelling drug.

Emma stood and held her hands out, palms up. "God, please. I was wrong. I want my wings back, please!"

Emma bit her lip and kept her faithful gaze on the sky, which clouded up with a fast-moving front. Tiny snowflakes began shaking down from the heavens. But no wings bloomed on Emma's back. She hung her head. She'd received her answer. The Devil clicked his tongue, and Emma looked at him across the expanse of white.

His voice was intimate and sexy, despite the distance. "He said no?"

Dean and Seriana, who had gathered around Emma, looked confused about what the hell this smoking, leather-clad entity had to do with any of this.

She looked angrily at the Devil. "My wings are busy right now. Thanks for that."

She knelt by Jason's side again, rearranging her jacket around him. "Jason, as soon as God takes care of Everett, I'll appeal to Him. I'll beg Him to fix you. The power Everett used against you was never meant to do anything other than purify a soul for Heaven. It hurt so much because you have a physical body, not just a soul. He's a bastard. I'll do whatever it takes. I'll bring you back to your family."

It wasn't her words that moved Satan, but the hand she kept on the half-breed's cheek, as if he could really hear her. Everett's fluttering had become agitated. The news that God was free must be burning his ass.

Then he called down. "Satan, what brings you above? Delivering Emma to me? I guess I get a Christmas present. Thanks a lot."

The Devil ignored Everett. He needed to end Emma's suffering, and he had a way. He wasn't proud of his weakness, but Emma's kindness was hurting the Devil's heart.

She stroked Jason's hair. She was busy thinking—trying to think. Jason's hands curled and trembled. Emma grasped one of them. "God, I know you're busy, and you have a lot of love going on up there, but I can't do this by myself," she prayed aloud. "Save him."

Dean hugged Seriana as the two stood a polite distance away, not wanting to disturb the scene.

Satan took a deep breath and held his hand in Jason's direction. He concentrated and pulled the suffering out of him, healing him in the process, closing his wounds. Satan absorbed the death that had Jason at the brink.

The Devil took a breath, hissing with the influx of agony. His hand holding the cigarette began to shake—the slow, steady stream of smoke breaking into Morse code for torment. *To protect Emma. To find Claudette*, he told himself.

Everett began to rain lightning bolts down on the clearing.

Satan dropped to one knee. He couldn't believe how much torture the half-breed had endured before succumbing to Everett. He glanced over again at Emma and found her looking back at him. He had to rally, and quickly.

For a moment Emma was afraid the Devil had been hit by something Everett had thrown. But when their eyes met, he gave her a saucy look.

"What I wouldn't give for my wings!" Emma shouted, drawing Dean and Seriana closer. "If I begged the Devil to give them to me, I could let the soul they're protecting in Hell be damned," she reasoned, looking up to find Jason's siblings staring blankly, unable to follow her argument. "With my wings I could do work. I could kick ass."

Emma looked down at Jason's beautiful face in repose, so innocent and young—or young-looking at least. "He wouldn't want that," she said, ending the debate with herself. "He's too good to punish even an anonymous soul. Crap!"

Seriana squeezed her shoulder.

Finally the Devil was able to close his fist, sealing the death he'd pulled from Jason inside his own body. Satan stood back on both feet, trying to find a place for the pain so he could think clearly. He had no time to ponder the irony that his healing power had been used for good this time. It was usually one of his most effective tortures in Hell. He'd resolve pain, only to reintroduce it tenfold. But he'd never kept the pain within himself before. Normally he held it just long enough to flame his anger and implement more viciousness.

But in this clearing—unbelievably, here on Earth—he'd rather have his hands shake with pain than see the pretty child cry. The Devil resolved not to let on that he'd healed Jason. *Let her think her God answers her prayers.*

Emma's brain and human body were almost spent. She couldn't imagine absorbing any more unhappiness. *I should really apologize to his family for getting Jason involved in this mess.* But just then, Jason's hands uncurled and his eyelashes fluttered a tiny little bit. Emma gave a cry of joy and turned to Seriana and Dean. "Did you see that?"

Immediately the half-breeds flanked her sides.

Jason's green eyes blinked open and took in the faces above him. "No, get out of here! That thing's too dangerous," he blurted the moment his pupils focused.

Dean gave a sigh only a relieved brother could make and patted Jason's hand. He looked at the snowy sky and its ominous attacker as he spoke. "We know, Jason." Dean grinned. "Seriously, brother, what do you think we've been doing while you napped?"

Jason smiled at Emma. "You're back? How was Hell? I wish my family could see you." He reached a hand up and stroked Emma's cheek.

Seriana hugged Emma's shoulders. "You mean this girl, here? We can see her."

Jason laid a hand on Emma's chest and felt the sweet, steady heartbeat. He sat up with his surprise. "You're human?"

Emma put her hands on his cheeks and gave him a tender kiss on his mouth. "It's a long story, but yes. I'm back, and I brought a souvenir."

Emma looked pointedly at Satan. She noticed the Devil's hand shaking slightly, the smoke from his cigarette inconsistent. His eyes met hers and for an instant, less than a blink, he let her past his hard exterior. She saw the soul beneath the swagger and sex. He was tortured, but he cared for her deeply.

Jason helped Emma up. The Devil looked at him and squinted. Emma felt a flare of alarm. Jason nodded and cocked his head, listening to words the Devil wasn't saying out loud. Then, grabbing Emma, he quickly rounded up his family and pulled them all out of the clearing into the trees.

He began talking immediately. "That *is* truly the Devil. He wants us out of here, the faster the better. I guess the angels are coming to get Everett, so we're going back to the house."

Emma followed as they began to move, but she shook her head at Jason. "You know I have to stay."

Jason paused. "I can hear his thoughts, like I was able to do on our trips to the past and future. Does that make sense to you?"

"Sometimes God gives us gifts," Emma said, remembering the Devil's observation before the battle. "I keep trying to convince you He cares."

Turning to Dean and Seriana she said, "God's restoring angels as we speak, so I would expect them very soon—like, now."

Even Dean, who always liked a fight, seemed to know it was more than time to run like hell. Emma leaned around the tree to look at the Devil. He was alone now, his smoke dissipated to who knew where. He took one last drag of his cigarette and flicked it to the ground.

Feeling more centered, Satan looked up to see Everett preparing another bolt, his eyes on Emma. The Devil gave a half-smile. His time as a bystander was about to end. He had to pick a side. Everett or Emma. Bad or good. His system accepted evil like a drug, but her blond curls had felt like home in his hands. And he hadn't had a home he cared about in so long.

As he exhaled, he held his hands open. In his palms grew horrific, purple-red fiery orbs. He smiled in Everett's direction while he tossed them like basketballs into the sky.

Dean and Seriana agreed to leave as Emma watched Satan fight, hardly able to look away. She finally turned and nodded at the pair while waving goodbye. Jason assured his family they'd be right behind them.

"You're so important to me," Emma said, returning her focus to Jason. "Thank you for coming back. I was scared I'd lost you."

Jason smiled and a bit of relief peeked through his stress. "I feel exactly the same way. Tell me, who is that Devil to you? I see worry in your eyes for him."

Emma wasn't sure she could put her emotions into words. "He's bad. I mean, obviously. But he might be a friend of mine. I can't tell if I can trust him."

Jason shrugged. "Right now, according to his thoughts, he just wants you and Claudette to be safe. Does that help?"

"I know I'm just human, but I don't want to leave until this is settled," Emma said. "You should go ahead with your family. I know where your house is. I'll come there when it's all done." She patted his shoulder.

"If you think I'm leaving you, you're crazy. Not again. Not after last time." Jason took her patting hand and kissed it.

Another sonic boom knocked them both flat, into the soft snow. Emma landed with her face turned toward the clearing. She saw Satan on his knees, holding his chest.

Jason's hand reach for her waist just as she noticed her wrists wrapped in snow-covered spider webs. She left the breath she'd been taking behind as her body was jerked to the sky. Everett was attached to the opposite end of the webs that held her, and before she could orient herself, she was cradled against his bare chest. He smelled of crisp snow.

He buried his nose in her hair and murmured, "Sweetness, I thought I'd lost you for good. Please tell me Jack kept his dirty hands off you."

Emma tried to wriggle free, but her body had relaxed despite the alarm in her head. He was using the ability angels have to put the dying at ease before their transition into Heaven against her.

"Who the hell is Jack?" Emma tried to bite Everett's finger as he affectionately touched her nose.

Everett leaned down and kissed her lips. She found when he lifted his mouth from hers she couldn't talk anymore.

Asshole.

"Jack is Satan, of course. Didn't you ask him his name? No matter. I need to change my plans. You, baby girl, may not live through this, but I would like the angels to side with *me* when they get here." Everett cuddled her like a teddy bear.

She looked down on the clearing from her psychotic new perch. Jack was still clutching his chest, and Jason stood directly beneath her, talking into his cell phone. The beat of wings in the distance whipped the sky into a blizzard.

The angels were coming in a flock.

"You see Jack? He's finally getting his due," Everett said with a smirk. "I'm making his heart turn any sin he has into poison. It's the first step to Hell, as you well know."

She could see the leaders of the flock. Seraph Gabriel focused on Everett, his eyes furious and righteous in their anger. But Emma knew there was one man Gabriel might hate even more, and he'd just fallen face first into the snow.

Chapter 13

Seraph Gabriel was handsome and furious. And he had eyes only for Everett. Emma was immobile and hating every second of it. *At least Jason is fine*, she told herself. Satan, on the other hand, was twitching in the snow. *Jack*, her mind corrected. Her heart softened as she remembered he once had been a man.

The angels' wings fluttered in unison, and each righteous face was etched with justice about to be delivered. Everett turned his back slightly to change his outfit, and in a heartbeat he'd replaced his tux with a crisp, white business suit when he once again faced the virtuous army, now gathering in a semicircle around him in midair.

Gabriel made the sign of the cross while the other angels surrounded Everett. Emma tried to plead to them with her eyes. Then Everett leaned down and tenderly kissed each of her eyelids. They were sealed shut. She was in complete blackness, but she could hear Everett's deception start on a course of no return.

"Brothers, sisters, it pleases me endlessly to see you," he began. "I have fought a hard, lonely battle. Many of you have been hurt by me, and for that I extend my deepest apologies." Everett repositioned Emma so her face nestled deeper against his chest, as if she was a resting babe. "God and I worked together to bring the Devil to the surface. It seems Jack was working with our beautiful Emma to bring destruction to our fair land."

Seraph Gabriel's deep, authoritative voice claimed the air. "Brother Everett, you would have us believe that tearing our wings from our backs and scattering us far from our home was part of a larger plan?"

Everett took a deep, pretend breath. "I know, kind Gabriel, my actions were drastic, but the implications were dire. God was trapped, and I had to save Him the best way I knew how."

Emma knew Everett's buttery words were supported by his glistening wings. The angels' desire to see good in their own kind made them easily blinded—and quick to find fault in those not from Heaven. None of them had made a move to rescue Emma, or even ask about her condition. "Of course, you all know about my affection for Emma, so I made sure she was not ended. She can start her life again, as a human, if the Council agrees. Every seraph deserves another chance." He began petting her hair like he would a cat. "Of course, she has lain with the Devil. Maybe she's even pregnant with his spawn, but I could no sooner condemn her than I could spit on God's feet."

The angels tittered amongst themselves, distracted by Everett's smooth demeanor and the scandal of another's sin. The proof was before their very eyes. Satan was reeling on the ground below. And they were now fully restored angels again, despite their brief, uncomfortable banishment.

"Well, God told us to listen to our hearts and make the best judgment we could," said Seraph Gabriel. He seemed to be weighing his options.

"He has infinite wisdom and loves all His children," Everett said, nodding. "I'll need your assistance to handle Satan. I'm surprised my heart-poisoning technique has contained him this long."

Everett shuffled Emma again anxiously and went for the killing verbal blow. "I know we all considered Emma to be an unconventional angel—maybe a little unworthy. If I'm to be brutally honest, as I feel I must be, her fall reflects poorly on all of us. But Gabriel, you would forgive Claudette any sin, and this is how I feel toward Emma." He paused dramatically. "Look quickly, the half-breed vampires are assembling. I'm sure hoards of them are on their way. They move so quickly. They're practically his children. We all know how evil the minion's spawn are."

Jason was reassured when his family reappeared in the clearing after his cell phone call. He had no idea how to help the writhing Satan, or even if he should. He looked up to see the angels in their impromptu sky gathering. *How can they ignore this pain here on the ground?*

Seriana held a hand to her mouth when she saw the Devil's torment.

Just then a small, brown-haired angel fluttered down softly and slowly, leaving the group above. She looked reluctant as she approached the Devil.

Jason motioned for Dean and Seriana to stand underneath Everett. Softening Emma's fall, were she to have one, would be their main job.

The small angel crept closer to the Devil and reached out a tentative hand.

Jason couldn't read the angel's thoughts, but the Devil's were one long, sure word as he endured Everett's torture: *Nooooo!*

"I'm here, Jack. Please allow me to pray over you." The little angel stroked his face. "Heavenly Father, please hold Jack in the palm of Your hand. Heal his pain, both real and imagined. He may no longer be in Your flock, but I know he's in Your heart. Let the truth shine through him and create the peace he craves. Amen" She smiled on the Devil and his muscles relaxed. She took his hand and Satan opened his eyes.

Jason expected a warm rush of pleasure to fill Satan's mind. Having an angel smile upon you was amazing—Jason knew first hand.

Claudette. My Claudette…

The Devil's thoughts were strangely tempered. He was warmed by her attention, but there was no rush of feeling, which seemed to confuse even him. Jason's jaw tightened as Satan then pictured Emma instead.

Now that he was no longer convulsing, the Devil propped himself up on an elbow. He scanned the sky and found Emma nestled in Everett's arms. Only then did he return his attention to his long-lost angel, now before him.

"Claudette, are you okay? Did that bastard hurt you?" The Devil pulled his metal flask out and took a healthy swallow. "I've missed you," he added thoughtfully as he wordlessly offered the flask to Claudette.

She shook her head. Satan shrugged and slipped the flask out of sight.

"If you're referring to Brother Everett, no. He did not hurt me," Claudette said, exasperated. "I find it hard to believe you would try to taint the face of Earth with your evil, Jack. I thought you were a better man than that." She sat back on her heels. Her gorgeous wings gently pulsed, sweeping the snow with every pass.

"I'm not a good man, cupcake. That's why I have the job I do. Is that Gabriel's pansy ass up there? Is he going to play tiddlywinks with the mutiny maker? That sounds about right for him." Satan stood and offered his hand to help Claudette. She took it, like Emma never would.

"Please, Jack, Seraph Gabriel's a good man. He's very fair." She hovered a bit above the Devil.

"Yes, he *was* very fair. I think he shared his dick with every willing female in Heaven." The Devil pulled out a cigarette and licked the end to start its fire. It became an easy extension of his hand.

Claudette looked down and crossed her arms. "I couldn't see you in pain. I don't like that. I never did. But I also refuse to lie to you. I love Gabriel. We've been lovers all these years."

The Devil took the news like a slap and quickly looked up at Everett before returning his gaze to Claudette. *It's not love. It's never been love.* His thoughts were sharp as they came to Jason. Satan shook his head, arguing with himself. *At least* she *never loved* me…

The angels' animated overhead conversation sprinkled glitter in with the falling snow. It looked like a rainbow was melting in pieces.

"Claudette, the girl he holds is in danger," the Devil said, scowling up at Everett again. "He's talking a bunch of smack. Honestly, I could give a rat's ass if the world blows up, or even if you all decide to take the douchebag back to base camp and crown him king. I want that girl on Earth with these half-breeds. That's the best, safest place for her. Tell them to do that, and I'll go quietly."

Satan met Jason's eyes. *I know you can hear me. Listen, things are going to get ugly. They're likely to take Everett's side. Can you promise me you love her? Do you love Emma?*

Jason had known angel Emma for a day, really. Maybe twenty-four full hours, but it felt like a lifetime. He knew he loved her. He knew he loved her when he tore off her wing. He knew he loved her when he came to and she was there, standing in his forever as a human girl.

"I do." Jason looked up at her in the sky.

Okay. No matter what, get her out of here. No matter what.

Claudette flew quickly and softly to rejoin the circle, but she seemed reluctant to report Satan's demands to her peers. On the ground, Jason pointed out different strategic places for his family to stand. Dean prepared to start tossing nature by snapping the branches off trees and gathering boulders.

The sky-high argument was escalating. Finally Claudette pushed Gabriel into asking for Emma.

Seraph Gabriel looked cautiously at Everett as he made his point. "Everett, it seems these are very unusual circumstances. Why don't you give Emma to Claudette, and you and I can go back to God and figure out what needs to be done?"

Satan met Jason's eyes and told him again, silently, *No matter what.*

Everett used his wings to pull himself away from the crowd. His arms tightened around Emma. His eyes were growing shifty, despite his wide smile. "I'm sure that's exactly what needs to happen, Brother Gabriel. But we need to handle the Devil first." Everett nodded down to the forgotten clearing.

Jack had one card left to play. He closed his eyes and opened his hands. The concentration took immense power. As he began the process of transforming, he drained the life from the surrounding plants. The trees that stood proud and true beyond the clearing turned into massive wooden raisins. With their roots shriveled and tapped, the trees came crashing down. Tree by tree, via a colossal game of dominoes, the clearing grew bigger.

Satan took deep breaths. He could feel the attention of the angels and half-breeds washing over him. He ignored them all.

He tilted his head back when he achieved the pinnacle of his power. Rings of trees stood dead, their lives offered for his needs. Satan shouted as his own wings grew and began to form behind him. The smoke that traveled with him now surrounded him like a tornado. His completed wings were massive and stained so inky black they were almost blue. Instead of endless magic and glitter, his wings shed red and black steam. He stretched them out and flew immediately. The angels were poised to fight, but their sweet nature compelled them wait for him to make the first strike.

"Hello, fucking fairies. Didn't know I could get my own ride, huh?" Satan had held on to his cigarette throughout his transformation, but he now took a drag and tossed it. It landed and exploded like a bomb in the center of the trees. "Everett. The girl?" Satan held out his arms.

Everett smiled. "Of course you know I can't give her to you."

"Can't say I didn't try, right?" The Devil turned as if to leave, then snapped back and threw a handful of invisible pain into Everett's face. He smacked Everett's arms as he winced from the onslaught to his senses.

Emma fell from Everett's grasp. She couldn't even scream as gravity took over.

The Devil dove immediately. He could hear some of the other angels pursuing her as well.

"Slow bitches," he scoffed. He reached her just before she got to Jason's arms.

Satan wrapped his wings around Emma and veered away from the ground. They looked like a feather-wrapped rocket and were going just about as fast.

He kissed her face and ran a hand down the length of her body. His touch freed her from her paralysis. Emma gasped like she was coming up from being held underwater.

"No. Oh, no. Please. Jack, that was awful. That was so awful." She reached around his neck and released a wracking sob. "To not be able to move…" Emma dug her nails into his skin.

Jack wrapped her waist in his strong arm and altered their flight path, swooping back toward the foliage below. He murmured to her, the world inside his wings so much quieter than the one outside. "You're safe. I've got you. Shh…" Jack stroked her hair with his other hand.

"I'm tired. This fighting—I'm so tired of it." She'd stopped sobbing, but tears still streamed from her eyes. Then, twitching as if she'd been prodded, she added, "Where's Jason? I—I have to save him."

"Don't worry, pretty child. It'll all be over soon." He kissed her forehead carefully.

"You have to let me talk to the angels," Emma said, her eyes locked on the Devil's once again. "I can tell them Everett is a swamp donkey." She took a few cleansing breaths.

"Wouldn't life be grand if it were that easy?" The Devil spread his wings. He hovered close to the top of the trees at the edge of the river. "I need to power up again. Can you hang on?"

Emma wrapped her legs around his waist and hugged his neck.

He closed his eyes and tilted his head back. "I'll be vibrating a little. Take advantage of that if you'd like to—and you can scream my name now that you know it."

Emma punched him in the arm, and he smiled. He did indeed vibrate as he sucked the life from the trees, and the river below bubbled like a pot on a stove. Fish rushed to the surface and bobbed there, belly up. The act of siphoning life off the land was silent, but the power it produced was fantastic. The Devil was a vampire on the soft neck of Mother Nature. As he finished, a slow, sexy smile revealed his white teeth.

"Now I'm ready to face anything. You need to tell me what you want, gorgeous," he purred.

"What I want?" Emma could hear the beat of wings. The angels were coming *en masse* from close by. "I want the fighting to stop. I want Jason to realize he's good. I want my wings." She paused, hoping what her heart told her would make sense when she said it aloud. "I want you to be out of Hell."

"Okay, I should have been more fucking specific," Jack shot back. "What you want for *your* forever—I can hand you one of two options." He seemed relaxed as he held her close, totally tuning out the steady cadence of the aerial army approaching. "You can stay on Earth or I can take you back to Hell with me. Choose wisely, my princess. The choice is permanent and the outcome is far-reaching."

Emma looked down and found Jason standing in the trees below, then gazed back at the Devil's sexy, very close face. She was shocked at how difficult the choice was. *I care about Jason—about saving him. Why can't I focus on that? Who would choose to go to Hell? An eternity with Jack, though... That would be something else altogether.* But then, for a divine moment, her mind cleared. She remembered the true nature of Hell—the Hallway, the darkness, the screaming. She just couldn't do it.

Satan smiled sadly. "Don't say it out loud, pretty child. I see the answer in your eyes."

She placed her hand on his cheek. "I'm so sorry. I wish someone could be what you need."

"Go with the half-breed. Get far away from here. Can you do that for me?" He looked down his nose at her, trying to bring a smile around.

Nodding, Emma turned until her eyes again found Jason standing next to a shriveled tree. He was waiting for her.

The other angels were almost upon them when Jack simply stilled his wings. He nuzzled her neck as they took a heart-stopping fall together. Just before they plummeted into Jason, Jack removed the hand that had been supporting her back. From his palm, a blast of power and fire halted their descent like a parachute.

When Emma looked back at him he wasn't even trying to smile anymore. He looked off into the distance above her head and opened his arms. Emma kissed his cheek gently, waiting to see if he'd meet her eyes, but stubbornly he wouldn't.

Jason held out a hand to her, and Emma took it.

"You two haul ass." Satan looked up at the angels now landing like falling leaves around them. "Everett won't bother you again."

Jason scooped Emma up, but she was still trying to figure out what the hell everyone was doing. The angels did seem to have sided with Everett, and they all began powering up at once.

Jason, can you hear me? Emma asked without speaking.

He glanced at her face and nodded as he ran. She began picturing the things about Satan that made her feel compassion.

The Devil—his name is Jack. He used to be a man, and an angel. And he's all alone if I leave. They're acting on lies.

Jason slowed to a walk. But Emma heard nothing from him—verbally or nonverbally—no matter how hard she tried. Now that she was human, Jason's mind was silent to her.

He seemed to realize this, because he spoke instead. "What could you do? How can you help other than doing what he asked?" He seemed patient and anxious at the same time.

I could speak for him, tell the angels to spare him.

Just then a huge explosion rocked Emma and Jason. He kept them stable and after a moment updated Emma on the Devil's thoughts.

"Jack's taking their blows now," he said. "They seem really intent on getting him back to Hell." The sky was illuminated orange and purple from the battle. Magic flew between the groups. The ground began to shake.

Jack doesn't want to go back to Hell.

Emma struggled and Jason put her down to walk. His jaw tensed. "He's giving us this opportunity to get away. His sacrifice will be for nothing if Everett gets to you again."

The trees around them began to wither like late-summer flowers. Jack was getting more strength. Jason shielded Emma with his body and covered her ears carefully as the crack sounded. It was as if a volcano had erupted.

What's happening?

"I can only read Jack. He's facing them all, but he'll only strike Everett. He's fighting valiantly." Jason watched her face. Emma put her finger on his lips. He kissed it, asking a question with his eyes.

I have to tell the other angels the truth. They'll never forgive themselves if they act on another's sin.

"Can't we wait until Everett has been defeated?" Jason spoke around her finger. His green eyes pled for her safety.

Emma hated her useless human form. She had nothing to offer Jason now, except to be his snack.

"The most powerful part of you has never been on the outside, Emma." He gently stroked her elbow.

Emma tried not to picture how her mortal life would be, how quickly it would end, but he saw it anyway.

"One day with you has been more important than a hundred forevers." He smiled. She still had a finger on his lips.

I knew you were good.

"Then I think we're a great match."

Jason looked to the sky, and Emma turned in time to see Jack thrown into the tie-dyed projection of the hate from the battle. One of his wings was missing.

"No! They're killing him. Jason, I can't just stand here. Please don't ask me to. I know you could make me. Please. He's not hurting the other angels?" Emma put her hands in her hair.

"No, his attacks are for Everett only. He's just absorbing the other blows." Jason put a hand on her shoulder.

Emma wasn't sure if it was for comfort or restraint. *Take me back.*

Jason nodded to her like the gentleman he was and carried her back to the clearing, now filled with broken life and wasted trees. They were just in time to witness Everett cracking Satan across the face while Seraph Gabriel and another angel held Jack's arms. Jason locked his arms around her.

She used her voice because it was all she had. "Stop! All of you. Stop! You assault the wrong man. I command you as a seraph!"

The other angels paused their beams of righteousness. Everett took the moment to knee Jack in the crotch.

"Everett lies to you. I'm telling you to let Jack be. He only sought to protect me." Emma looked from one beautiful face to the next.

Everett created two lightning bolts and held them like swords. With every word he spoke he sliced into Jack. Though there were no physical wounds, Jack convulsed as if a million volts were coursing through him. They probably were.

"Don't…listen…to…her… She…has no…wings." Everett was merciless in his onslaught.

Emma begged Jason in her mind. *Let me go! You didn't bring me here to watch. Let me go!*

His arms untwisted, and she stumbled forward. Everett added thunder to his lightning, and Jack's head lolled on his neck. Emma knew Satan would no longer have his feet under him if the seraphim weren't holding him fast.

Emma fell with the thunder. Everett had overestimated, and Gabriel and the other seraph reeled from the blow as well. Jack's arms were free, and he snapped to attention immediately. Emma's slow feet carried her to the scene, Jason at her side all the way.

Jack licked one of his hands like a cat and then the other. Soon he had two mini suns at his beckoning. He tossed them right into Everett's face. The evil angel fell to his knees on the ground. Jack laughed at his agony and pushed Everett's face effortlessly into the snow.

He grabbed each of Everett's wings and settled a sturdy motorcycle boot between the angel's shoulder blades. Jack's pure concentration radiated from his face as he ripped the wings out of Everett's back like they were stubborn weeds in a garden. The fallen angel screamed with horror and torment.

The angels reacted to the Everett's pain and aimed beams of angry blue light at Jack once again. Satan tossed the wings aside and moved through the quicksand of their crippling combined forces. He stepped up to stand on Everett's back. Under the Devil's full weight, Everett dissolved into the ground like melting ice.

Jack fell to his knees as soon as Everett was gone, but still the angels fought for all they held holy. He stood quickly, fencing the space around him with a tsunami of angry flames.

He can't keep that up forever, Emma thought urgently. *When that curtain falls, they'll send him back to Hell.*

Jason put a hand on her shoulder. "That's where he belongs. He is *of* that place."

Emma shook her head. "He's been alone for the longest time."

Seraph Gabriel spoke in his clear, prophetic voice. "Human Emma, step away from the half-breed. You may come here to us."

The way he moved and spoke made it obvious Seraph Gabriel was very used to getting his way. Righteousness, and his status as a seraph, gave him authority.

Jason took a step away from Emma, but kept his eyes on her face. "They don't trust me? Do they think I'll hurt you?"

Emma tried to remember what being endlessly right felt like. She took a step back and could feel the fire on her shoulder blades. *Always with the freaking fire.*

She gasped as the Devil's tattooed arm wrapped around her waist and dragged her backward. As quick as Jason was, she was through the wall before he could get a grip on her. She began kicking as Jack pulled her against his chest. The angels' blue light ricocheted off the flames. She could glimpse them through the inferno, but they couldn't see her, just as she hadn't seen Jack until he pulled her through.

Jack set her on her feet.

"Ouch," he winced, shoving his remaining wing out of the way. His voice wasn't full of the vibrant cool she'd come to recognize in him.

"Did they hit Jason?" Emma tried to walk back through the flaming barrier, but met a solid wall.

Jack watched her as she turned to hear his answer. "No. They won't hurt him if he doesn't attack them. You know that."

His hand shook as he wiped his brow. She *did* know that. The angels would never hurt a soul on purpose—without stupid-ass Everett egging them on.

"Why were they firing?" Emma searched through the flames until she could see Jason. He was talking animatedly with her old co-workers.

Jack put one knee and one hand on the ground to steady himself. Maintaining the wall seemed to be costing him everything he had left.

"I took Everett out before he could prove what a shitball he was. Doubt blooms strong in the virtuous. They were trying to get me, if that makes you feel better." Jack put his other knee on the ground.

He was pouting about her choice, Emma realized. She brought herself closer to him. Alluring as he was, and despite the goodness lurking deep within him, now that she'd made her decision, her defenses were up. Hell defined him—made him who he was. Its essence was within him, whether he wished it so or not. She tried once, then twice, and finally on the third attempt, she made herself comfort him by putting her hand on his head.

"They would have gotten me too," she told him. "I guess I don't garner tons of trust." Emma kneeled so she could see his face, her heart softening once again.

He put his other hand down as well. Finally this mighty being was on all fours.

She pushed his hair out of his eyes. "What are you doing?"

He seemed to be mediating. "I'm trying to get up some courage, and I'm going to need a little fucking time to make that happen."

Even now, she could feel the force of his potential power rippling through her.

"Are you going back to Hell? Can't you go back?" Emma tilted her head so she could see his eyes.

"Stop giving me kindness. Can't you see it hurts me?" He was angry, but too weak to fight her.

She waited. The force flowing through her backed down an octave.

"Emma, I can't go back there. I know what my job would be, and I can't face it." Satan pushed himself to kneeling.

He tried reaching for one of his cigarettes, but his hands were shaking too much to get them out. Emma pushed his hands away and dug into his pocket. She pulled out the hand-rolled paper tube. The Devil puckered up, and Emma put the cigarette to his lips.

He touched the back of his hand to the tip, and it glowed orange. Their small tent of fiery protection shuddered with an explosion. She looked up while the Devil just kept looking at her, his hands stuffed into his waistband. The angels were flying now. Their whirling gusts of glitter and magic were beautiful and furious. They were tossing bombs of light.

Emma desperately wanted the angels to stop getting it wrong—getting everything wrong.

The Devil looked from her to his mouth and back again, refusing—or maybe lacking the power—to use his own hands. She understood what he wanted and pulled out the cigarette. He blew smoke at her, and it turned into a hand that cradled her face.

"Toss that butt into the wall of flames." Jack smiled, his white teeth reflecting the warm glow of the fire.

When she did as he requested, the cigarette caused a tiny explosion and revived the fire around them.

"Pretty child, my Hell will be the same as always. I'll be in that smoky room, and in between the tortures I dole out, I'll have just enough time to greet all my female guests." The pulsating fire steadied his hands briefly, just long enough for him to replace the ghostly smoke with his real hand. "And those women? They'll always look like, but not quite be…you."

Emma felt her eyes well up, and she covered his hand with hers. "I can make them stop. Let me go out there and make a case for you."

"They'll never forgive me for what I do next. I hope you will, someday. Maybe you'll get it." He stood and held out his hand.

She got to her feet on her own and hugged him.

"But if not Hell, then where?" Emma put her head under his chin. He smelled so delicious.

He petted her hair softly. "You know the answer to that one as well. Are you stalling?"

"But to just end? To stop existing altogether? It's so final." Emma looked at his face again.

He looked exhausted and drained and…done.

"There are worse things. To want is worse. To want you? Impossible." Jack looked around at his withering protection. Emma began patting a gentle rhythm on his chest. The rhythm he would have in his heart no longer. He tilted her face to his, lifting her chin and running his thumb along her jaw. "I knew hope. Before I was gone I knew hope because I knew you."

Emma shook her head, trying to tell him how unacceptable this outcome was.

Satan lifted both his hands and outlined her face. He stilled her movement. "I consider this a gift. From me to you, Emma. Make your forever as happy as you dare."

She closed her eyes, expecting his soft kiss. It was just his style. But when she felt nothing, her mind began to race. *Maybe he was just getting a rise out of me before he went back to Hell. Maybe it was all a joke and he plans to take us both to eternal damnation with his next breath.*

Emma opened her eyes to find Satan still standing there, but she could feel the fractures in his armor above them. The loud pops and bangs increased, and she shut her eyes tightly again. Maybe the angels had reinforcements. Then suddenly her entire being was consumed by his lips, his kiss.

She gasped as the feeling rolled through her. Her knees went weak as she orgasmed. He grabbed her harder and deepened the kiss, his tongue tasting hers. Every part of her body tingled, exploded.

She moaned and tried to get closer to him, though their chests were already touching. He placed one foot on either side of her body, and before she knew it she was on the ground. He lay on top off her with his delightful weight pressing her, holding her down. She'd never felt anything like the sensations that coursed through her now. She panted as he stopped the kiss.

Her eyes snapped open as the flames shattered around them. He covered her head with his arms and didn't react when the flames landed like molten glass on top of him. He was already in tremendous pain.

Emma's body went numb. He'd taken something from her and poured in something else during their kiss.

He smiled through his agony as the angels fluttered above him. White and perfect, they bonded together and their combined power hit Jack squarely in the back.

Emma wanted to wave them away, she wanted to talk, but there was only numbness.

Jack grew brighter and brighter, glowing as if from within. She kept her eyes on his. He never flinched, just tried to sustain his smile and keep his gaze on her throughout the chaos around them.

Jason pulled her out from under Jack, just as Jack became as white as the face of the sun. Jason cradled her carefully in his arms, but she still couldn't move. He was speaking to someone else, trying to keep his voice calm.

"She's dying. Dean, he tried to kill her. Her heart's slowing."

Emma noticed, belatedly, that the numbness was affecting her organs as well. She could hardly take a breath. She wanted to look back at Jack, but she couldn't move her head. Then the blackness claimed her. She never saw the epic ring of warping power that ended the standoff.

Maybe the noise would have killed her anyway. Surely her human skin would have crumbled off at the tiny, abrasive blasts of ice that detonated as Jack parted with his existence. His soul was long extinguished when Jason laid her carefully in the snow.

Jason pictured the first time he'd found her, fresh from her fall from Heaven. He wondered if he'd always been destined to hold a dying Emma.

Dean's face was completely bewildered as he knelt next to Jason. Something about Emma seemed oddly familiar. Seriana was the first to sense the change. She touched Emma's chest and felt a slow, off-kilter beating, much like the one within her own.

"Jason, she's changing. The process has started. I think Emma's becoming some sort of vampire!"

CHAPTER 14

When Emma gasped and opened her eyes, everything around her was crisp and clear. She felt…good. She looked around at the room: clean, neat, and mostly empty except for a bookshelf laden with volumes of all colors and sizes. Jason smiled as her gaze landed on his beautiful face.

He reached out and touched her, insisting, "You're the beautiful one."

"Oh yeah—you can hear my thoughts. That's going to get awkward." She smiled back at him. "Where am I?"

"At the back of our house," he said. "That's Dean's ridiculous library. You know—he's obsessed with understanding the human body, and his *un*-human body."

Jason seemed unflappable as Emma ran through the last bits of her memory.

"Shall I fill in the gaps?" he asked, recognizing her struggle. "Will that give you peace or pain, Emma?" He extended his hand, and Emma took it, pulling herself to sitting.

Sunlight poured through the window, and she knew she was altered. She was still in the clothes Jack had created for her, but Emma knew she was no longer human. She wanted to hear him say it.

"I believe you're some kind of vampire now. Or *like* a vampire… I'm not sure. How do you feel?" Jason looked worried as he waited for her response.

She looked puzzled. "Great."

Jason laughed, and Emma wanted more of his joy immediately. She answered him honestly in her head.

I feel wonderful. Thirsty, but this is exquisite.

She flexed her newly strong arms. Jason stood and quickly walked with her through the house and out the door. Evidently being a vampire was much like being an angel. She flapped her wings out of habit, and then hung her head at their loss. She had only a phantom sense of mass where they used to be.

Jason pulled her into a gentle hug. "I'm so sorry, Emma. If I'd just been able to get to you sooner…"

Her thirst was overwhelming her coherent thoughts, but she needed to explain. *I think this change is a gift.*

Jason looked sadly into her eyes. "I hope the adjustment won't be too horrible."

Jason's care and concern, despite his lack of humanity, amazed Emma once again. She knew being here with him was right.

God loves you. You're better than wings.

He kissed her forehead.

"Let's get you fed before we ask you to make moral judgments about vampires—half-breed or otherwise." Jason took her hand and led her to the woods.

Emma tried to listen to Jason's handy, helpful hints on feeding, but she kept tripping over the thought of Jack burning white in the glow of the angels' wrath. Jason soon quieted. It gave her peace that she wasn't alone with her thoughts. Her gaze lingered on the trees as they walked briskly through the woods that surrounded the Parishes' home.

"Blood is a refined taste," Jason explained when she tuned back in. "We may have to catch a human and open him up before you have any interest. Though honestly, I expected your instincts to take over your mind."

Stepping in front of her, he grasped her shoulders and looked deeply in her eyes. "Food."

Emma pictured a fluffy green tree.

"It should be blood. When I say 'food,' your primal response should be red. It should color all your thoughts right now." He stepped back.

Am I broken?

"No, it's just that you were changed by…him. And as far as I could tell, he wasn't a vampire." Jason put a thoughtful finger to his lips.

He nodded at her flood of thoughts. They were coming toward the same conclusions.

The Devil tricked me? Maybe I don't have a food source? Will this be my Hell? Endless thirst?

"I heard his thoughts before he was gone. He didn't wish you any ill. Maybe try closing your eyes—let's see where your tastes lie."

She did as he suggested. Emma tried to empty her mind and let her primal needs take over, but she was worried. As an angel, she'd been used to protecting humans. Now what would she be?

Jason stood behind her and murmured softly in her ear. "I won't let you kill anyone. You're safe with me. I promise."

Trust him.

She opened her eyes and the bark of the tree in front of her was so appealing. She could feel the hunger pooled on her tongue. Soon she could take her thirst no longer and jumped on the moss-covered trunk. Her teeth sharpened as soon as her lips touched the bark, and she sank them into the tree, filling her mouth with its sweet sap. She closed her eyes with relief. When she finally opened them, the tree that had been so magnificent was crumpled into a pile of black ash. And her thirst was satiated.

Jason looked pleased and surprised.

I feed from trees?

"Apparently. Now that is a true gift." Jason held open his arms and Emma walked into them, curling her hands in his shirt.

She felt him chuckle in her hair. "Don't worry, angel, I'll see to it that ten trees are planted for every one you drain."

She smiled into his chest. *Thank you.*

Jason led her to a gentle stream and sat next to her on a boulder. For further proof, they watched a family of deer lapping nervously at the water. Emma felt no impulse to attack them. Instead she reveled in her heightened senses. The fawn's white spots were so clearly defined.

"Where's your family? Is everyone okay?" Emma hated that she'd forgotten to ask until now.

"It's fine, Emma. Adjusting to new a lifestyle takes a while. They're back at the house. They wanted to give us some privacy." Jason put his hand on top of hers.

Emma looked up at the morning sky. It seemed like a normal day. It was as if the world hadn't been on the brink of destruction.

How long ago?

"Two weeks. You saved the world two weeks ago." He lifted her hand to his lips and kissed it softly.

Emma nodded at the rightness of the white snow and the harmless, puffy clouds.

"We saved the world together. I would've never been able to do it without you." She pulled his hand to her lips and kissed it in return. *Jason, can you tell me what happened?*

"Okay." He took a deep breath. "When the Devil dragged you behind the flames, I tried to get you, of course, but the barrier was impenetrable. So I turned my efforts to the angels and tried to describe to them what I believed was going on."

Jason indulged in the sight of her calm face. She looked into his green eyes and felt such peace in his gaze.

"The angels have a few prejudices. Half-breeds trying to do the right thing seems like a foreign concept." Jason sighed as Emma remembered their first meeting and the insults she'd thrown at him. "That worked out eventually, so it's fine. Anyway, they took to the skies and began pelting your shelter with weapons. I could hear your mind, so I knew you were safe."

He looked away from her face to the stream. The deer family had bounded off, leaving only hoof prints as their memory. Emma knew she was blushing.

He clarified. "The Devil, Jack, had only beautiful thoughts before he was eliminated. He was a changed being."

She pictured the smile Jack had worked to keep in place for her though his agony. There was a quick, sharp pain as she felt the loss of him. His gift to her had the very makings of a blessing.

"I think it is a blessing," Jason said. "He gave you the only way you could ever deal with being a vampire. I would thank him if I had a chance." Jason hopped down from the boulder and waited as she did the same.

He grasped her waist in case she needed steadying, but she was sure-footed. "So being a tree eater is going to be wild," he said. "I guess it's just like eating huge broccoli?"

Jason was lightening the mood as best he could. She turned slowly and glanced up at his magnificent lips.

Kiss me, Jason. I need to feel alive.

His eyes changed to a deeper green as he moved her hair away from her face. "I'm so glad you're here. Thank you for going to Hell and back."

He leaned slowly until their lips almost touched. She took a deep breath to inhale the moment, the perfection of his intentions. His lips tasted of her own desire, her own forever. He comforted her with his strong embrace. When he ended the passion, he hugged her softly to his chest, cradling her head and smoothing her hair.

She had only contentment in the center of his world. *Thank you for making Heaven so unappealing.*

They hugged for a long time, just enjoying the lack of urgency, the sound of the winter birds making up for their dull color with vibrant songs.

"I could stand like this—just like this—forever," he said. "With you in my arms I may never need another thing."

Emma hugged him hard around the middle. She pictured the moments they'd had during her angel's pause and leaned back to see his face.

"Yeah, I'm going to need that for sure," Jason said.

Emma laughed, loving that she influenced him with her less-than-celestial impulses. *Shouldn't we tell your family we're fine?*

Jason was busy changing her mind while his eyes smoldered. She felt a chill of anticipation race up her spine.

"You'll like it very much. I promise." He trailed his hand up her back in an exact replica of her chill.

As a lover he'd be absolutely in tune to her slightest whim, and the thought made her gasp. She had flashes of him plugged into her fantasies and was rewarded with his sigh in response to her thoughts.

"Oh." Emma had nothing better to say to his overwhelming sexiness.

Emma heard the crunch of snow behind her and whirled around. Jason placed a calming hand on her shoulder. "It's just Dean. I'm sure Seriana was worried and wanted an update."

Emma felt a little embarrassed about her quick reaction.

Jason placed his hand on her hip and spoke softly. "We all have to adjust to the fast reflexes—except for Dean here. His were slow from the start."

Jason ducked as a snowball from Dean missed its mark. "I heard that! Get your butts back to the house so Seriana will leave me alone."

Jason nodded, and his brother jogged off with a wave to Emma. "I guess we'd better head back. Dean will be fascinated by this turn of events. He loves anomalies, and a vampire-angel feasting on trees definitely qualifies."

He offered Emma his elbow so he could escort her through the woods. She smiled and took his arm.

If Jack isn't the Devil anymore, then who is?

"I heard the angels talking during the battle," Jason said. "They seemed to think there'd be an epic battle in Hell. The strongest, meanest creature would win the job."

They reached the break in the woods and could see his house.

Emma remembered her time in Hell—the smoke, the monster she'd seen behind the first door in Hell's Hallway.

"Everett'll win. He wants it bad enough, I'm sure," Emma said, rubbing her eyes with her hand. "And then he may be sorry he did."

Jason stopped and tilted her face toward his. "Hell was awful. I'm so sorry I couldn't be there to help."

You did help. Honestly, I needed you to believe in me or I'd still be there.

The memory of her experience in Hell overwhelmed her, and she shook her head. The trauma was so raw, so close to the surface. Jason looked troubled.

"Let's go meet your family again," she said. "Last time was sort of hurried." Emma forced her mind to jump past the tortures of Hell to focus on now.

They closed the remaining distance to the house, and Jason held the door for Emma. She entered to find his family waiting for the new vampire in their clan. After the formal introductions, the ladies went into the kitchen so Seriana could grill Emma about Heaven. She was endlessly curious.

Just a short time later, all the Parishes went on alert at the same moment as the distinct sound of truck tires approached the house. A few moments later the doorbell sounded, but they all stayed frozen until the UPS man had left the package at the door and departed.

Dean opened the door to find a small package wrapped in brown paper and labeled *Emma c/o Jason Parish*.

Emma stepped forward before Jason could pick up the box. "Don't. I'll get it. It's addressed to me."

She had a million suspicions, but only one made sense. From deep in Hell, Everett had found her. And whatever was contained in this inconspicuous, brown wrapping couldn't be good.

Jason shook his head and insisted on retrieving the package himself. He brought it to Emma, and the two took seats on the couch. Emma couldn't stop the sinking feeling about where it came from. No one who'd known her when she was alive existed anymore as a human. The dust of their bodies had long been recycled into other living things.

Dean and Seriana excused themselves to give Jason and Emma privacy. Jason protectively took the parcel back from her. He cradled the small brown mystery in the crook of his arm and held his hand out to Emma.

I've no clue why it's here.

"We don't have to open it. I'll see that it's destroyed."

Emma took his hand and squeezed gently. "I'll always wonder. I can't even fathom what it is."

Jason pulled Emma closer and kissed her forehead. "Whatever you wish. I'll stand beside you."

How can you have lived so long and still be so decent? I've been to Heaven and still think you're a miracle.

Emma spoke for the benefit of the other vampires in the house. "Let's get outside. Just because it's small doesn't mean the contents are harmless."

Jason's siblings stepped back into the room noiselessly.

"We'll come with you. You may need support," said Seriana, looking distrustfully at the package.

Dean shook his head. "No, I think they want to be alone with this. May I suggest the beach?"

Jason nodded and opened the door for Emma.

While leading her to the path that would take them to the beach, Jason shared his knowledge. "I'm pretty sure I know who sent this, and we have nothing to fear from your package."

Soon enough they were standing on the smooth sand of the beach. It was still early evening, but the winter demanded the sun's decline almost before night had properly begun. Jason handed Emma her parcel.

"Please, open it. It's from a friend." Jason put his hands in his pockets as he set Emma at ease.

The brown paper was easily torn and not magic in any way. The white box's lid slipped off as well. Emma gently touched the contents. She'd been a vampire for mere weeks, and aware of it for only hours, and yet the trappings of angels now looked foreign to her. Extraordinary to her.

The paper was almost transparent and had the consistency of spider web. She lifted the note out and tilted it toward the setting sun's warm show.

The writing was very masculine and terribly messy, but the ink was lovely. Angels wrote notes with quills dipped in liquid diamonds, and their scribed words were wondrous to behold. Emma's vampire eyes missed not one facet in the letters.

It was from Jack. She could feel his concern soaking through her fingertips. Her mind's eye saw him again: illuminated seconds before he ceased to exist.

Emma read his words, feeling tremendous hope that he might still be somewhere in the universe, experiencing joy.

Pretty child,

It will be over for me soon, this reure of evil. I wish you the best. Tell him to bite that lovely bottom lip of yours — it makes you pant.

— Jack

The box was heavy. He'd given her a gift. *Another* gift. When Jack was able to accomplish this, she didn't know.

Jason quickly gave her an answer. "I was listening to a lot in those final moments, and he did create something during his alone time behind his wall of flames. He was doing *this* instead of fighting back." Jason inclined his head respectfully toward the box.

Emma pictured Jack in the middle of the chaos creating the delicate note now in her hands, tapping into his latent angel powers to make something beautiful for her. She lifted the tissue in the box and smiled. The gift was another remote control. This one was gold and its buttons were onyx.

He must have been a Christmas Angel, once upon a time, Emma thought, smiling at Jason. *And he never pressed his pause button. I'm not surprised. He seemed like a full-steam-ahead kind of guy. But to save it? To give it to me? For us?*

Emma's words morphed into feelings. Compassion, thankfulness, and loss.

Jason lifted the controller from the box. It looked sensual in his strong hands.

"I was going to bite your lip before he asked, so he wasted time and words choreographing my plans for your passion." Jason's eyes told her he was remembering the last time the world had stopped just for them.

He read her teary thoughts and changed his approach. "Emma, sometimes a soul is forced to continue beyond its vessel's desire to live. Jack's stint as the Devil prolonged his agony much longer than he wanted. He was ready to go."

Tears welled up in Emma's eyes as she listened to Jason's words.

"I do know he had compassion again in the end," he continued. "He cared for someone besides himself, even when he was disappointed by his Claudette. Just a little time with you changed the Devil."

Emma smiled and put her hand to his face. "And yet *you've* taken *so* long to realize your worth. Even the Devil changed his mind more quickly. You certainly play hard to get, Jason Parish."

He chuckled. "Yes, I think I've been too harsh. For an angel to choose me over Heaven? For you to want to stand next to me at all should bring me to my knees. This beach should be the church where I beg forgiveness from God for taking even one breath for granted. Every second I've been given has led me to this. To you."

Jason set the box gently on the ground. He put one hand behind her neck, buried the other in her hair, and kissed her.

Emma felt the soaring perfection of two souls connecting. Belonging. She melted into his chest. He pulled away from her lips, his face full of intention.

Emma looked down and watched the note as the wind caught it and cartwheeled it away. The transparent scrap landed in the surf and melted. The seawater tinted red for a heartbeat before the message was washed away, clean and clear. The pang of loss pinched her heart, she turned and faced the man in front of her.

Emma took the remote from the box and handed it to him. "Press pause, Jason."

Jason kissed Emma again as his long finger pressed the pause button. They could feel the Earth grind its endless rotation to a halt and laughed out loud when their heartbeats sped up as they became human again.

They looked around, alone together with no eyes above or below to judge how thoroughly they wanted to bless each other's bodies.

Emma stepped away and twirled. "Look, Jason! You paused the snow!"

The flakes that had been gearing up to add another cold layer of nature to the soil now hovered like beautiful jewelry in the sky. As each flake melted on Emma's warm body, she created a tunnel with her twirling.

"Emma, you have to see the sunset." Jason caught her quickly and motioned to the sky as if he'd painted it himself. The gathering clouds were painted deep purple and red with the very tip of the sun still peeking above the horizon.

It's amazing. Perfect pause. I do believe we have some love to make. She raised one eyebrow with her taunting thought.

Jason gave her a wink. "Remember, by reading your mind I can learn just which touch you like best. And then I will do it over and over and over."

Emma gulped and smiled. He promised lovely luxury, and her body responded. Emma stepped away from his tempting mouth and walked backward toward the surf.

He watched her playfully, but as she got closer to the water, his expression grew concerned. He ran to catch up and wrapped his arms around her waist. Her heels were just a hair's breadth from the edge of the hushed water.

"You're human in the pause. You might get cold if you get wet." Jason kept her firmly in his grasp.

"Half-breed, you worry too much. We could be mostly naked by now." She touched his lips, and he kissed her fingers.

She pictured her intentions, and Jason bit his lip. He watched carefully as she freed herself from his hug.

Emma stepped back and when her feet met the water, instead of sinking she was able to walk along the surface. *Everything's suspended, lover. Come get me.*

Emma spun on her heel and ran toward the sunset. Jason fully expected to sink when he tried, but his shoe behaved as if it was touching ground and supported him in the usual way. He couldn't help laughing as he trotted out behind her. He stopped laughing when he almost stepped on her discarded jeans. His eyes traveled from the pants to a trail of Emma's clothes, each item a little miracle on the sea.

She had her back to him, and her beautiful shape was silhouetted against the sky, completely naked. She was framed in snowflakes as she peeked over her shoulder and looked shyly at his face. Her eyes were startlingly emerald. Her unlikely food source had colored her eyes to match the leafy green she drained.

Jason took a slow, deep breath. *Wings or no wings, she's still an angel.*

Time was already stopped, so the only noise Jason could hear was his own temporary heartbeat. As he caught up to Emma she turned her face to the sunset, which seemed impossibly close.

She had a chill—he could tell from the small bumps on her perfect skin. He put his warm hands on her hips. He felt his way to her backside, smoothing her skin as he went. She leaned her head back against his chest, and her hair tickled his hands.

He was too much of a man not to look down at her breasts. They were perfect and cold as well. He let his fingers travel to her shoulders and turn her around. He tested the size of her waist and skimmed her belly button with his thumbs.

She shivered.

Jason was fascinated at her response to his thumbs' pressure and used them to trace a line to her nipples. She hissed a breath in through her teeth, and Jason had to stop so he wouldn't take her right then.

I promised slow. I promised slow.

His mantra almost failed him when Emma wrapped her arms around him, kissing him deeply.

In his arousal, he was sorely aware of the fabric between her sex and his pleasure. *She'll be so warm inside.*

Her lips still tasted like angel cake, and Jason couldn't blame the Devil for wanting to keep her.

She began unbuttoning his shirt, and every inch of his chest revealed was treated to a caress from her hands. *When you just breathe on me, I want you. Being in your arms will melt me. Being naked with you might kill me.*

Emma's thoughts made him growl. She fumbled with the buttons on his pants, and he quickly unfastened them for her.

Kill me, Jason.

He kissed her and scooped her into his arms. There was no bed, so the water would have to do. It molded to her gently, and its cool was a gasping contrast to her hot skin. He made sure to kick off his shoes and socks. The water below her was so clear he could see his reflection as he covered her body with his own.

She was still shivering.

"Are you cold?" He began to mentally dress her out of habit.

He started with her feet because the rest was too pretty to cover. He gave her stiletto heels and white, fuzzy leg warmers.

She shook her head. *Not cold. I just want you so much. Stop putting clothes on me and get inside me.*

"Your wish is my command," he said

He had wanted to take more time. He wanted to outline every part of her with his tongue. He wanted to sink his fingers inside her and hear her thoughts as she came. But the pause wasn't endless, and the whole world had halted so he could enter this woman right now.

Jason lined up his hips and pushed inside. He looked at her face, and her eyes had a sheen of tears. She batted her lashes and smiled at him as he began a rhythm that could bring only joy.

You are with me, Jason.

The stilled water was the perfect surface for lovemaking, and Jason used it to his advantage. He touched her everywhere he'd dreamed he might someday, and she rewarded him with gasps of pleasure and moans of delight.

She climaxed first, and he could feel her legs tremble. Then his brain turned white and even his teeth tingled when he was spent. He remained inside her, staring at her flushed skin—so alive, so sated. She reached up and pulled him down for another kiss. He hugged her and kissed her cheek.

The beeping had started, and this time Jason knew it signaled the end of their pause.

"Are we going to…" He looked up at the stationary snowflakes and grimaced when they began twisting and swirling again in the wind.

Fall? Go in the drink? Hell, yes!

Jason watched as the waves freed themselves and began their endless swaying climb to crash on the beach. He grabbed Emma and tossed her over his shoulder, the water already feeling less solid by his feet. He ran as fast as he could, but gravity claimed them when they were still a few steps from Emma's jeans.

The vampires were swallowed into the sea with a splash. Underwater, Emma laughed and swam away from Jason.

He loved her mischievous smile and realized she'd planned the impromptu swim when she chose to tempt him on the water. He saved her clothes and swam to her, a pair of vampires once again. They swam until they could stand, but when Jason tried to offer Emma her pants again, she swatted them away and pulled him closer.

Make love to me again, half-breed.

CHAPTER 15

*A*s the months progressed, Emma blended easily into the family. The close-knit threesome found they enjoyed having another personality in the mix. Emma gave them the opportunity to interact with someone beyond themselves without any of the danger relationships with humans could bring.

Despite this closeness with the siblings, Emma stayed in the guest room at their home—a bit distanced from Jason. He insisted she spend her nights alone, kissing her sweetly at her door each evening when it was time for bed. He wanted to make her new life as "normal" as he could, he'd explained. He wanted her to find her own way. So he was being a gentleman—as much as possible—and giving her some space.

But tonight they had a date. Emma pulled her hair into a high, sassy ponytail, and walked down the stairs to find him waiting.

He looked up, and his eyes climbed from her heels to her smile. When she stood before him he pulled a bouquet of daisies from behind his back.

"You make every room the place I want to be," he said with a welcoming smile. He held his hand out to her.

"You're smooth, Mr. Parish. You *do* know we're living together? No need to court me." Emma took the flowers and winked.

"I disagree. A lady deserves to be wooed." He leaned down to kiss her cheek.

Emma found a vase in the kitchen and added the blooms to water. "So are you going to tell me where we're going tonight," she asked. "Or is it still a surprise?"

Jason motioned for her to step into the living room. Emma reached for her jacket hanging in the foyer, but he beat her to it and held it open for her arms.

He slowly fastened the buttons, littering her neck with small kisses. "It's still a surprise," he said, his words tickling her skin.

From the couch Dean and Seriana rolled their eyes and pointed to the exit in unison.

Jason laughed as he opened the door for Emma. In the driveway was a perfect red convertible.

"Where'd you get this?" Emma spun to face him.

He shrugged. "I rented it for us."

After walking her to the passenger side, he held open the door as Emma slid into the comfortable seat.

"I've never had a ride in a topless car." Emma traced the edge of the windshield with a finger.

It was standard transmission, and as they took off, Jason's forearm rippled when he shifted gears. Emma lifted her face to the deep night.

The air sped over the car, and Jason drove just fast enough to give her a thrill, but conscientiously enough to keep her feeling safe at the same time. When they came to a stop, it was at the top of a beautiful cliff overlooking the ocean.

Emma turned up the radio and slid her seat back so she could only see stars. Jason mimicked her actions and reached for her hand. The stars were outdoing themselves. The slight chill in the atmosphere had polished them to a high sheen. Jason's hand in hers was warm.

She broke the silence. "I didn't get a lot of time under these stars before I was walking among them," she said, thinking of long ago.

Jason turned his head to look at her, and she met his eyes. "I know," he said.

He was thoughtful to want her to experience the simplest of Earthly pleasures, but she needed to change the subject. Emma felt slightly claustrophobic at the unknown of her future. *Will I be an angel again?*

"So, you guys are endlessly running from your grandfather, right? That must be tiresome."

He looked away from her and at the sky. "Sometimes it feels pointless. We've been here longer than we've been anywhere, and it just doesn't seem worth working up the fear to move on. I have a nagging sense he'll find us eventually—like when we run we're only postponing the inevitable."

Suddenly Emma could feel Everett's eyes boring into her back from his place in Hell. "Yeah. I think I know what that feels like."

They were quiet again, easy with each other.

"You've got to enjoy the moment you're in," Emma added. "That's what my father always said. If you're not having a good time, it's your own damn fault." She sat up.

Jason tucked his hands behind his head. "And how would you suggest we make this moment any better?"

Emma pretended to think, raising one eyebrow. "Well, we could count the stars. Or even skip some rocks from the cliff."

"I hate to rain on your parade, but you have to be closer to the water to get a stone to skip." He gave her an adorable smile.

"Well, then I'm all out of ideas." Emma flipped her ponytail, pretending to be stumped.

Jason sat up and touched her face. "I could kiss you." He placed his lips gently on hers and breathed into her. "And kiss you." He removed the tie from her ponytail. Her hair blew all around them. Jason touched his forehead to hers. "And kiss you."

Emma straddled him in the driver's seat. She turned her face so the wind blew her hair out behind her like a flag. He was so perfect, so handsome and ready to be hers. She closed her eyes when her traitorous memory called up Jack's deep eyes, his sinful mouth.

She kissed Jason deeply, determined to replace her every memory of Jack with the reality of Jason.

A good man was right in front of her, not perished in a burst of white light. The right man, she told herself, despite the ache lurking just below the surface that told her otherwise.

Over time Jason had found that his ability to read thoughts—his gift from God, or at least one of them—was diminishing. After a few more weeks of random flashes in the silence, he was once again alone with just his own silent musings. Emma always smiled at him, for him, but he had concerns.

There were days when she stared at the sky for great chunks of time. She was fascinated by the birds, whose wings were so reminiscent of the ones she seemed to covet. Jason was afraid to ask if she missed being an angel. There was nothing he could do if her answer was yes, so he avoided the topic altogether.

It was summer when he found her sitting by the creek, turning a stone over and over in her hands.

"Hello, beautiful. Thinking about rocks as an appetizer before the trees?" He sat next to her.

"You're hilarious." She smiled, but the sparkle never quite made it to her spectacular green eyes.

Avoiding the topic of Heaven wasn't a solution. Jason knew that. It was easier, but all the things that went unsaid built walls. He picked up a stone of his own.

"Can I help you?" He didn't need to be specific. The issue she was contemplating left no room for anything else in her mind.

She sighed. "I really love being here with you. I do," she said. "But I have trouble getting Jack out of my mind."

Her words were a knife in his chest. Before he'd lost the power to read her mind, he'd seen much of Jack and Emma's time together in her memories.

"Are you reading my thoughts?" She put her hand on his.

"I can't. I mean, I haven't been able to for a while. That power seems to have worn off." He grasped her hand and felt her smooth skin.

She took the information with a nod. "Well, I just can't stop the guilt I feel about not trying harder at the end. At his end."

"There was nothing you could've done differently. You did speak to the angels, but for the most part you were behind the fire wall. Why was protecting him your responsibility?"

She was quiet for a bit before she answered. "I believe people are put in our paths for a reason. I can't believe I was destined to pull Jack out of Hell just to protect what was important to me." She dropped his hand and stood, hugging her arms. "I should have spoken up more. I should have demanded to be heard."

Jason stood as well. After a moment, he hugged her.

"I feel like you're not remembering the incident correctly," he said. "Don't forget, you were human at the time. And there wasn't a moment where you were given the floor to deliver a speech. The angels were whipped into a frenzy—like cats with catnip." He rubbed her arms. "They didn't want to listen."

She nodded. "You're right. I have to quit thinking about it. Maybe I'll pray instead."

She opened her arms and returned his hug. He breathed a sigh of relief.

Emma tried to throw herself into the vampire lifestyle. Dean, Seriana, and Jason complimented her often, and they were thrilled that she was able to accompany them on feedings. Blood didn't call to her, so helping *them* sustain their lives was easy. She could count to five and pull the predator away from the prey without having her lips curl around her teeth in anticipation. Eventually she went out with each family member alone, so the others were not tormented at all.

In spite of all this, one of the siblings had seemed tentative around Emma for a while now. As she walked home with a rosy-cheeked Seriana one evening, Emma found out why.

"Do remember anything about the souls in Heaven?" Seriana looked sheepish.

"Did Jason tell you not to mention Heaven to me?" Emma asked, wondering why Seriana was so unsure.

The half-breed let her long brown hair cover her face like a sheet, embarrassed. She mumbled, "I'm sorry. He did. I shouldn't have said anything."

Emma stopped her with her hand. "It's okay. I'll tell you everything I can remember. Do you have a question?"

Emma led Seriana to an empty park bench and they sat together.

"Do half-breeds go to Heaven?" she asked and without pausing for Emma's answer continued. "Stupid question, never mind. Of course not."

Emma looked into Seriana's eyes as she registered the importance of her words.

"Wait. Please don't jump to conclusions like that. I'm actually not sure about half-breeds. When angels arrive in Heaven they're sort of washed of their previous identity. I could only recognize those I'd known in life if they crossed my path. I need to emphasize how big Heaven is. Some angels are merely collections of positive energy, not recognizable as their former selves at all. That's how they're happiest." Emma waited as Seriana looked down at the street.

"I mean, we drink blood. I would've killed many times if it wasn't for my brothers—and now you." Seriana shuffled her feet.

"I don't have all the answers, but I do have my compass." Emma tilted Seriana's chin so she'd look her in the eyes. The former angel placed her hand on her chest. "When I think of you my heart feels warm and bright and refreshed. You're so very important, Seriana. I trust my heart, and I believe half-breeds can live a true life. I know that's what your mother wanted for you."

"Do we die? I mean, do you know that?" Seriana bit her lip.

"I can tell you that half-breeds cease to exist when their spirit gives up the will to live." Emma had to be honest. She was providing Heavenly advice after all. "Sweetheart, a half-breed vampire's life can be very long, but they don't usually have a bond with other half-breeds to help them navigate the world. Many sort of become mindless, endless animals."

Seriana looked toward the sky and took a step away from Emma, gathering herself. "I guess I knew that, deep down. We've been like this for a while, and we haven't come across many others like us. And the ones we met, they weren't, they weren't capable of much more than feeding anymore."

The two sat in silence, absorbing this information. Emma thought perhaps the conversation was over when suddenly Seriana spoke again.

"Was my mother in Heaven?" The words bubbled out of her like they'd been resting on the edge of her tongue for a while.

Emma adopted the comforting demeanor she'd once used when she returned to Earth as an angel to collect souls. "Oh, sweetheart. There are so many souls up there. I wouldn't be able to tell you that."

Seriana's hands clenched one another. "Of course not. It was silly of me to ask."

Emma grabbed her hands. "Seriana, look at me." She waited until the woman's childlike eyes were on her face. At times it was hard for Emma to believe how many years Seriana had been on earth. "I have a sure-fire way for you to find out if your mother's in Heaven."

Seriana looked at Emma eagerly, clearly expecting a magic trick or some hidden tool.

"Close your eyes. Good. Now, I want you to picture your mother. Try to remember her touch, her smile."

Emma gave the image a few moments to form in Seriana's mind. Finally, she nodded, eyes still shut tight. Emma touched the center of Seriana's chest. "Tell me what you feel in your heart, right now."

Seriana replied, "Love. The strongest love. But I miss her so much." She opened her eyes.

"Your heart is your compass. It will always tell you about someone's true nature. If your heart is soaked in love at the thought of your mother, she's in Heaven—if she's no longer on Earth. But I have to tell you, mothers always leave their love with their children. Always." Emma pulled her in for a hug.

Seriana wrapped her arms tightly around Emma. "Thanks. I've wanted to ask you that forever, it feels like."

When the women resumed their walk, Seriana had a little skip to her step. Emma decided she'd ask Dean if he had any questions as well. Jason was trying to protect her, she knew that. But helping Seriana just now had given her a phantom tingling where her wings used to be.

Their conversation had opened a floodgate of questions from Seriana. "Do you guys wear clothes up there? Do you really walk on clouds? Are pets in Heaven?"

Emma laughed out loud before answering. "Yes, we wear clothes—usually of a soft, white material. You can walk on whatever you fancy. If you like clouds, that's what will be under your feet. And are pets in Heaven? God loves all his creatures. Could you imagine a Heaven without fuzzy, four-legged fur balls?"

"Wow. Is it hard to be down here?" Seriana walked more slowly now, trying to prolong her alone time with Emma.

"I love being with your family, and the Earth is so beautiful—truly God's favorite masterpiece. But I do miss Heaven. My job there was satisfying, and I did it well. I just think I needed a break." Emma looked to the stars, remembering how she'd once seen them from the other side.

At that she was lost in her thoughts, but eventually they drew her back to what was now her life. The present. How scary it must be for the Parish siblings to face this unknown and try to keep their partial humanity around them like cloaks.

Emma and Seriana finished their journey home quietly, though Emma rubbed her new sister's back from time to time.

A few weeks later, Dean was absorbed in the evening news when suddenly he rocketed off the couch and began pacing the living room. When he'd calmed down enough to explain, the others learned he thought the details of a recent murder sounded like the work of half-breed vampires. The deaths of humans at vampire hands always set the Parishes on edge. Their mother's lessons ran deep, and they took every instance of vampires killing as almost a personal attack. While Jason, Dean, and Seriana gathered around the computer to see if they could track down more than a brief, bone-chilling description, Emma let herself out and went for a walk in the woods.

Her feet took her to the clearing where she'd begged for her wings in the heat of battle. Temperature didn't matter much now that she was a vampire, but as she looked around, she could smell the snow in the air. *Winter again.*

Emma felt restless and unsure of her purpose. Her little half-breed family needed guidance, and she was doing her best, but was that it? All there was for her in this life? She decided to pray. Emma pictured God in the form He'd last taken: jolly old Santa.

> *Dear God,*
> *I'm trying to find pieces of you everywhere here on Earth. I'm worried I'm not doing my best because I'm longing for Heaven. And I feel unfulfilled about Jack. I know it's not my job to know the outcome of every event—but he had hope, he was caring. To see the angels end his existence has really shaken me. I don't even know what I'm asking for here. I just miss You.*
> *Love,*
> *Emma*

Her prayers were met with silence. No wonder it took such faith for humans to believe. Asking and never knowing if you shall receive was a hard thing to do.

Emma bent down and picked up a charred rock. This part of the woods was a testament to Jack's power, how he'd protected her and didn't retaliate against the angels who attacked him.

My impulses have always sucked. I lived a quick life as a human because I ran into a burning building after my horse.

But she couldn't find it in her heart to regret her decision to try to save Feisty. The huge brown eyes and sweet smell of her horse friend were still more things she missed.

Emma tossed the black rock into the center of the clearing. She should be getting back. Dean was up next for his feeding. Then the scent of crystallized rain halted her, and she smiled into the sky as the tiny flakes began dancing from the clouds. It looked a bit like angel-wing glitter, and Emma stuck out her tongue to see if it would have a taste.

Her mouth stayed open as a swirling white tornado fell as gently as the snow. It could only be an angel. The smell of cleansing rain and honesty made Emma take a knee. Her prayers were being answered in a very solid way.

Emma rose when she'd recovered her wits, curious about the angel who now stood before her.

"Former Seraph Emma, greetings," she said.

The angel was gorgeous, of course. The draping on her angel gown was elaborate and simple all at once. Emma knew wearing it was like an elegant hug.

"I'm Claudette," the angel added, hoping Emma would make the connection.

Raising her eyebrows, Emma accepted the welcome with a nod. *Jack's Claudette? Must be.* She certainly didn't have to use the title "Seraph" to refer to Emma now that her wings were long gone. It was a sign of respect...and flattery.

"Angel Claudette, greetings." Emma tried not to let her gaze linger on the glorious wings. Her back hurt briefly, remembering her own feathers.

Emma let the silence build between them and noticed Claudette seemed anxious. *Hmm. That's a wonder. What does she have to be worried about?*

"Emma, I shouldn't be here. Gabriel will be furious, but I couldn't think of anyone else who could help." Claudette's wings fluttered as if she might take off.

Gabriel was a good seraph, but he was very rigid in what he believed was right and wrong. There was no gray area for him.

"Claudette, I'm no longer in possession of any powers that can help you, though I would gladly give advice." Emma held out a hand.

Angels were a close-knit bunch in Heaven, quickly forming friendships. Emma took the same approach here on Earth, hoping to set Claudette at ease.

"During the battle, we had much debate amongst ourselves about the fate of Jack." Claudette bit her lip, taking Emma's hand.

She had regrets as well. Emma could see that much from the position of her wings.

The angel's corkscrew curls ruffled with the gentle breeze. "I was against ending him. I love Gabriel, but Jack had changed."

"Are you convincing me or yourself?" Emma tried to stifle the anger that suddenly flowed through her like lava. For Jack's sake, she forced herself to continue holding hands with Claudette.

"Both of us, I guess." Claudette met Emma's eyes briefly, and Emma drew a breath to pronounce that *she* needed no convincing, when Claudette abruptly continued. "There have been developments recently. I went to confession and told God of my regrets. He became chatty and explained that Jack was in Purgatory." Claudette now looked deeply into Emma's eyes.

The angel was trusting a vampire. Angels never revealed what went on in confession. It just wasn't done.

"Jack still exists? How is that even possible? I saw him leave." Emma dropped the angel's hand to pace with this new information.

"I wanted to go to Purgatory to find him, to find out about his condition." Claudette began pacing with Emma, but she hovered just above the snow-speckled ground. "So I went to August and asked to see the book."

Emma pictured the skinny, serious angel in charge of Purgatory. August always seemed disgusted with her job of keeping track of the souls there. Emma was willing to bet she was smiling now, with the former Devil in her charge. The prestige must be heady.

"She's quite proud, as you can imagine." Claudette seemed to feel the same dislike. "So she let me see it." Claudette stopped her pacing and caught Emma's hand again. "August told me Jack has to decide the state of his own soul, and he's just not doing it. I'm sure Heaven has little appeal after we attacked him, and Hell is, well, Hell. Purgatory isn't doing him any favors. He trusts no one. Not even God. The only thing I could think to do is bring you to him."

Her cards were on the table now, and Claudette waited. Emma tried not to let having power over an angel overwhelm her. It felt a little like her old job. She shook her head to clear it.

Jack still exists.

He was the heartbeat of so many of her regrets.

Jack.

She already knew she would go. God wouldn't have let Claudette get this far if Emma wasn't supposed to face this challenge. Emma was about to nod, giving her assent to be transported, when she heard the crackle of a leaf behind her.

Jason.

He watched as Emma whirled around, surprised. She'd been wholly involved in something, or she would've heard him before he was standing so close.

The snow behind Emma had an unusual pattern—almost as if an umbrella blocked the flakes.

"Are you okay? I heard you speaking." Jason stepped closer again.

Hearing her thoughts would have come in handy once again. He saw indecision in her face.

"You can't see her." Emma motioned to the snowless space.

Jason shook his head. He hated how happy the pronoun "her" made him. Why he had an irrational fear it would be Jack, he wasn't sure. Emma closed the distance and hugged him. He kissed her hair, and it smelled like Heaven again.

"Is that an angel?" Jason tried to hold Emma closer.

"Yeah, that's Claudette. She has some good news and some bad news." Emma looked in his face, and he was trapped by her beauty — and by the determination he saw in her eyes.

He nodded and tried to appear encouraging.

"Turns out Jack still exists! But he's in Purgatory and needs my help." Emma had her hands on his chest.

Jason's jaw tightened at the Devil's name. *He's back again. God, I just can't be rid of him. He's in her memories and maybe in her heart.*

Jason knew he was supposed to be sympathetic. Jack did seem to have some goodness there in the end. Now he was supposed to encourage Emma and wait patiently as Jack needed her, yet again.

Instead he clutched her tighter and spoke words he was afraid were too selfish. "I don't want you to go to him. Stay. Stay here with me."

At that, a door shut somewhere in her head. He could almost hear it. It wasn't just Jack. He knew she'd always be the first to rush in when someone needed help. He thought of her horse, her eagle, himself.

"Please tell me you understand. I can't just ignore Jack." Emma tried to pull away.

Jason wanted to keep her close. He knew the inevitable outcome. She would do what she thought was right. That might even be the reason she chose to stay with his half-breed family in the first place. Surely an angel would never be allowed to fall for the Devil.

He blew out a frustrated breath. His embrace now felt like he was trying to hold an unwilling cat. He would wait for her. He knew he would. But he wasn't quite ready to give in.

"I *don't* understand," he said. "I say someone as old and experienced as Jack can help himself. But I know you'll go, and before you do I need you to know I love you." He opened his arms, but she didn't step away.

"Jason?" She seemed shocked.

"You know I love you. And I'll pray that you come back to me, and I'll wait. I'll wait forever if I have to." He had spoken his truth.

Emma reached up and touched his check. She smiled, but her eyes were sad.

"Are you sure you're talking about me? Emma? Not the angel left in me?" Her doubt was louder than her words.

"Yes, it's you. Just you I love." He put his hands in his pockets so he wouldn't grab her up and run far away from the floating temptation he couldn't see.

She put her bright green eyes on his. "I'll be back. This isn't goodbye."

Emma stepped backward until she was right next to where Jason supposed Claudette was. Then quick as a wink, Emma was gone.

Jason punched the closest tree. It was still weak from the battle a year ago and crashed spectacularly. He wished he had something to fight, like he did the last time she left. Being in his head was going to be awful.

He looked at the sky, sure she was up there somewhere. She was without her wings, with only his love.

CHAPTER 16

*C*laudette placed a soft kiss on Emma's cheek, and then they were traveling, angel style. Emma closed her eyes and tried to enjoy the rush, but all she could see was Jason's eyes, helpless and hating that he had to let her go.

She felt free, and that made her a traitor in her own mind. The half-breeds were her job now, her purpose. Leaving them was a personal failure.

In the sky with Claudette's wings so close, Emma could almost taste the goodness of being a seraph again. *But I probably wouldn't even have my job anymore.*

"I do believe you'll always have your job, if you should want it." Claudette's voice was soft and almost like a song.

You're listening to my thoughts?

"It's part of what we do." Claudette set Emma down on a hard, white path.

You're my Christmas Angel? Aren't you a little early?

"I had to fudge a few documents and wiggle a few requirements out of the way, but yes. I'm your temporary Christmas Angel." Claudette patted her beautiful gown. "I have to go, though. I barely have time to let you in. Your half-breed is a chatty fellow."

She produced a key—a slim, silver hint of a needle—and wiped clouds out of the way until the door to Purgatory was revealed. The keyhole glowed white as the key came close, and the door hummed as Claudette inserted it. When the door opened, Claudette quickly pushed Emma through.

"You're not coming in?" Emma was surprised.

Claudette peeked through the crack as she closed the door. "No, I have to run. Gabriel is looking for me. Good luck." She banged the door shut in Emma's face.

"And how am I supposed to get out? Claudette?" Emma pounded on the door, but there was no response.

Great. Well, Hell was a picnic. Can't wait to see what the waiting room is like.

Purgatory was white laminate. The floor, the ceiling, the walls—they all looked the same. Emma stepped farther into the room and when she turned back around, the seam that had indicated the door a moment before had disappeared.

She turned again and the room was covered in little circle-shaped holes. When Emma peeked in, she found they were windows, and the people she could see in the rooms behind them seemed deep in thought. Then there was a smooth *whoosh*, and the doors to all the rooms materialized and slid open. Suddenly lightheaded, she sank to the floor and had to hold her knees for a few seconds. The setting reminded her of the Hallway in Hell a bit too much. She shook it off, stood up, and kept walking, peering in each doorway she passed.

After a moment she came to a room that contained a face she recognized. Jack was wearing white scrubs, and the sight of him made her smile. She couldn't help it. Emma had to duck to get through his low, rounded doorway. As she stepped in he sat on a white couch. He stared right at her and said nothing, but one hand trembled slightly, as if to silently protest its lack of cigarette.

"Jack?" Emma sat in the chair opposite him.

He looked her up and down thoroughly from her boots to her jeans to her white sweater. By the time he looked in her eyes, she had tingles everywhere.

Damn, that man knows how to look at a woman.

"I guess the choice was made for me," he said snidely. "Bastards. It was a set-up after all. 'Choose Heaven or Hell, it's totally up to you.'" Jack made a fist.

Emma held out her hand tentatively. He seemed confused. Jack's forearm muscles grew more defined as his anger increased. Once again, she wasn't entirely sure he was safe to be around.

You're a vampire now, Emma. Suck it up. You'll be fine.

"Jack, I'm here to help you make that choice." She stayed standing, agitated by her concern and unable to sit still.

He stood as well and advanced on her. She bit her lip as he wrapped his arm around her waist. His lips were so close, and he still smelled so damn good. She knew her eyes were half-closed at the sheer nearness of him.

"They did a great job this time," he said appreciatively. "Usually, the girls look just a bit like my paramour. But this decoy is outstanding—except for the eyes." His moving lips were as mesmerizing here as they'd been in Hell.

She had to snap out of it.

She spoke to him like she would have on Earth. "Hey, jackass, when you made me a tree-eating vampire my eyes turned green. So blame yourself for that one."

"Wait. What?" Confusion brought the light that was definitely Jack back to his eyes.

His slow, sexy, white smile made her knees go weak. He wrapped his other arm around her for support.

"Let me try something." Jack gave her the softest, sweetest kiss on the mouth and licked his lips. "It *is* you. Emma."

"You're so dirty. Couldn't you just have asked me a few telling questions?" She hugged him back hard. He was so solid. He could still be saved. Her angel's heart soared, and tears came to her eyes.

"No, pretty child, I'll always ID you by taste. How did you get in here?" Anger flashed in his handsome face as he looked around. "Are you in Purgatory too?"

"No. No, calm down. Can we sit? I think I'm a visitor."

Emma sat on his couch, and he sat next to her, slinging his arm around her shoulders like they were on a date. They looked at each other and smiled at the same time. He was so happy he was almost vibrating. His eyes danced, and Emma had a feeling hers were dancing too.

"Tell me why your choice is so hard to make. Why are you brooding in here?" Emma touched his jaw, trailing her thumb along his scruffy skin.

He put a hand on her thigh. She shook her head and rolled her eyes.

"The choice is obvious to you, Emma? Where would you have me go?" His eyes transformed from delighted to leery.

She responded too quickly to be lying. "Heaven again. Of course."

He took his arm from around her and stood. She noticed he still had his old motorcycle boots.

"Such faith so quickly. Your seraph heart beats true, even if that particular muscle has slowed." He nodded as if to say she was doing a good job.

"It's not the Heaven in me that makes that choice. It's who I believe you are," Emma countered. "I didn't want you back in Hell. Losing you has tormented me. I should have done more. I could have done more." She sighed in frustration.

He batted his eyelashes like the professional flirt he was. "Tell me more about the torment. Was it mostly below the waist? I'm betting it was."

She ignored him and tried again to help him see the light. "When you were in Heaven you were misled. It can happen to all of us. I know what you did in that clearing. Jason told me he could hear your thoughts as you took his pain." She stood and held his hand, loving that it was within her grasp. "You wanted me to believe God had answered my prayers."

Emma had to touch his lips to get his attention. He was trying valiantly to get away from his good deed. "And I said prayers for Jason's safety, but also for yours. Now to see you here and know that God had a plan for you — I just…I'm overwhelmed."

"I have that effect on you, I know." His words were teasing, as he intended, but his voice was husky as he touched his forehead to hers.

They stood like that, so very close and holding hands. Each breath he took was her next one.

Finally he kissed her nose. "How long do I have you for?"

"I have no idea." She pictured Jason's sad eyes, his declaration to wait for her.

"Your half-breed is treating you well?" Jack could sense the change in her and dropped her hands, giving her space.

"He is. I'm a great help to them. Seriana in particular seems to need the assurance I can give her." Emma tucked her now-lonely hands in her pockets.

"You best get back," Jack said. "I have no idea when I'm getting out." He seemed to be looking for a cigarette, but his scrub pocket was empty.

"You just have to decide on Heaven. I mean, it's that simple, right? I know you hated Hell. And Everett is most likely the Devil now. You couldn't go back there to face that." Emma tapped her foot.

This is such an easy choice. What keeps him here thinking?

"Everett? I would school him so quickly it would be a joke." A look of deep regret crossed his face. "Pretty child, pain and hate have been my best friends on many occasions. Remember, I've been the Devil longer than I've been anything else."

"And I've been an angel longer than I've been anything else, and I know good when I see it," said Emma. She gave him a look that clearly said *touché*.

"Princess, no matter which way I go, seeing you isn't an option. That's what makes this hard." He looked at her so wistfully he almost missed an opportunity for the obvious innuendo, but at the last second he pointed to his crotch and raised his eyebrow.

"You don't think I'll ever go to Heaven? Thanks a lot…but at least you don't think I'll go to Hell." She took her hands out of her pockets and ran them through her hair.

"Don't," he growled.

She didn't know what he was protesting until he'd crossed the distance between them, punching the wall as he moved. The door to his cubicle sealed shut as he gathered her roughly in his arms.

"Don't do that again. I can't take it. The smell of your hair, the curve of your breasts." He began whispering in her ear. "Don't…move…at… all." The words tickled her cheek. And her reason and good intentions melted like ice in hot water.

"This pull I feel for you, it's not natural," she said. His chest was against hers, and all she really wanted to do was kiss him deeply, free his long hair from its leather bindings.

He gave her a half-smile. "I'm twitching for you. I just want you. And hell no, it's *not* natural."

Damn it.

She undid the simple knot, and his hair framed his face. He closed his eyes as she ran her hands through the waves, just doing something to him, for him. Her stomach fluttered as he reacted to her touch.

"Don't tempt me. I'm actually begging you. You're all I think about, and to have you want to touch *me*…" He shook his head, his eyes sad and tormented.

She kissed Jack because she needed to, because she wanted to see his eyes dance.

It was selfish, and it might be playing with his emotions, but he was so intense. He kissed her back but opened his eyes and curled his fists tightly, restraining himself.

His lips were hot, and his skin tasted like sin. She ran a hand up his chest, inside his scrub shirt, and down again. She traced where she remembered his tattoo to be with her finger.

"Emma, step back." His voice was a warning she wasn't sure she wanted to heed.

I promised Jason I'd be back. I have to get a hold of myself.

She did as he asked and apologized. "I'm sorry. That wasn't nice of me." She had more to say but no words came to express her regret. If it was even called regret anymore.

He nodded and patted his scrubs for a cigarette again. It wasn't there. "You know, you come to Purgatory with nothing but your thoughts and memories to help you make your decision. But I'd kill at least ten of the people in here for a pack of my smokes." He sat in a hard-plastic lawn chair, one of many seating options strewn around the room.

Emma sat on the couch again. She put her fingers to her lips, which were tingling. She wanted more. Jack began tapping his foot—too much energy to sit, but he didn't seem to trust himself standing either.

"I wonder if you're a test for me or I'm a test for you?" he said. "You know this place is convoluted sometimes." Finally he stopped his movement and just let himself stare at her.

She looked back at him, wondering about his question, when she realized something was jabbing her in the back. Puzzled, she stood up and reached into her back pocket. She pulled out a slim, hard case. Its glitter and sparkle denoted it as an angel's.

Claudette slipped this to me? Sneaky little thing.

Emma popped open the clasp and resting in white velvet was one hand-rolled cigarette and a Heavenly looking lighter.

"Sweet Jesus. Please tell me that's what I think it is." Jack was out of his seat and in front of her, looking determined and a little scared.

She hid the stash behind her back. "You know how I feel about smoking."

He stepped into her personal space and tried to peek over her shoulder. "Oh yes, I remember. It kills, yadda yadda."

He grabbed her waist and tried to turn her. She stood fast. He gave her a longing look. "Well, at least I know it's really you. Stealing my smokes is just your style."

She loved playing with him, teasing him, here where they weren't in any danger.

She brought the goods out in front of her and smiled. He watched dangerously as she put the drug to her lips. It tasted like him. Surely this vampire body could take a puff or two to torture him without coughing.

"You wouldn't." He bit his bottom lip.

"Wouldn't I?" She lit the end of his favorite habit and let it glow. She inhaled and held the smoke in her mouth.

He took a deep breath. She leaned up and kissed his lips again, letting the smoke fill his mouth. His half-closed eyes registered pleasure, then rolled back in his head with the intense release.

Jack took the cigarette from her and held it in his fingers. He took a drag and blew the smoke in his well-practiced way. It formed a heart-shaped ring. He grabbed a handful of her hair and kissed her solidly, his hands no longer shaking. He held tightly and moved her head to one side, then the other, as he tasted her mouth. She moaned and gave up caring where she was, who she was pledged to.

This man, his touch, his sex — Emma wanted it all.

The Devil was, of course, an expert at knowing when a woman would submit to him. The way Emma was breathing, the intense look in her eyes — he could have her, and God, he wanted her. He looked away for a moment to give his conscience time to catch up, but it didn't move as fast as his lust.

"Pretty child, brace yourself." He had to warn her, give her a chance to come to her senses. She didn't. Her eyes met his and smoldered.

He pivoted and pushed her against the cold, white wall. He heard a little growl of pleasure in the back of her throat and tossed his cigarette into the corner of the room. She could easily fight him off now. She was so strong.

But she just waited with her new green eyes anticipating his next move.

His hands went everywhere. Just when he was feeling one delicious part of her yet another called to him. She bit his neck, just a little, but he had to stop himself and hold still. Her naughtiness made everything in him fire up. If he didn't hear her sigh with the satisfaction of his cock buried in her, he might choose Hell after all.

He reined himself in and slowed down, holding her face in his hands. She smiled. *Fuck! She's smiling at me.* He kissed her slowly now, nibbling her bottom lip.

The wall that had propped up their passion gave way, and Jack had a dizzying bout of instability. He pulled Emma close and rolled so when they hit the floor she'd have a softer landing.

He did hit the ground and knew, when her vampire body was warm and soft and very human, that they were in a pause. An amazing angel's pause. Jack figured Claudette was behind their extended time and silently gave her more credit for being thoughtful and a little mischievous.

Emma took a surprised breath and clutched his chest as she came to the same conclusion. She was human again for a little while.

Jack knew the drill. He'd stolen quite a few pause buttons back when he'd been an angel. He quickly used his imagination to fill the space around them with the setting of his liking.

"Pretty child, I'm perfectly all right with you using me as your bed, but do you mind if I grab some rum first?" She was so close he had to kiss her, and she still tasted like angel cake. Human Emma was his favorite. He loved her soft skin and gray eyes.

"We're in a pause? Crap. I'm going to mess with the time-space continuum if I keep this up." She rolled off of him onto the floor and looked puzzled at the smoky bar he'd conjured up around them. "You picked a place filled with bottles and smoke? Seriously, you're a glutton for punishment."

Jack got to his feet and held out his hand, but she ignored him and got up on her own. His outfit was predictable as well: leather jacket and jeans with a skull and crossbones belt. He closed one eye and thought for a moment. Soon enough he had "Emma" written across his chest in a very real-looking temporary tattoo.

When she started laughing, he wanted to find the pause button, smash it into a million bits, and just keep her forever. That would be his choice, if he truly had one to make. Not Heaven, not Hell, just a small place to be with her, to spend eternity making her gasp and laugh.

Emma eyed him, waiting to see what he'd do here in a pause. She loved that there was no urgency between them. She wanted to hang her guilt and morality at the door and just have a date like a real girl.

Her human life had been short and full of Everett's tinkering. Her seraph lifetime was absolutely paramount in its importance. And her brief vampire life had been focused on making those around her happy and safe. Even with Jason, sweet Jason, she had to be cautious. Responsible. To live just for a few moments in complete hedonism appealed to her—but it was wrong, of course.

Jack began pouring his rum into a glass, then shrugged and drank his fill straight from the bottle.

"Yes!" He exclaimed after wiping his mouth with the back of his hand. "Can I get you a glass?"

No. No drinking here. It's hard enough to walk the straight and narrow with him around.

"I'll take wine." She shook her head at her own disobedience.

"Light and sweet or spicy and deep?" He motioned to the shiny wood bar like a magician.

"I like sweet. I'm not even sure what kind of wine that would be." She shrugged and waited.

"I've got the perfect thing." He snapped and pointed. A bottle and glass appeared, and he poured the liquid like it was gold. The rose-colored drink swirled, and he stared intently at the motion. Then he sniffed the contents and nodded before taking a small, hissing sip.

"That's my drink! Quit sucking on it." Emma stomped her foot and finally noticed her outfit.

Jack had chosen a colorful sundress with skinny straps and a pair of cute sandals for her attire. He watched as she discovered her clothes.

"This is actually pretty. Thanks." She held out a hand for her glass, and he pressed his chest against hers as he handed it to her.

He watched her drink as if watching a porno, and Emma blushed when she finished.

"Did you like it?" He was smiling again. She could tell he knew she loved it.

"It was all right," she said coyly. "I've had better out of a box." She'd never had boxed wine.

"Liar. You would drink a vat of it." He ran the tip of his tongue over his teeth, delighted that she was so playful.

"Can I have more then?" She pouted at her empty glass.

He laughed and snapped his fingers, and the wine bottle hopped back into his hand. He poured more and stood so close she had to turn her head to raise her glass.

When she moved the glass away from her face, he was waiting. "God-damn it. Angel cake dipped in wine. Girl, you will kill me."

He leaned in for a kiss.

"You're rum painted with sin. Goddamn it. Boy, you will kill me." She mimicked his sentiments in the hopes of a thorough sexing within the next manufactured heartbeat.

But he nodded and stepped away. "Do you know how to play pool, angel?"

There was a well-used pool table set up in the empty bar. The balls were already racked up. The overhead light illuminated Jack eerily as he walked over and chalked his stick.

"No, Jack, I don't know how to play." Emma dropped her glass on a table as she passed.

She walked by him, trailing her hand over his shoulders and plucked a pink stick from the wall. After she chalked and lined up on the cue ball, she broke with such force that he laughed and slowly began to applaud. Two stripes went in.

"I only know how to win," she trashed-talked.

"Oh, is that right? Well now that sounds like a challenge. Are you willing to bet?" He put his stick behind her back and used it to pull her against him.

She wanted to be snarky and funny, but he was close again, and there was such heat radiating from his chest. She nodded instead.

"Okay, if you win, I'll let you imagine the scene." He motioned grandly to the surrounding dingy bar. "If I win?" He nuzzled her neck for a moment. "I get to see the panties I put on you."

He whispered the word panties in her ear, and it tickled her brain.

"That's impossible," she said.

She looked in his eyes and found them crestfallen. She'd wanted to be fun, and he'd taken her words as a rejection. His deep, brown eyes reflected a knowing. The knowledge that an angel would never choose the Devil. It just wasn't done. She touched his chest and outlined her name.

"It's impossible because I already imagined they weren't there any-more."

Emma watched the victory and hope bloom on his face as a huge smile. She couldn't lie to herself anymore. It felt amazing to make him happy.

"Game on, pretty child. Now get out of my way so I can concentrate." He did a wonderful job of disrobing her with his eyes while he sunk one solid ball after another.

"You know, you should at least give me a shot." Emma twirled her pink stick.

"Absolutely not. You stole the break. Take your spanking like a big girl." He winked at her as he sunk the eight ball last.

She stuck her tongue out. He set down his stick and sauntered over. A sexy song suddenly blared through the speakers. She held her stick out in front of her to keep him at bay. He pulled it from her hands and snapped it in half over his knee, tossing it aside.

"Are you ready for me, Emma?" He stood close, but he wouldn't touch her. Yet.

She looked from his beat-up boots to his sexy eyes. God, he was here in front of her, and with all this playfulness she felt right. Human. Like a lady who could do whatever she wanted.

Emma wrinkled her nose and started to lift the hem of her dress. He shook his head.

Confused, she arched an eyebrow. "I don't welsh on bets."

"I don't deserve you. If you belong to another man—I mean *you do* belong to another man. You're sweet to humor me, to try to make me feel like more. But after a while? A man can't stop thinking about you, and I have to ask you to have mercy on me."

He stepped back a bit and bent at the waist, almost a bow. "Do you think I didn't want to bed you the minute I knew we were in a pause? I care too much to compromise you. And I know he's better for you. I'm a regret. I'm always a regret."

He held his own hands with this declaration. He was revealing all his weaknesses and begging Emma to protect his heart. From her.

She could only be honest. Soon the beeping would start and reality would collapse this bubble that was just theirs. She wanted more time that she knew she didn't have.

Stepping closer, she held his hands. He looked at them like they were poison. A poison he desperately wanted to take.

"I should choose him. Jason. The right thing to do should be obvious. He said he would wait forever for me. Who can turn her back on that kind of devotion? But you have already been a regret for me. Always I feel you tugging on me. I can't stop berating myself for what happened. I mourn you every day. I should have done more. *That's* my regret when it comes to you." She squeezed his hands more tightly, trying to figure out how to put into words what she was feeling.

He searched her eyes and spoke. "Stop. Let's just go. What you say now will play on a loop in my head always, and his name is already among your words." He tried to let go of her hands.

A faint beeping began to sound.

She tried to ignore it and dropped his hands to hold his face. He looked at her lips and wouldn't meet her eyes.

"Damn it. Hear me. Look at me. Now." The beeping was getting louder, and her eyes filled with tears.

He did, but he looked like a condemned man waiting for the execution.

"I'm not humoring you. I just want to breathe you, all the time. When you look at me, I feel like my skin has words written all over it just for you." She put her lips on his and spoke right into his mouth, louder to compete with the noise that now overpowered their music.

"You're in my heart. I want you between my legs. I want you to just be with me. Laughing with me. And it's all wrong, but I can't stop wanting you." Her tears fell, and she kissed him knowing they'd open their eyes back in Purgatory again.

As if her words had released something in him, he grabbed her roughly. He lifted her to straddle him. She could tell they were moving, but she needed to get closer to his skin.

When he set her down and pushed her away, she felt a jolt of surprise. He seemed frantic, and they were right next to the source of the loud alarm. Emma was completely confused as he began kicking the wall. Then he picked up the pool stick and slammed it with all his might into the spot where he'd been kicking. One final punch and the sound was silenced. He turned, smiling.

"Where were we?" He grabbed her waist and put her on the pool table, scattering the leftover balls as he climbed on top of her, leaving her no choice but to lie back.

"Wait! What the hell did you do to that thing?" She had to hold his face to keep him from kissing her neck.

"I jammed the fuck out of it. Shh... The sex? It's gonna happen. Now." He started on her neck again and she began to squirm.

The music played without interruption now, and he was talented and determined. When her dress skimmed the top of her thighs, she had to bite her lip to convince herself to make him stop.

"Okay, one more thing?" she said.

He growled and lifted himself away from her with a push up. "Yes, pretty child?"

"I didn't even know it could be stopped." She looked past him to the busted wall.

He sighed and eased himself to her side. He twirled her hair around his finger. "That's because you follow the rules, princess. I never do."

He was looking at her again in that way he had. Like she was a drink of water and he was dying of thirst. It made her feel adventurous and sexy.

"Can I take you somewhere now?" she asked. She wanted to see him in the sunlight, see him free from smoke.

"You lost the bet. But because you have spectacular breasts, I'll let you do whatever you want." He reached out and felt one lovingly. She lost her train of thought until he clicked his tongue, frustrated by waiting.

She curled into his arms and felt him kiss her hair as she began picturing her gift to him. When she opened her eyes, she was surprised to see just what she'd imagined. They were in a sunlit forest. The trees wore their most glorious fall colors. They were lying on a big, fluffy bed in the middle of a patch of sun. The music he'd imagined for the bar continued to play, but softly now so they could hear the birds chirping and the wind rustling the leaves.

She looked up at his face. "This. You in the sun. That's my dream come true."

He reached down, found her hand, and kissed it in appreciation. She touched his chest, and he rolled onto his back, the white linen shirt he now wore falling open. His skin absorbed the sun gluttonously and felt warm under her fingers. Emma traced her name on his chest again and added more ink with her fingers and imagination.

He lifted his head and saw that he was now a sexy billboard emblazoned with the words *Emma was here!*

"You little sneak."

The tickling began immediately, but just when Emma laughed so hard she couldn't breathe or fight back, he stopped.

He straddled her and spread her hair out around her. Emma smiled and rolled her eyes as he touched her face and bit his knuckle.

"If I get nothing else for the rest of my days, this sight is enough. More than I deserve."

It took her a second to talk around the lump in her throat. "Kiss me, Jack. All these promises you've made? Threats to please me? Make them come true."

He set to work immediately, obviously battling an internal clock and a plan to touch every inch of her skin. She pulled off his shirt, and he had to back up a bit so he wasn't kneeling on her dress.

With a sassy smile, she stood up on the bed to take her dress off, bouncing slightly for good measure. She tossed the dress high, and it caught on a low-hanging tree branch, where it swayed gently as testament to Emma's decision to please this bad man with a good heart.

He knelt before her as if deep in prayer. "You skipped the panties, I see," he breathed. He nuzzled her stomach and gave a gentle nipping bite to her thigh. She shivered and put her hands in his long hair. He ran his palms from her ankles to her breasts. He watched her carefully as he explored inside her with his fingers.

His fingers were long and knew exactly when to curve or rub harder. She knew instantly she would come like this: with him watching her, supporting her as she stood and he knelt.

When she thought she could come no harder, he pulled her back down to the bed and added his mouth to the blissful mix. She could die here, with the trees swirling in a blur above her, and that would be okay.

She was unmotivated to do anything other than breathe, content with her ridiculous pleasure, when Jack stood. The sound of his belt unbuckling made her pay attention and remember there was more. Of course, there was more.

She watched him get naked in front of her and gave a low whistle of appreciation. She wasn't even sure she could fit him. He was everything he'd promised in his dirty voice.

"Don't be afraid, pretty child. I won't let it bite you." He stood for a second more before taking his place between her knees.

"I think I would be all right with that." She was languid and a little slow. He'd overwhelmed her, and now he wanted to do it again. "Wait, you. I should get to you first."

He shook his head. "Sweetheart, you're not in any shape to get on your knees."

Then his hands were everywhere again and she had to almost fight him to get to his manhood. When she held him he stilled.

"Seeing you like this? It was worth a thousand years in Hell."

She looked into his eyes. "Seeing you like this? It's like finally seeing the truth."

With that he pulled out of her hands and entered her. She arched her back as he hit a place she didn't know existed. But he clearly knew exactly where it was because he twisted and turned her legs and hips so he could hit it again and harder.

She went feral with him inside her, biting his shoulder and scratching his chest. His eyes rolled, and he went faster still, slipping a hand between them to rub her so quickly and perfectly all she had left to do was scream.

So she did. And soon after she felt his warm release as well.

CHAPTER 17

He cuddled this woman, this angel, to his chest. She was purring and moaning, so he knew he'd done a masterful job. That she would imagine him in the sun, that she would give herself to him — it was everything. If only she knew that, and maybe she did. His heart hurt in his chest.

It suddenly occurred to him that he'd never before been with the one he loved. Maybe that's why he'd never really fit in in Heaven. He hadn't known where in his body love flowed from. Turned out it *wasn't* his dick. This whole situation was doomed, though. He did know that. But he listened to her contentment and felt the sun on his skin and thought maybe, just maybe, things wouldn't change.

He reached down and pulled the fluffy blanket up from where it had landed on the forest floor to cover them both. She had her head on his chest, and he could feel her deep breaths blowing across his skin.

He knew he should get her dressed. The last time he'd busted a pause button there had been a legal hearing in Heavenly Court. Those righteous types were *such* sticklers for the rules. That was shortly before he'd been condemned to Hell a thousand years ago. His only defense had been that he had a really great hand of poker and wanted to play it through, which didn't go over so well with the other angels.

Emma's skin pressed against his was more addicting than any of his other vices.

Finally she peeked out from under the blanket. "Will we stay here forever?"

"I don't think so, princess. I should let you get dressed. But first…" He slipped his clever hand under the blanket and brought her even more pleasure. When she was done again, he sighed. He refused to let her be embarrassed in front of the impending angel crowd and closed his eyes. He imagined her in a crisp white business suit, complete with inappropriately high heels. He twisted her hair into a fall of curls on top of her head and secured it with a diamond clip.

"Am I going somewhere special?" She tossed off the blanket to reveal his choice for her attire.

Without answering, he began dressing himself. He got as far as the leather pants when a very different alarm sounded. It was more of a fire alarm and he pulled her to his chest, hoping they'd end up in the same place.

"Deny me. When they ask, I forced you to come with me. Your presence was against your will. Promise me."

She looked confused as they both began to disintegrate. When the anger reached her face they were gone—separate.

Jack landed with a hard thud in his Purgatory room. It was empty. He could still smell her scent on his hands, and he hugged his middle. He'd never been a fearful man, but he got it now. Fear came when you had something to lose.

Or someone.

Emma tumbled, dressed to the nines, and landed in front of two very official-looking chairs. She recognized the elaborate clawed feet immediately and picked herself up from the cloudy ground.

It was Heaven, and it was good. She was still human, which confused her. But at least the view was one she'd seen many times before. The angels milled about, mindful that their wings didn't touch one another. There were little clear spots on the ground where portholes looked to Earth below. This was Heavenly Court, and Emma was disappointed to see Seraph Gabriel occupying a throne.

He caught her looking at him and acknowledged her with a nod. *Probably because it's less awkward than openly shunning me*, Emma thought as she nodded in return. She went to brush the dirt off her Jack-imagined suit, but of course, it looked cleaner for having touched Heaven's clouds.

The second throne was empty. Emma held her shoulders back and tried to be as proud as those around her. It was hard to be human. The angels had a certain magnificence.

Seraph Gabriel started the proceedings and the angel audience stilled to watch. He was always a stickler for titles and conforming to the rules. Emma really wished God were here instead.

"Former Seraph Emma, you've been brought before this court for participating in an illegal entry into Purgatory. Once there, you enabled the pause, after which you and your accomplice proceeded to disable the timing mechanism."

The angels standing around tittered at the outrageous allegations. There was a shuffle and a parting as Jack was dragged into the scene, wearing just his leather pants and no shoes. The angels on either side looked down their noses, as if just being near him was a torment.

Jack only had eyes for Emma. When they locked gazes he mouthed, "Promise me."

Subtly shaking her head no, Emma let him know she would not deny him. She would never abandon him.

The next set of angels walked a very scared Claudette into the circle. Emma couldn't help but give Gabriel a hard stare. *The woman you love? Your partner? To bring her here like this is the ultimate slap in the face.*

Emma was thankful she'd once run these very proceedings, sitting in the chair Seraph Gabriel now occupied. The second chair should have contained another seraph, and she wasn't exactly sure why it was vacant.

Jack was already shouting in her defense. "No! I forced her. I tricked both Claudette and Emma. They aren't to blame. It's me, Gabriel, you limp asshole. Let the women go."

Seraph Gabriel wouldn't look at Jack, insulting the former angel by refusing to acknowledge his words.

Just then a loud peal of thunder announced Everett's arrival. "Sorry I'm late. Looks like I missed some good stuff," he said, surveying the circle around him. "Emma! Hello, whore. Jack, you bastard. Claudette, I sensed weakness in you last time we faced off. Gabriel, I bet your balls feel huge right now sitting in God's chair."

Everett wore a black silk suit that looked like pajamas. He seemed completely comfortable in his role as the new Devil.

Guess the place hasn't started to get to him yet. Emma wanted to whip her heels at Everett, ninja style, as he leered at her. Jack was running an endless stream of curses at him and straining against the angels.

You can do this. You were a seraph. You are a seraph. Then it came to her, what she would do, and she felt peace. She nodded calmly in the midst of the chaos. The current Devil was here to transport the former Devil to Hell, obviously. She ran through the Angel Offenses law book in her head. Claudette would be stripped of her wings and demoted to a spirit, possibly a ghost on Earth. She knew Seraph Gabriel would administer the harshest possible punishments, and that meant Emma's sentence would include becoming a ghost as well. Maybe even Hell. There was no breaking and entering tolerated in Heaven, particularly with Gabriel in charge.

Claudette was shaking as Everett settled into the second judging throne.

Calm, peaceful… Get your angel sense back. Having a panic attack wouldn't keep the others safe, so Emma stood even prouder.

She looked at Jack's angry face and smiled. As if he could hear her love, he raised his eyes to look at her again. "Jack, let me do my job. Trust me." She wanted to say more but they had witnesses, so she just nodded her thanks when he stopped his cursing.

Emma turned to face the judges. Seraph Gabriel seemed pleased at the return of decorum. He spoke in an official voice. "I shall hear the truth from each party involved, starting with Claudette."

There were no angel lawyers. They weren't necessary. When the truth was demanded, angels would never lie. Claudette was shaking and whimpering, but the words came tumbling out of her like water from a leaky faucet.

"I felt bad for Jack in Purgatory. He'd been there so long… I wanted him to make a choice. I visited him, but he wouldn't speak to me." Claudette kept her eyes on her feet, which were buried in wafting clouds.

Emma watched as Gabriel's wings tinged red with his anger. Claudette's deception was bringing out the worst in him.

He's harsh with her because he's jealous. What a hypocrite.

"I knew he had feelings for Emma, so I brought her up here to help him make his decision," Claudette continued. She looked painfully in Emma's direction, knowing now that her choice had been a poor one.

Emma was grateful for her time with Jack — just the opportunity to know he still existed. But she couldn't convey this to Claudette. She had to seem in control, professional.

"I pressed the pause button I received when I became Emma's Christmas Angel because I wanted to give her more time to convince Jack." Claudette abruptly stopped talking because she was finished outlining her sins.

Although she wanted to, Emma didn't point out that Claudette was acting out of concern for another's soul, which was a very angelic action. She had a plan, and she needed to stick to it.

Seraph Gabriel listed Claudette's actions more formally. "You, Angel Claudette, admit to manipulating the blessings of a Christmas Angel to aid and abet the destruction of Purgatory and a pause button." At least Gabriel had the decency to look a little sad as he added, "You shall be justly punished by this Court."

He then turned to the next defendant. "Jack, former angel, former Devil, and current human, I shall hear the truth from you." Seraph Gabriel looked more than angry. His powerful hand gripped the chair's arm like he wished it were Jack's neck.

Jack would be tricky, Emma realized. As a human he could lie. He was not bound by his previous stint as an angel and his experience as the Devil probably gave him extra power to fib in Heaven.

Jack smiled at each woman involved and then leveled his eyes at the thrones. "Gabriel. You can suck my dick. You're a traitor to your lover. I actually can't think of anything worse than you right now—even with that ball-less wonder Everett sitting next to you."

Seraph Gabriel held up his hand to stop Jack's words, but it would take more than a gesture now.

"I'm the Devil," Jack raged. "That asshole is just keeping my place warm. Do you think a silly angel or a stupid vampire is any match for me? My powers of persuasion are legendary. *Legendary.* Neither one stood a chance. I could've had them both at the same damn time wearing devil horns if I wanted to. They had no will. Punishing them just makes you a big tool. A jerk. A fucknob." Jack gave Claudette and Emma withering looks, meant to seem demeaning.

Nice try, Jack.

Gabriel looked perplexed. If Jack was telling the truth, the only correct thing to do was forgive the women and return the man to Hell. He waved in a few angels for a consultation.

Emma was grateful she had a plan. Jack was trying to warn her with his eyes, silently begging her to agree with his testimony. He hoped she remembered she could lie—she was still human.

She tried to thank him for his efforts with her smile. This would be the last time they saw each other, she knew that. She had to tell him, even if it didn't matter. She waited until Jack looked in her eyes again. Then she said it out loud. In Heaven.

"I love you, Jack." And her eyes filled up because his did.

The jig was up. He knew she was planning something big. She'd been too calm during this whole song and dance.

"I love you right back, Seraph Emma." Jack's jaw was tight as he used her most prestigious title.

An angel and a Devil had admitted their love. This was cause for much upheaval and excessive commenting among the spectators. Even Claudette stopped looking sad and nodded in approval. She was a true angel and more love in the world only made her happy.

Everett's snicker could barely be heard above the din. But Emma caught it and looked at his horrible face. There was rage, as usual—there might always be. He moved his hand in a suspicious way and Emma was the first to notice Jason hovering, trapped in yet another cloud coffin. He'd been a silent witness to the proceedings.

Everett's smile was huge as he watched her die a little inside. She'd not anticipated Jason—with his beautiful, hurt face—having to witness this, her confession of love for another man and the shame of being judged in Heaven.

Damn it. Jason will never believe in good again. I've failed.

She took a few steps in Jason's direction and was chained instantly. The silver handcuffs were so beautiful, they looked more like jewelry. Everett tipped an invisible hat to her, his eyes merry.

Now what she needed to do would hurt Jason as well. Emma closed her eyes in rage, envisioning all the possible ways she could kill Everett. Her calm was cracking and her hands began to shake, making the elegant chains clatter. She took a breath.

When she opened her eyes she was ready for the next part. Her testimony.

Seraph Gabriel used his deep, most intimidating voice, as if he could scare her. "Emma, former seraph and current human, I shall hear the truth from you."

Everett jumped in. "The truth shall set you free, Emma. Oh, wait—no it won't. I feel like it's my birthday and I'm having an orgasm." Everett clapped his hands in delight.

Ignoring him, Emma began. "First, I would like to point out that Satan has brought a kidnapped victim to the proceedings." Emma pointed to Jason with both her hands because they were lashed together.

"Pish. If I remember correctly, the Devil is afforded the protection of a companion any time he's commanded to enter Heaven. That's Jason, my pal. He's a half-breed minion, and they're scum." Everett pulled Jason closer to the circle of angels.

Wings rustled as the angels scrambled away from the half-breed as if he had a contagious disease. Emma's heart skipped at the forlorn look on Jason's face. If her plan worked, she reminded herself, he would be okay too.

"Second, I would like to postpone proceedings until God is available to sit in the judging chair." Emma stopped herself from motioning with her hands again. She didn't want to call any more attention to her handcuffs.

Seraph Gabriel seemed flustered by her professional demeanor, so she knew she was doing exactly what she needed to.

Finally he answered her request. "Denied. God is handling an influx of souls from a natural disaster. The presence of Satan forces me to expedite the hearing so as to remove him from Heaven as quickly as possible."

Emma nodded and felt her soul deflate a bit. She'd really been hoping for God. But she forged ahead.

"Okay, as you're God's emissary today, I'm sure He told you of His promise to give me back my wings someday. Well, today is that day. I would like my wings before I'm judged." Emma felt everyone's eyes on the back of her head. What she was asking was unheard of.

Gabriel was obviously torn, as Emma knew he would be. A seraph would be forced to tell the truth, but he didn't want to grant the accused such a huge honor.

"I am unable to grant that request, as you well know," he finally replied. "If God had promised you, you'd have your wings by now, I do believe. He's far too busy for our petty disagreement." Gabriel nodded and waited expectantly for her to start her testimony.

"I find your answer unsatisfying, Seraph Gabriel. Surely you aren't submitting to your own fear of Satan's presence. Justice must be served." Emma stepped closer to Gabriel, daring him with her words.

"I do not fear Satan. If you want your wings back, I suggest you take a moment to pray. If God sees fit to answer, He will." Gabriel shrugged and waited.

Emma nodded and bowed her head, but she knew she was lost. If God had wanted her to have her wings they would have emerged when she first set foot in Heaven. She tried not to think about the time she'd begged for her wings during Everett's attack on Jason's family. She glanced up and caught the half-breed's eye.

Jason couldn't speak, so he mouthed his words. "You are an angel."

"Thanks," Emma whispered. And she tried not to let what she was about to do kill her any more than it already was.

> *Dear God,*
> *I'm sorry to interrupt you, as I know you're doing important work right now. The only way I can save Jason, Jack, and Claudette is if I have my wings. I promise I will only do good with them, and I'm pretty sure I'll lose them again soon anyway. I'm not sure you're even listening to me anymore, but I can't regret what happened with Jack. I love him. And even if I'm not to be granted this blessing, please know I am forever your servant, no matter where I dwell.*
> *Love always,*
> *Emma*

The crowd had gone quiet, respectful of prayer—except for Everett, who kept snickering.

There was nothing. At first she just listened to the Heaven around her. It didn't matter if she had wings or not. She intended to tell the truth.

She prepared to do so when it started from the ground—the love, the embrace. She kept her eyes closed, but she knew it would be phenomenal. God was with her, even though He was handling the whole world. He trusted her with wings. He believed in her. She knew then she would be successful, because He'd heard her after all.

The wings were beautiful, and being an angel again was glorious. She opened her eyes and saw the awe in the audience's face. They might have doubted her, but God didn't. And neither had Jason, despite what he'd heard. She smiled at him and heard the handcuffs clatter to the ground. No seraph would be bound in Heaven.

She turned to examine her wings. She could tell from the breadth of their extension and the pattern in the feathers that she was indeed still a seraph.

Seraph Gabriel cleared his throat and addressed her. "Seraph Emma, God has granted your request, which surprises me. Of course you know you cannot lie."

Emma heard Jack cursing again. She nodded in Jason's direction and released him from Satan's coffin. The half-breed stumbled a bit, but then stood strong.

Emma addressed the court. "Pardon me if the rest of you can stand by and watch, but I can't have an innocent soul suffering in front of me as long as I have my wings."

Even Gabriel looked abashed.

"And yes, Seraph Gabriel, I fully intend to tell the truth."

Emma fluttered her wings for the pure joy of it. It was magic. She turned and smiled at Jack again, and he had to smile back. Her joy was catching. She was completely confident now, for the rules were written in actual stone. She could not fail.

"I did enter Purgatory with the aid of Claudette," Emma began. "I did enjoy the pause button, which she must have pressed. I was a party to the disabling of the timing mechanism." She refused to leave anything out or duck her head in shame as she told the next part. "And I made love with Jack during that pause."

Again there was a cacophony of gossip and talk. Emma stood straight. She could have left that out—it wasn't part of the charges—but Jason deserved the truth, and Jack deserved to have someone proud to be with him. Emma didn't have the heart to look at Jason now. He had promised her so very much.

She waited until the last of the noises had calmed. Then she continued. "Seraph Gabriel, as I'm sure you are aware, each punishment you dole out will be according to, but not exceeding the crime. Jack will be sent to Hell, and Claudette and I shall be stripped of our wings and demoted to ghosts."

She waited as Gabriel motioned for the stone tablets to be brought to him. He was careful to check her words, and he was probably doing it slowly because he was starting to dislike her wise demeanor. However, eventually he had to agree, for it was the law.

Everett began rubbing his hands together and wiggling his eyebrows at Jack.

"And you will further note that a seraph may take the punishment of the accused at any trial onto herself, if she so chooses." Emma paused, as Gabriel looked confused.

Jack began shouting. He'd put it all together, and Emma discreetly made a fist to hold his voice. He then fell silent because he had to.

"You'll find that in the Seraph law book if Josephine would be so kind as to bring it to you." Emma refused to look at anyone, instead searching the clouds with her gaze.

Everett sat on the edge of his seat looking too scared to even hope he would get to have Emma all to himself.

After more slow perusal of the antique pages, Gabriel nodded. "If any seraph should want to assume the guilt of an entity, she may do so in Heavenly Court."

Emma had seen it done once and had read that very law aloud. Of course, the infraction had been very minor—that seraph had saved his angel brother from a loss of power for three years.

"I would like to accept the punishment for Jack, Claudette, and myself." Emma looked down so Gabriel would feel the choice was his, but of course it wasn't.

Seraph Gabriel debated with the other angels for a moment, but Emma felt their decision before he spoke.

"Very well. You are well versed in the laws of the Court, and that's testament to your dedication and years of service here in Heaven. The Court will adjourn briefly as I construct an acceptable sentence for Seraph Emma." Gabriel stood and stepped behind his judging chair.

Everett began wolf-whistling, and Emma pointedly ignored him. She had but a few brief moments to set up the people she cared about.

She flew to Claudette and immediately set the tearful angel at ease. "Claudette, you did the right thing. I'm very proud of you. As a seraph, I grant you Earth privileges." Emma bent her head and touched Claudette's shoulders with her wings. Claudette looked confused but accepted the honor.

Emma stepped in to hug her and whispered quickly, "Jason will need safe passage back to his home, and I don't trust anyone here but you to treat him with respect. Jack will be returned to Earth as a human, if I get my way, so transport him as well. I need you to take me from Jack and Jason's memory. Let them live like men. Do you understand? This couldn't be more important." Emma looked anxiously into the pretty angel's face.

"Seraph Emma, you honor me with your trust, and I am humbled by your selflessness. I will be a servant to these words you speak for the rest of my existence." Claudette looked teary but fierce, and her promise would have to do.

Next Emma flew to Jack. He was furious—like an angry bull with no outlet for his rage.

Emma blocked out Heaven, Jason, and Everett and touched his face. "Forgive me, my love. I couldn't see you in Hell again." She tried to soothe him with her hands. It didn't work. She kissed his angry mouth, letting him have his voice again.

The angels still held Jack tightly, despite his human condition. She hugged him, imagining his boots and leather jacket on his body, and her wings fluttered vigorously in his captors' faces. Jack smiled a bit at their discomfort. She patted his pocket and filled it with cigarettes. It was her gift of the drug she disliked so much that made him realize he would never see her again.

His eyes grew wide. "Let me go to Hell. Life without you will be worse. Please. Don't make me miss you, Emma. Love feels amazing. Go ballistic! Fly with me from here. Do anything—do something!" His voice was harsh and desperate.

She refused to cry, though she wanted to curl up with this man and sob into his chest. She had to be brave.

Jack tried again. "Emma, Everett has the Hallway. I can't disable it from here, like this. I won't let you go back there."

He began fighting the angels, who happily used more force to hold him. Emma stole his voice again, keeping her personal Devil quiet for the remainder of the proceedings.

She had a serene look on her face now. Perhaps no one else understood, but she knew this was the only choice.

Seraph Gabriel returned to his throne, and Everett seemed to be using all his control to remain sitting. He was happily clenching and unclenching his fists.

Emma pulled her chin up. She would hear her sentence with her head held high. God would expect nothing less.

Gabriel couldn't meet her eyes. "Seraph Emma, you have admitted to sins and have agreed to take the punishment of the other accused entities as your own. I sentence you, with the power invested in me by God, to serve a tenure in Hell for the period of one thousand years."

Emma blinked at the harsh number, picturing the white heat of the invisible fire. She needed to be strong. Tears would make it hard on the others. Despite her best intentions, her vision took on a golden sheen and she felt the moisture of her fallen tears. She knew her cheeks would be streaked with telltale hints of gold.

Everett began hooting and hollering like his favorite football team had won the Super Bowl.

"Your wings will be torn from your back and destroyed. After the period of one thousand years, if your spirit still exists, you shall spend the rest of eternity as a ghost in the cemetery close to your human house. Do you have any last request or words?"

She had to take a few breaths. She didn't want her voice to crack. "Who removes my wings?" She bit her lip. It was a petty question, but she just didn't want Everett to take Heaven from her.

"I do, of course, my sweet honeysuckle." Everett popped out of his throne and rubbed his hands together.

Seraph Gabriel stood as well. "Stop, Satan."

Everett's feet were frozen in place.

"Whoever volunteers may remove Emma's wings." Seraph Gabriel sent a gracious hand over the audience.

Emma looked out over her angel witnesses. Their numbers had doubled, maybe tripled, since her trial started. No one would accept the offer to maim another angel. It was against everything in them, and they didn't like to be reminded of the pain it was possible, however remotely, they could actually endure. But they would certainly stand there and watch as Everett gleefully did it.

Emma was tempted to beg—to point to angels and call their names—but her pride refused to let her. She looked just over the top of Everett's head. His smile was blinding. She knew it without focusing on his face.

After a reasonable amount of time, Gabriel nodded. "No one offers? Very well then. Satan, you may—"

"I'll do it."

Emma gasped quietly in her relief. Jason stepped forward, so brave in this unknown world.

Everett's feet had been freed by Gabriel's permission, and he now stepped closer to Emma. But Jason stepped between the Devil and the angel. He pushed on Everett's chest to make room in front of Emma. Everett was immediately ready to fight. Jason assumed a defensive posture, and Emma knew he would fight them all for her—Everett, Seraph Gabriel, any and all of the hovering angels—if that's what it took.

Seraph Gabriel was embarrassed by the lack of order in his court. "Satan, to your seat!"

Everett was pulled as if by a string and slapped back into his throne.

When Jason felt certain Everett was going to stay put, he turned to face Emma.

He repeated his words quietly now, just for her. "I'll do it."

She nodded, unable to thank him, though she desperately wanted to.

He reached up and wiped away her tears. "Don't cry, beautiful Emma. Don't let them see you sad."

Instead of pulling off her wings, he faced Seraph Gabriel. "I'd like to address the Court."

There had never been a half-breed at a Heavenly trial before. Seraph Gabriel had to set a precedent. He certainly didn't want the Devil allowed to commit violence on a seraph in Heaven. It seemed wrong. The judge decided to placate his unusual volunteer. Gabriel nodded. "Keep it brief, half-breed."

Emma spoke up, angry after her tears, and ordered, "His name is Jason, and you shall address him as such."

Jason turned to her, touched her face, and ran his hands down her wings. "I wondered what you looked like with both wings. I have to say, you're a sight I never want to forget."

Then Jason spoke to everyone, but he held her hands and looked into her eyes. "This seraph doesn't deserve the punishment you deemed fit for her. You all stand here, watching with morbid fascination as she readies herself to be mutilated. And yet you are considered angels? I hope if there is a God that He sees you all for what you are right now. Of all these accused people, Emma is the one with the least guilt and the biggest heart. And yet she is given the harshest of punishments. If this is Heaven, I want no part of it."

He paused and Everett broke in, still angered that he would not have the release of pulling Emma's wings from her back. "Half-breed scum. You *do* know the object of your devotion was spreading her legs for that bastard over there, don't you?"

Jason didn't turn. He only looked at Emma. "I did hear that she fell in love. Jack has had a hold on her heart for some time now. It kills me… but I'm glad she found the joy she sought. Her human life did not include many pleasant memories."

He stepped closer to her and lowered his voice, not talking to Everett any longer. "I wanted to be that man for you. I don't know what's next or how this even works, but I meant what I said before you left. I'll wait for you — forever. I don't know how to do it any other way."

Emma reached up and hugged this beautiful soul. "Don't give up on Heaven because of this. I've made mistakes, but this is a wonderful place. I want your soul here someday."

"Still you try for me." He shook his head. "Emma, *you* make me good. Only you. Not this place. Not these fake angels. Kiss me, Emma."

Jason asked so sincerely that she couldn't deny him. She hoped her kiss would convince him Heaven was good, that this was just a bad moment. Jack was surely growling, but as the soft kiss ended, Jason came away holding her wings.

"I did it with love, so it wouldn't hurt."

Her wings disintegrated in his hands — two beautiful puffs of glitter. She put one hand to her mouth and nodded. Human again, Emma knew she should thank him, but she could only pat his shoulder. It took the crowd a few seconds to realize what Jason had done. Some began crying. Others had their mouths open in shock.

Seraph Gabriel spoke again, ending the proceedings. "Satan, you may remove Emma and take her with you. Now I have to think about what to do with these men."

Emma spoke loudly, though her voice was harsh and human now. "Just a suggestion, of course, Seraph Gabriel, but how about letting Jack remain as a human on Earth? His actions can dictate the correct place for his soul when the time comes."

Gabriel considered Emma's words as Claudette stepped forward.

"Seraph Gabriel, I will transport the men to the surface." Claudette's voice was steady, her purpose sure.

Gabriel waved his hand in her direction, and Jack was freed from his captors.

Claudette touched Jason's arm and said, "I'll take him first."

Emma waved, and they were gone. No proper goodbye, but she wasn't sure what the right words were supposed to be anyway. Claudette would carefully erase Jason's memory. She'd pluck any stray thoughts of Emma out of his mind and leave him as he was before the Christmas Eve she'd crashed into his life.

Jack reached her and twirled her quickly. His voice had been restored by a thoughtful bystander. "This is going to work," he said eagerly. "I'll start killing people the minute I get to Earth, and I'll be in Hell in no time. We'll toss that asshole out and then we can stay or leave together. I was worried there for a minute, but you're so smart!" He was practically dancing in anticipation, and he began kissing her and touching her arms, rubbing them to keep her warm. She hadn't noticed she was cold.

"You're such a romantic, Jack. Nothing like promising to be a serial killer to make a girl's heart beat like crazy." She was having trouble meeting his eyes.

She was such a bad liar.

"Wait. Wait. What?" He tilted her chin up so she had to look at him. Her tears gave her away. "That's the plan, right? I go to Hell with you? I'll go fucking nuts right now if I have to."

He started to pull away from her, intent on his immediate evil.

"Jack. Say goodbye to me. You won't remember it, but…" Emma paused to remember his exact words. "It will run on a loop in my head—always. It will be what I have." She held out her hand.

Claudette had returned. She nodded subtly to Emma, confirming Jason's mind wipe.

Jack looked from Claudette to Emma and back again. It clicked. Her plan. He'd been an angel after all; he knew all the tricks.

"That's why you gave her access to Earth while you still had the power as a seraph. I say no to that. It's unacceptable to forget you. Don't make me." Jack's every muscle was clenched.

Everett was closing in. Emma wanted Jack gone before her existence was claimed by the Devil.

"Tell me goodbye—and make it count," she said, trying to sound commanding. Emma's heart was beating so fast.

Jack hugged her tightly. "But I just found you. All these years, and I found you. I won't say goodbye. I won't forget you. I will get you out of Hell. That's the only promise I'll make."

Everett began his annoying clapping. "This is so touching. But I'm on a tight schedule. She has a Hallway with her name all over it."

Jack whirled on Everett and started punching, but the angels were too quick and held him down. Claudette rushed over, reached into the scuffle, and touched Jack's boot. In an instant they both vanished.

Emma had no idea how much strength she'd been getting from Jack's presence until he was gone. Embarrassingly, her knees gave out as Everett got closer.

He pulled her to her feet by her hair. The angels winced as Everett then tossed her back to the ground, in the direction from which he'd arrived on the scene. Emma's human body betrayed her as she groaned in pain. Finally Everett bent down and scooped her up.

He slapped her ass and smiled at the audience. "Well, thanks for the present, guys. How holy do you feel now?"

His laugh lingered long after they'd disappeared.

CHAPTER 18

*C*laudette moved so fast that Jack had a head rush when she set him down. He knew it would take Claudette just a fraction of a second to change his whole world. She'd make him just a regular Joe Blow: no Devil past, no angel past, and worst of all, no Emma past. So he staggered a bit and came up talking.

"Listen, C, I need you to let me remember Emma—unless you think you can save her by yourself?" After Jack made sure he could still picture Emma's face, he kept talking. "Let me stay here on Earth as a human. I'll find the half-breed, and we'll figure it out. That Hallway? It's my best work and she'll die in it—even if she has to continue enduring it after that. Please tell me your conscience won't let you condemn her to such a fate?" He had to take a breath. He begged her with his eyes, and she looked torn.

"I promised her I would wipe your memory," Claudette said, wringing her hands. "It's what gave her peace before her sacrifice." With that, Claudette seemed to settle into her decision.

But Jack wasn't finished. "She's in Hell for us both," he said, looking at her pointedly. "Not that I'm not grateful, but it was *you* who got Emma into all this. She's being punished for a chain of events *you* began."

Claudette looked stricken. Jack was relentless. "She won't make it to the spirit realm," he said. "He'll shred her to bits—all the time, every minute of every day. Claudette, he's so much worse than me." He ran a hand through his hair.

As he looked down he noticed the ridiculous *Emma was here* tattoo still inked on his skin. In all the craziness, no one had cleaned it off. He zipped his jacket to hide the words. Maybe they could help him remember her. It strangled his heart to think of her facing the Hallway, being forced to act at Everett's every whim.

Claudette was just opening her mouth to speak again when they were both surprised by the appearance of a second angel. When Seraph Gabriel's face finally became clear, Jack knew something was about to happen. It probably wasn't going to be good.

When Emma found herself standing back in the smoky room with all the bottles, she pinched her arm. She wanted it all to be a horrible nightmare.

Everett had changed into a crappy replica of Jack's usual attire. His way-too-new-looking boots made a squeaking noise on the floor.

"Look how it all ends, you little whore. You get the men to dance around at your feet, but you always wind up back in front of me." Everett sat on the chaise lounge she'd escaped from once before.

A lifetime ago.

Prayer had helped then, and maybe it would help now. Closing her eyes, she tried her best, but when there was nothing but silence as an answer Emma knew this was her destiny. To be at the feet of this horrible man. She then resolved to let the room's surroundings remind her of Jack, of what she was protecting him from.

"On your knees, whore," Everett snapped, and her knees automatically bent.

This is going to suck.

"I think this room has a little too much of the past resident in it. You will clean it while I watch." He wrinkled his nose and her outfit changed from the simple white gown she'd been wearing to a tiny French maid's costume.

She looked at her hand and found a small bag in it. There was no way all these bottles would fit there.

"Get started. Bend at the waist. Look over at me and bat your eyelashes every third bottle." With that he crossed his legs and reclined in his seat.

She tried to tell herself this wasn't that bad. It could be worse. It could be the Hallway.

When she bent and slid a bottle into the bag it promptly disappeared to make room for the next one. Everett was getting an eyeful of her ruffled panties. And every third bottle, as commanded, her head would turn and her eyelashes would flutter rapidly, despite her every effort to stop them.

He would break her, she knew. But fight rose up in her, even in this hopeless place. She held desperately to that hope as she bent for bottles under Everett's rapt attention.

Jason walked home scared, yet he had not one clue what he was frightened about. When he opened the door and saw his siblings' faces, still the fear did not leave him. He was missing something. Somewhere awful things were happening, but he couldn't place it. His family was fine. Then he looked at his hands. They were covered in glitter.

Seriana watched him inspect himself. After a while, she realized he wasn't going to say anything.

"Jason, what's up? Where's Emma?" She looked past him for their fourth family member.

"Who's Emma?" Jason wondered aloud.

Dean appeared in the doorway and looked at Seriana with questioning eyes. "Who's Emma?" Jason repeated, annoyed at being left out of the joke. His siblings' expressions morphed to alarm.

Dean came closer and put his arm around Jason. "Brother, Emma's your girlfriend. You went to go find her."

Jason slowly shook his head and shrugged. Seriana grabbed one of his glittery hands, inspected it for a moment, and took off out the door.

Dean led Jason to the couch and began to talk. Hours later, when Seriana returned, he'd told his brother everything he knew about Emma. "I couldn't find her," Seriana said as she trudged back through the door.

"Don't feel bad. I can't even remember her," Jason said, running a hand through his hair. "I can't recall any of the things you've mentioned, Dean. But I feel this hurt, this dread." Jason put his hand on his chest.

"But I do feel bad," Seriana said. "There's nothing we can do for Emma unless we find out where she's gone."

Jack waited less-than-patiently for a man he hated to make a decision that affected the woman he loved.

"So, Claudette, you're saying Emma asked that Jack's memory be wiped… She did seem to know what she wanted at the end of the trial." Gabriel reached over to place a hand on Claudette's lower back.

The angel stepped away so she couldn't be touched. The two held a second conversation completely in body language.

"Gabriel, you pretentious bastard, I need to get moving." Jack began stepping backward, hoping those two had too many of their own problems to worry about him.

"Jack, you need to stay put. Maybe we should take him back up and put this to counsel. I'm very curious to see what the law says." Gabriel stretched his huge wings and held out a hand to Claudette.

"The law? Really? That's all that interests you?" Jack interjected. "What kind of evil are you, Gabriel? A courageous woman stood up to defend Claudette when you wouldn't, you flying pansy, and now you're too stupid to help her?" Jack wanted to pick his words carefully, but his temper was too hot. Every second Emma was down there, Everett was doing God knows what to her. He decided just to go for it and add more flames to the fire.

"I've seen a lot of nastiness in my day, as you can imagine," Jack continued, finding his rhythm. "And what you're doing right now? It would score some serious points in Hell. This is evil, angel. I know it better than I know my name. I hope your God is proud of the spineless wimps He has running the joint." Jack punched his own hand. "All I'm asking is for you to give her a shot. Leave someone alive who can try to help her. Crap, throw her a rope, you bastard. You already pushed her off the ship in the middle of a hurricane."

The trio waited in the woods—each for the other to choose a path or make a move. Then the former Devil did something he'd never imagined. He prayed.

> *God,*
> *This overgrown monkey doesn't know his ass from his wing.*
> *I know Emma's good. She made even me have hope. She's like a*
> *miracle-maker. Let the punishment fit the crime. Hell, let me take*
> *her place. She believes in You. She trusts You. Don't put her through*
> *horror just because she loves me.*
> *Jack*

He opened his eyes and found that even though he'd said the words in his head, the angels looked shocked. He didn't give a rat's ass. He'd do anything for her.

Seraph Gabriel nodded. "Very well, former Devil. You can keep your memories of her, though I can't imagine what good they will do you now that you're human."

Then he turned and gave Claudette a direct order, because she wasn't responding to his overtures of affection. "We fly, angel."

They were gone in a swirl of glitter, light, and brilliance.

"Fucking angels," Jack said, looking skyward. "So pretty, but so damn useless. Tossing their best to the wolves like chumps."

He put his hand in his pocket and pulled out a cigarette. He lit it, thinking of her hand patting the box into existence in his pocket.

I'm coming, Emma. Hang in there.

Emma waited because she didn't have a choice. Everett had commanded her to stand still. He was so close she could smell his musky, gluey odor. She hated him, yet she was still as a statue as he began licking her neck. She shivered with revulsion.

"Did Jack have you here too? I bet you bent over in a quick minute when you saw his handsome face." Everett was talking at her, to her, and into her. "I guess I'll take you here first then. Make my mark. Whore." Everett picked her up and tossed her roughly onto the lounge.

She couldn't talk. He'd taken that from her. He pranced around her like a proud turkey, ridiculous in his excitement.

"Panties off." He snapped his finger, and she closed her eyes.

I will not cry. I will not cry.

She heard it then, while she was trying to be anywhere but in her body. Overlapping prayers. She couldn't smile, but she wanted to as she heard Jack's horrible — yet apparently effective — prayer twirling in and out of Jason, Seriana, and Dean's combined Our Father.

She realized that despite Everett's commands, her ruffled panties had not budged. She opened her eyes to find him snapping and pointing and snapping. Nothing was working. She felt the thrill of victory and the tremendous relief of being clothed in front of this horrible man, even if it was just for a few more seconds.

The panties were so stubborn that even when he tried to pull them off, they stayed put, as if she was a doll with her delicates painted on. When he commanded her to take them off herself, she also had no luck.

Thank you. Thank you all for praying.

"Speak. Do you know why this is happening?" He got up in her personal space again.

She started laughing at him then. She couldn't stop herself. "You're the worst Devil. You can't do anything right, assbag."

Everett hauled off and slapped her. She stopped laughing.

"Really? Would you like to see effective? Come with me then." He grabbed her arm and she had no choice but to follow.

When he opened the door she knew where they were heading, and she hated that she started shaking. The tears that sprang to her eyes were Pavlovian — the sight of the cement had brought them without her bidding.

He held her arms and shook her, spittle escaping his thin, angry lips. "I know how to hurt you — your sharp tongue and disobedient ways. Don't forget to thank your Jack. He's got a real knack for design."

She tried to hang onto him — and that was saying something. It was as if he was tossing her off a cliff, except this was much worse. He gave her one last shove and she fell backward into her greatest fear.

Jack didn't hesitate, and he didn't knock. Which in hindsight was a crappy idea. Three half-breeds versus one even tremendously bad-assed human was shitty odds.

The three were standing and ready for trouble when he burst into their home, and they quickly surrounded him. They'd been preparing for their grandfather's surprise invasion for years, so they moved fluidly together, and the intruder was treated to a brutal restraint. His protests didn't faze them in the least, but they relaxed slightly when they heard Jack's loud, demanding heartbeat. They had nothing to fear from a mortal.

"You were the Devil," one of them finally said, peering carefully at his face.

The female — Seriana, if he was remembering correctly — recognized him. Jack pulled his arms from their grip and straightened his jacket.

"The ladies find it hard to forget me," he said, nodding. "You're welcome." He lit another cigarette, thinking he should pace himself. These stupid things were his last gift from Emma.

"Emma has been sentenced to Hell, and we need to bust her out," he said, hoping he sounded authoritative. "I don't have a clue how we're going to do this, but we have to." He inhaled the tainted air and exhaled a tiny cloud.

Jason looked puzzled as Dean filled him in on Jack's role—as far as they knew. Jack grudgingly supplied a version of the drama from Heaven, which left out huge events, such as the fact that he'd screwed Jason's girlfriend. The half-breed would fight harder for a girl who hadn't cheated on him. Jack was sure of that.

Dean nodded and seemed to want to take the leadership role. "Okay, great. Well, thanks for dropping by. We'll do our best. Do you have a number where we can call you if we free her or need any more information?"

Jack shook his head and tossed his butt on their living room carpet. He considerately stomped out the burning end, but Seriana's mouth dropped open when she saw the burn mark his random vandalism had wrought.

"No, *you're* helping me. Not the other way around. I'm stuck as a freaking human, but I'm more devious than all of you put together. Let's roll." Jack headed for the door and was surprised when none of the half-breeds followed.

He rolled his eyes and tapped his wrist as if he were wearing a watch.

Jason had been quiet—too quiet, Jack now realized—through the whole encounter, and finally he had something to say. "Jack, I have such a burning hate for you right now I want to pop your head off and drink you like a cheap beer. Can you tell me why I want to kill you? Because I haven't a clue."

Truth or dare? Jack wasn't sure how to make the half-breeds follow him, factoring in their considerable brawn. He walked back and stood on top of his burn mark as if it was a stage marker.

"Assholes and pretty vampire, did she tell you about the Hallway in Hell while she was with you?" He scanned their faces. The brother and sister looked genuinely clueless, but Jason had a shadow of knowing he was obviously trying to grasp more firmly. "I designed it, and I was incredible at what I did."

Still seeing doubt in their eyes, Jack laid out the plagues, and Seriana held a hand to her mouth. "If you think it sounds horrible, imagine living in it," Jack said. "That's where I believe he'll take her. That's where I think she is right now. I have to get to her."

Jason was pensive. "You didn't answer my question, and none of us is coming with you until you do."

Jack could feel the time ticking away. Seconds alone with Everett—he could melt Emma's brain, kill her spirit.

"I love her. Emma and I love each other, and it broke your heart. But you still acted like a stand-up guy even though you knew she'd been with me." Jack looked at the ceiling. He had to give Jason his due, but he had hated the kiss he'd witnessed between those two. "You took her wings off very kindly, when Everett had been ready to cause her some serious damage."

There was silence as Jason registered this information.

Jack covered his eyes because he hated to beg, and he knew he had to. "Please help me. I'll do anything you want. You can kill the crap out of me when all is said and done. Whatever you need."

Jason stood. "We'll help." His voice turned slick and deadly as he smiled a hunter's smile. "And I might just take you up on your offer. I have a feeling Emma is a woman worth fighting for."

Jack walked to the door and flung it open. "On that happy note, let's make tracks."

They all clamored into Dean's suv. He started it up and turned on the headlights. The night was electric with their determination, but the vehicle didn't move.

Seriana turned to face Jack. "Um, where we headed?"

Jack lit another cigarette and took a long pull before answering around his exhaled smoke. "There's only one person I can think of who might be able to help, and I'm not even sure she's alive anymore."

Her screams were music to his ears. Why her pain had always been a soothing balm to his soul, Everett didn't know. He honestly didn't care.

He sat on the couch amidst the empty bottles and thick smoke. He'd left the door open so he could hear her beautiful suffering. And it *was* beautiful. Hearty even. He tried to gauge which plague she was facing now. He lifted his glass of wine to the Earth, silently toasting his predecessor. What a masterpiece the Hallway was.

She was choking on a scream and he tilted his head, concerned for a moment. He nodded when the bloodcurdling noise began again. Everett pretended to hold a conductor's baton as she hit a particularly excruciating high note.

His plans for her were vast. He could give a rat's shit about the rest of his Satanly duties. All his prayers had been answered, and God was indeed good. Emma had been right about that after all.

CHAPTER 19

*V*iolent checked her mailbox. It was stuffed with nothing but advertisements, and she closed the door without removing them. She hated the sight of all the printed paper. Really they were tree corpses.

Violent ignored the blisteringly beautiful sunset and walked through her front door. She'd seen way too many to get excited anymore. She poured herself a tall glass of water and went into the living room. Her blue denim couch was waiting for her, and she sat on her side. In her mind, Giovanni still sat next to her.

When she'd pulled herself up to the soil from Hell all those hundreds of years ago, love had spurred her on. She hadn't been wrong. Her painter had recognized her from his dreams when she found him in Italy.

Violent took a long gulp of water. Her eyes flicked from one of the paintings on her wall to the next. She liked to follow the progression of the art from their dream meetings to the joy of their first actual embrace. She closed her eyes and relived the moment for the millionth time.

Violent had waited, standing in Giovanni Fontina's line of vision and blocking the landscape he was attempting to paint. He'd been focused on the canvas, smearing and blurring the lines in front of him to match nature, so she was able to take him in while he worked. His strong forearms were splattered with paint and his nails were dirty. He looked grubby in this reality — and perfect.

Violent had spent enough time standing there to begin to doubt. Would he think himself mad when he saw his dream come true? Would her purple eyes scare him? Would he somehow know she was a creature from Hell?

She curled her hands into fists, and Giovanni paused as if he heard something. He turned his head slowly, and his smile spread when he saw her. She bit her lip with worry. He tossed his brush to the side and sprinted. When he gathered her in his arms she almost knelt in relief, but his mouth was too frantic—kissing her and offering beautiful Italian words in praise of her beauty.

Giovanni's gorgeous dreams had been an excellent gauge of his character. And his art had lived in his soul as well.

She smiled now, sitting on her couch as her eyes filled. They'd been so happy. He had delighted in her every word, and at night they'd escaped together into his dreams. His art was already full of her, but now she could hold still and pose for him. Giovanni had grumbled often that there was no purple pigment to truly capture the light in her eyes.

He was such a good, true man that Violent had trouble remembering that she herself was evil. He called her *"il mio Cielo"* or "my heaven." She let him believe she was his personal angel, never revealing the truth.

Soon enough, she was expecting his child. He spent nights crooning to it within her belly and throwing excited hands in the air when its movements under her skin were visible. Violent had to hide her fear. She was petrified of what they might create together. When the pains came, late one night, she touched sweet Giovanni's eyes gently so he would remain in a dreamless slumber while she gave birth.

Violent met her offspring under the stars, deep in the woods. She'd chosen the spot because it could serve as a burial ground, if the need arose. But Celeste was too beautiful and too wanted by her father to come to a murderous end at her mother's hand. Instead Violent found room in her heart for her daughter.

Giovanni woke in the morning to find their child suckling from his love's breast. Violent would never forget the softness and pride in his eyes. His dreams were true and touchable, and he said often how greatly he was blessed.

One week after Celeste was born, Violent grew concerned when she saw a tickle of blood from her daughter's mouth. After a close inspection, she determined her daughter was not injured. She leaned over the girl, puzzled, until she saw a dot of blood on the white bed sheet, then another, then another. Violent looked for the source and cringed when she realized the crimson came from her breasts. Instead of mother's milk, she was feeding her newborn with blood.

She tried having a wet nurse for Celeste, but the girl rejected all other types of sustenance. Violent should have handled the situation herself, but she'd been weak and sought advice from Giovanni. He looked from his listless daughter to his love and back again. When he lifted his daughter to be fed, she could deny his trusting eyes nothing. Violent knew everything was changing as her daughter sucked eagerly and her skin pinked up. She felt a shift in the world as she held Celeste's warm body.

Violent looked across the room at the picture Giovanni had painted a few weeks later. Celeste was the tiniest little thing, and she was also a vampire. There had been no words for it then. When her breasts had dried of their nourishing blood, Violent had fulfilled her daughter's need by killing and dragging bodies back for her little one to feed on. It was grisly business, but Violent's experiences in Hell had given her much to draw from. The hardest part was keeping the feeding schedule—and precise method—a secret from Giovanni.

She just wanted to love him, but they had to spend more and more time apart because of Celeste. He seemed to have put the fact that his offspring had suckled blood instead of milk far from his mind. His feigned ignorance kept him happy, though Violent knew it was a charade.

Violent still lost her worries in his arms at night, and soon she was pregnant with twins. The staggering responsibility of more little vampires forced her decision. She could not do this alone. Giovanni was going to have to help her and understand what they were creating.

It was this cowardice that had killed the only man she would ever love. She told him then of her actual origin. She had scared him with her strength and shown him some of her vast powers. When she was done, he believed. He knew she was from the depths of Hell.

Violent's heart clenched into a ball again remembering his screams as he fled their house. Instead of chasing him down to keep him safe, she let him go. She was too heartbroken at his instant fear to do anything but weep.

Two weeks passed.

When one of Giovanni's friends finally revealed that her love had been murdered for being a wizard, she didn't believe him. The friend insisted Giovanni had claimed to have lain with the Devil and said his child drank blood. They had no choice, the man said. Giovanni was crazed and dangerous.

So she'd gathered her little monster baby and found her love lying in a ditch in town, covered with a blanket. When she uncovered his form, he had a knife in his chest, piercing his beautiful heart.

Violent pulled out the knife and set her daughter down. Rage consumed her, and she let her minion strength take over. She killed every single bystander. They wanted crazed and dangerous? They got it. When no one else was moving, she looked for Celeste. The girl was hugging her dead father's chest.

Tears fell as she went to comfort her daughter, but her compassion quickly turned to revulsion when she saw that Celeste wasn't hugging her dead father, but drinking his leftover blood.

Violent squeezed her water glass so hard it broke. She didn't know why she punished herself with these memories. She'd been on the Earth almost four hundred years, and the remembering never got any easier.

Giovanni had been the only human worth anything, so she spent a good two hundred years procreating. Half-breed vampire after vampire she bore, hoping her descendants would wipe out the humans altogether.

Violent looked at the knife on her mantel. It had caused her untold pain, but she'd made it a symbol. It kept her focused — the knife that had ended Giovanni's life.

She needed to breathe, to be away from the art his hands had created. Violent walked out her back door and into her gardens. She lived for her plants now. Her trees, her flowers. She needed to tend to them so they'd make it to the next season. The humans were killing the plants now too.

She leaned down and plucked a brown leaf from one of her babies. Sometimes removing the parts consumed with death gave the rest of the plant a chance. Celeste had started it all. If Violent had possessed the strength to pluck Celeste from the Earth, she and her love might have had more time together.

She looked up at the stars poking through the murky sky. Really it was her own fault for wanting to know the beauty of Giovanni's dreams. Satan had even warned her. He'd known it was a selfish choice to go to Earth and find her painter. She could almost smell the smoke from his cigarette as she remembered his words.

"Beautiful minion, take my sword. It is your fate to choose. This painter you love? If you make it — and I don't think you will — he gets a piece of Hell for his very own. Is that a gift or a curse, Violent?"

It *had* been a curse. She hung her head. There was no changing things now. She'd tried to kill herself so many times before. She longed to get out of her own head. Maybe she'd prefer Hell now. Dealing with the humans was arduous, and the memories of her lost love had become more painful than any of the tortures she'd experienced in Hades.

She could still smell Satan's smoke. It was so vivid she searched her backyard. The small orange glow from his cigarette gave him away. She could hear his crisp heartbeat now that she was paying attention.

"I'll bet you were thinking about me, gorgeous. How right am I?" He tossed his drug into her plants.

Violent strode over the soil he'd defiled and picked up the lit trash. She popped it in her mouth like gum, chewed it, and swallowed.

His only reaction was to raise an eyebrow. "Violent. Still as charming as ever."

She rubbed her forehead. "Satan, you being here can't be good news. Did you get evicted?"

"Something like that. Call me Jack, for now anyway." He stuffed his hands into his pockets. "I need your help."

Violent shook her head and turned her back. "I don't help humans. Sorry. Leave a message after the beep. *Beep.*"

"You owe me, Violent." His voice was quiet and desperate.

She turned and watched as he walked into the pool of light her kitchen window created in the garden. She recognized the look on his face. He was willing to face anything—a sword as long as his leg, a dragon, crawling to the center of the Earth, anything. The man was in love.

"What's her name, Jack? Does she know she'll get a piece of Hell for her very own?" Violent smiled a bit as she repeated his warning to her.

"Emma. And I'm not sure she'll have a mind to know anything by the time I get her out." He made a fist and gripped it with his other hand.

There was a discreet cough from the dark. Jack rolled his eyes.

"Pardon me." He held up his hands in surrender. "I meant when *we* get her out." He nodded to his left.

A half-breed stepped into view. Violent looked him over like she always did when she met one of her descendants. This one looked a bit like Celeste. She instantly disliked him. A female joined him. She favored the twins. The last stepped into view and Violent covered her mouth with her hands.

She crossed to him so quickly he didn't have time to seem alarmed. "You look just like him." She took the liberty of touching the half-breed's face and smiling.

Jack cleared his throat. "Well, I guess I'll introduce you guys."

Violent ignored him, gazing into Dean's eyes and gripping his arms tightly.

"This angry, jealous asshole next to me is Jason. The pretty little beauty over there is Seriana, and the dude you're manhandling goes by Dean."

Violent grabbed Dean's hands and pulled him into the light. "None of my children have resembled Giovanni this much. It's like seeing a ghost. A beautiful, perfect ghost." She looked excitedly at his hands, thrilled to find them dirty and splattered with what looked like red paint. She brought them to her mouth and kissed them. After licking her lips she realized it was blood on his hands—no doubt left from his last feeding—which sobered her a bit.

She stepped away from Dean but kept her eyes on his face. "In all the art he painted, he never added himself. All these years I've had only myself and my spawn to look at. But now…"

Jack stepped between Violent and Dean, drawing Violent's eyes reluctantly back to his own, at least for a moment. "Well, as creepy as all this is, we don't have a shitload of time. I need you to tell me how to get to Hell. I already went to the place where I came out and fought the dragon with Emma." He paused and seemed to have to gather himself. "But there was no entry we could find. And these giant mosquitoes can dig pretty fucking deep." He motioned to the half-breeds with his thumb. "Unfortunately Mr. Alzheimer can't remember shit about how Emma got to Hell the first time."

Violent raised one eyebrow and Jason looked at his shoes.

"So, Violent, take me to your leader and make it fast." Jack cracked his knuckles and lit another cigarette.

Violent tore her eyes from Dean and looked at Jack again. "You *were* the leader, last I checked. And as far as owing you anything, I'm not so sure about that. All I caused Giovanni was pain and death. How do your friends feel about the lot in life I handed them?"

Jack ran his hand through his hair in frustration. She squinted at his discomfort. He punched a tree and bloodied his hand.

Jason stepped forward. "Ms. Violent? I believe we're related. It's nice to make your acquaintance." He held out his hand. Violent crossed her arms. "There's a great need for you to assist us. We would appreciate it very much." He looked so earnest.

She shook her head. "Half-breeds are evil. I know. I raised a bunch of 'em. No matter how nice you are now, blood speaks louder when the time comes.

Jack cursed and stomped on her plants.

Violent was ready to dropkick the ex-Devil when Dean spoke. "Violent."

He wasn't speaking Italian, but his voice was deep and familiar. She walked closer.

"Did you love Giovanni?" Dean reached for her hand this time.

"So much." Her eyes clouded with tears. "But it all ended so badly, and look at what you've become. You're a result of that horrible love."

"This is a burden I happily bear, knowing now that you made an impossible love possible, even if only for a short time." Dean smiled broadly.

Violent knew he was playing her. He was using his striking resemblance to unbalance her.

"We're fighting for another good person. Emma's just like your Giovanni. She's good, and she's dying a little bit every second she's in Hell. We can save her. Do it for impossible love, Violent. Do it for Giovanni. Make him proud." Dean patted her hand.

After a moment she nodded. Even though she was answering Jack, she spoke to Dean. "Okay. For Giovanni, I'll help you find her."

Dean opened his arms and she stepped into him, closing her eyes and thinking of her past love.

Jack tapped her on the shoulder. "All right, Grandma. Let's get to work."

ACKNOWLEDGMENTS

This book is the direct result of being loved by my wonderful husband. To my children, I revolve around you. To Mom and Dad, no dream is too big thanks to your example. To Mom and Dad D, your hearts are limitless. To Pam, let's always laugh. Karen, that place in Boca will wait for us. To Kim and Jo, tons of thanks. Shannon, girl, I don't deserve you, but I can't quit you. Angels and Vixens, you keep it hot. My Bookshelves Girls, we'll all get there. Alice, thanks for slapping me in the head and motivating me to give Jack room to run.

Jessica Royer Ocken, many thanks to you for your pretty edits. My words adore you. Coreen, thank you for the gorgeous and creative layout. To the exquisite Omnific staff, your heart and dedication is in everything you do. Thank you!

Most of all, to my beautiful, smart, wonderful pre-readers. This story is dedicated to you.

ABOUT THE AUTHOR

There's always been place in Debra Anastasia's mind that contains other worlds, other people, and endless outcomes. As a child she played there often—the door was opened by reading. But eventually time and responsibilities clouded this place with cobwebs.

But now... Oh, now. Writing has helped her open that door again, and she was thrilled to find everything still in place and ready to play.

Debra now lives in Maryland with her family, and when she's up late at night, stories leak from her fingers onto the keyboard. You're invited to share her imagination, and she promises not to waste your time. "Let me tell you a story," Debra says. "It is an honor to be your author."